BEYOND THE GATE

Sequel to "Another Kind of Loving"

The theme is the effect of war on succeeding generations. Of three main threads, the first concerns an Australian, Jake, who sees a close English friend and fellow prisoner of war die by friendly fire in Germany. He eventually takes his friend's widow and son to Australia. Fifty years later, when she learns of this, his granddaughter travels to the UK to research family history and find the truth behind her troubled growing up.The second is Luke, whose adored grandfather was badly damaged in the First World War. The third is Minkie, a young Bosnian woman who has returned to war-torn Sarajevo after being fostered through her teenage years by a couple in a village in middle England.
This village of Daerley Green in Oxfordshire is where all three threads come together as the truth of the various circumstances unfolds and unlikely relationships are made or broken.

By the same author

The Young Traveller in Finland	Phoenix House, 1962
The Young Traveller in Yugoslavia	Phoenix House, 1967
Travellers' Guide to Yugoslavia	Cape, 1969
Travellers' Guide to Finland	Cape, revised 1977
Welcome to Yugoslavia	Collins, 1984
Welcome to Scandinavia	Collins, revised 1987
The Big Muddy *–A canoe journey down the Mississippi*	Oriole Press, reprinted 2006

Fiction

Another Kind of Loving	Antony Rowe, 2005

Educational Aids

Assassination at Sarajevo	Jackdaw Publications, 1966
Caxton and the Early Printers	Jackdaw Publications, 1968
Scott and the Antarctic	Jackdaw Publications, 1971
TheVikings	Jackdaw Publications, 1976

BEYOND THE BROKEN GATE

Sylvie Nickels

Oriole Press

Published by Oriole Press in 2007
26 The Daedings,
Deddington,
Banbury OX15 0RT
Tel.01869-338995

ISBN 978-0-9518670-1-3

Cover supplied by Melinda Sandell

Printed and bound by CPI Antony Rowe, Eastbourne

To Bill W. and all his friends

The present contains nothing more than the past, and what is found in the effect was already in the cause

Henri Bergson, L'Evolution créatrice (1907), ch.1

NORTHERN GERMANY, April 1945

After weeks of marching, first east, then west, then east again they resumed a westerly course. The whole world seemed to be on the move: retreating German soldiers, entire communities emptying in panic ahead of the advancing Russians, and the occupants of scores of prisoner-of-war camps herded this way and that for no clear purpose.

They were all starving and exhausted. Hunger was as much part of them as drawing the next breath or putting one weary foot in front of the next. Jake's septic foot was worse every day. Pete carried his pack most of the time. They'd supported each other for two years in the camp; there was no question of them separating now. Anyway they were far back in the column. The guards had stopped haranguing them for they were hardly in a state to try and escape even if there were somewhere to escape to. Jake reckoned the guards, poor bastards, were as keen for the end of the war as they were. Earlier there had been deep fear among the men that they would be shot before they could be liberated. Pete still fretted he would never see his Annie again, but Jake was upbeat enough for both of them.

Unexpectedly, miraculously, there had been a delivery of Red Cross parcels at the village of Gresse on the rim of Luneburg Heath. At the edge of the village, the two men sat on a grass bank to examine their spoils. There was bully beef, some very hard tack, some dried milk which Jake mixed with ditch water from his flask. The silence between them was of the kind that grows when all there is to say has been said.

Jake thought back to the day Pete had been marched into the camp: a shit-scared rabbit trying to act out a brazen fox.

He'd kept himself to himself, rebuffing overtures, became the butt of jokey comment. "A Midlands farming lad," someone quipped. "What would he have to talk about anyway?"

Jake found him one evening squatting, his back against the wall of the barracks, and eased down beside him. "They give me stick, too, for my Aussie accent," he commented. "I guess like me you miss the countryside."

"It's the night skies I miss. Thick, black and stuffed with stars. But I suppose yours'll be bigger."

"Not where I come from," Jake said, settling more comfortably. "Rain forest area at the top of New South Wales. Trees shutting out sky. But I'll tell you something. You can walk for days and see nobody, hear nobody: just the parrots and the kookaburras, maybe wallabies. And skinks. Plenty of them skinks."

"Whatsa skink?"

"Kinda lizard. Hard skin, cold eyes. A bit like the camp ferrets sniffing out escape tunnels." A pause then "That's what's creasing me, mate. All these bloody men and nowhere to go."

"That's what's creasing me too," Pete said.

They became inseparable: Holy Pete (because his surname was Gideon) and Jayjay (because his surname was Johnson), sharing everything whether it was food or bits of tinder for heating water for a brew, or news, good or bad. In the end, it was Pete who was the more talkative. Jake learned about his home village of Daerley Green in north Oxfordshire; how his parents had been killed in an accident; about the girl Annie he'd married soon after the outbreak of war, and of little Matt conceived during his last leave. The leave before he was shot down.

Pete had worked on a farm, Annie served in the village shop, her Dad was tenant landlord of a pub called The Trumpet. Pete had produced well-thumbed snapshots of the village green and its chestnut tree and the rolling farmland that encompassed it all. It looked quintessentially English and in time Jayjay felt he knew the village by-ways and the characters that peopled Holy Pete's growing up.

But Annie came over as a right selfish Sheila and Jake didn't much like the sound of her. Of course he hadn't said anything, but he couldn't help comparing his vision of Annie with the reality of Kerry, his own feisty Sheila. God, how he missed her. The sex, of course - didn't they all? But just as much, the comforting familiarity of the freckles on her snub nose and the dimple that flickered on and off her left cheek as she talked. They'd met at college where he was doing history and she was on a psychology course. Then came the Dear John letter that had ripped him apart.

*"I know this will hurt (*like hell she did) *but we've always been straight with each other. I've met this guy, invalided out after his plane was shot up. He's sweet and we love each other; you'd like him, Jake, though I guess you won't see it that way* (too right). There was a lot of other stuff, but the long and short of it was that they were having a baby, getting married, probably were married by now.

He'd ripped the letter into shreds, saw the surprise, then instinctive comprehension of Pete's expression. It was a while before either of them referred to it, and then it was Pete who broached it as though it were the continuation of a long discussion on a subject now put to rest. Only then did Jayjay rant on and on and on about sodding women and the sodding war, and Pete let him until he had run out of words and anger had tempered to sorrow,

Soon after this Pete suggested they both joined a class. There were quite a few of these, run by the prisoners, books provided – if erratically – by the Red Cross. The choice of subject had been Pete's. Neither of them fancied a language course, the most popular; and art or music appreciation seemed to belong to an unimaginable kinder lifetime, But natural history?

"Maybe we'll get on friendlier terms with the bed bugs,"

Holy Pete suggested.

For a while it was the big joke of the barracks and a steady trickle of entomological specimens, usually squashed beyond recognition, turned up on their bunks until the novelty wore off. But the class itself developed its own agenda, its dozen or so participants from different parts of the UK, indeed of the globe, contributing from their own experience. It also added a new dimension to their days – and nights. "Wassat?" Jake hissed one night, reaching up to prod Pete's leg in the bunk above. But he was already awake, lying on his back listening to the fluting, trilling concerto that soared above the snores and mutterings. "Nightingale," he said quietly.

By day they would seek each other out to share the glimpse of a firecrest or hawfinch in the conifers closest to the perimeter fence. During autumn and spring migrations they watched aerial ballets of waders or formations of swans or geese trumpeting or honking their way cross the sky.

Just before they started the march Pete had a message from Annie saying little Matt had measles.

"God wouldn't let him die before I get back, eh Jayjay?" Pete said now, catapulting Jake back into the uncomfortable, painful present.

"Don't be bloody stupid," Jake said, not at all sure that He wouldn't. "We'll be home in a few days."

That seemed to satisfy Pete. He looked up at the sky, buzzing with even more activity than usual. Ahead the track followed the edge of a wood, but here it cut across open fields.

"Hey, look at ours!" Pete exclaimed. Circling above them several planes became recognisably Typhoons, the red, white and blue circles clearly visible. God, it must be great to be flying up there, free. Jake watched as they began to peel away, bank, turn, lose height, one behind the other.

Pete stood up, legs akimbo, arms raised in greeting, head back, cheering. Jake heard him shout "We're going h-o-o-o-me." In disbelief he saw the puffs of smoke from under the wings.

"Get down Pete, for God's sake," he yelled, but Pete was still standing, cheering when he was hit in the stomach, spun round and fell, his head in Jake's lap. Death must have been instantaneous.

"Bastards," Jake screamed. "Bastards, bastards, bastards."

He cradled Pete's head, shifting his weight to ease the pain in his bad foot. And saw his tears of fury and grief fall on to his friend's fair head.

Oxfordshire – Spring 1948 / Jake

Jake stood at the window of Mrs Benson's b. and b. on the outskirts of Banbury. The small room's most outstanding characteristic was its anonymity: blue candlewick cover on the narrow single bed, Utility wardrobe, dressing table, a chair, blue curtains to match the bed cover, a matching bowl and jug decorated with red roses for his morning ablutions.

"Come down for a cup of tea when you're ready. I expect you could do with one after that long journey." Apparently he was the first Australian Mrs Benson had met and she took it for granted he'd come straight off the boat.

From the window he looked out over rolling farmland: healthy green rows of some legume crop and the wheat already well-established. Then he turned his attention to the sky: uniformly grey. It was a habit developed during the war. It's what he and Holy Pete had spent acres of their time doing during those months in the camp: lying on their backs, sharing hopes, sorrows, frustrations, looking up at the sky. It was the one way they could avoid seeing the barbed wire, the watch towers and the goons parading the perimeter fence.

Down in Mrs Benson's living room, his hostess served tea in pretty cups each with a rose at the bottom. Clearly roses were her thing and this was her best china tea set.

"So you were stationed here during the war, Mr Johnson?" she prompted him.

"Well, not quite here, but I had a lady friend not too far away." Before Mrs B. could jump to wrong conclusions he added hastily, "She married someone else, and anyway I had a girl back home." No point in mentioning she'd married somebody else, too. "But I had a great mate – went through p.o.w. camp together, only the poor ba…" he caught himself in time, "poor bloke was killed right at the end of the war. Makes it hard to believe in a God when that happens."

Mrs Benson's expression clouded. "I would prefer you did not call on the Lord's name in vain in this house, Mr Johnson."

"Sorry ma'am. Pete, my friend he was quite a follower himself. In fact, we called him Holy Pete." Under the table Jake crossed his fingers and hoped that whatever God there might be would overlook such a distortion of the facts. "Anyway Pete's wife lived near here, a place called Daerley Green. Thought I'd see how she's getting on, and the little one."

Mrs Benson's expression clouded again, this time in commiseration. "Terrible for those young women left to bring children up on their own. Yes, Daerley is about eight miles away."

Jake doubted that Mrs Benson's commiseration was deserved. From his only distant glimpse of Annie Gideon she seemed to be managing widowhood very nicely, thank you. Memories of those first days of peace were still too painful to revisit more than briefly. Dominating them was his grief and anger at the loss of Pete, the only enduring relationship in his life. Then there had been the physical pain of his septic foot, the days in hospital followed by the limbo of facing the totally unstructured rest of his life. He had filled forms, been interviewed, shuffled from one transit camp to another.

One of the camps in the Midlands didn't seem so far from Holy Pete's village, so one week-end he had hitchhiked. It wasn't hard to find the cottage – he'd seen the dog-eared picture of it often enough, with the pretty woman with fluffy fair hair leaning on the gate. That Sunday afternoon he saw a little boy playing in the garden and his heart contracted at the thought this was the son Pete had never had a chance to see. He'd been about to push open the gate and speak to the child when he heard a woman's laughter through an open window, followed by a teasing "Now stop it, Billy!" And through the window he saw a dark-haired young man, his arms entwined round a pretty woman with fluffy fair hair, his large hands cupping her buttocks as he pulled her against him.

Jake made a hasty retreat. A few weeks later they sent him back to Sydney. He felt like a soul adrift. Though the war had brought suffering and loss back home too, it had not brought the immediate threat of devastation on the civil population. He found himself resenting the very sight of the healthy young, easily bored by stories of hardship and loss. There was no one to share his feelings with, and the streets of Sydney still held too many echoes of Kerry and a world of pre-war innocence.

A letter came from one of the few people he kept in touch with: Greg a fellow inmate of the hospital in Northampton where they had treated, indeed saved his foot, though he was left with a slight limp.

"*I don't want to worry you, mate,*" Greg wrote. "*But I got a glimpse of your pal Pete's widow on a visit to my in-laws in the Midlands recently. Imagine – found she lived in the next village. She didn't look in good shape, nor the kid.*"

Jake couldn't get it out of his mind. His father became impatient. "You going to moon about your dead pal's wife for the rest of your life, boy?"

"You don't understand," Jake shouted, seeing and hearing yet again Holy Pete's exuberance, arms raised to the sky, the roar of the plane, the dreadful rat-a-tat. And Pete spinning like a monstrous top, crashing into his lap.

"Too right," his father shouted back. "Too right I don't. I was only in Gallipoli, didn't get further than a trench a few yards above a god-forsaken beach, living, breathing in a lifetime's stench of filth and death. Calling truces so we could bury our dead. Had more in common with the god-damned Turks than the buggers at home who'd sent us out to fight 'em."

Across the room Jake's mother caught his eye and shook her head. Dad had never talked much about Gallipoli, and it was only when he studied it at school that Jake began to guess at what he must have gone through. Even then he couldn't really associate it with the man who scowled across every meal table, mostly spoke in monosyllables. It had been different for his sister Harriet who was a touchy-feely person, prone to fling her arms round you for no apparent reason. She'd always been Dad's favourite, Jake knew that, and maybe now he could understand better how Harriet's undemanding affection was easier to handle than his own teenage stand-offs.

Now, too, he could understand how his father could no more talk about his own particular hell hole than Jake could speak of Pete's head, warm on his lap, while his guts spilled out on some god-forsaken track in north Germany. He wished Harriet were still around, but she'd married and gone to live in W.A., in a suburb of Perth. There was a son called Jake after him, and another child on the way.

He missed Pete more than he could ever have imagined "When this is all over," Pete had said. "We'll go into business you and me: I'll run the market garden, with Annie helping of course; and you can do the building and decorating. And we'll find a girl for you. There'll be a great need for a lot of building and decorating after all that destruction."

"And in which hemisphere will this be?" Jayjay asked. "Or are you planning six months a year in each?"

"Oh, we'll work it out."

Would their friendship have survived civvy street, he wondered, or his instinctive reservations about Annie? So why now, half a world away, did he feel responsible for her and the child?

The fact was that under the Repatriation Scheme he had been trained to teach history to a classful of kids, but had gained no instruction on how to fill that big inner hole of who the hell he was. A string of brief affairs didn't provide any answers either, except to demonstrate that a returned airman with a limp seemingly represented an attractive challenge. Usually they soon dropped him as too serious – "you've gotta start forgetting all that war stuff". He missed Pete more than ever, and those silences in which they had some of the greatest companionship. Maybe through Annie and Pete's child he might find some sense of continuity or purpose.

So he'd found himself a job on one of the merchant ships carrying beef and butter to the war-weary motherland, and found a degree of peace in that limbo of the several weeks journey. Greg had met him off the ship in a Southampton crouching under grey skies. It was Greg who had found Mrs. Benson's b. and b., and who put him up for a couple of nights in Clapham first. He had changed greatly since their sojourn in hospital: looked fit, had a job in his father's hardware store, a wife who clearly adored him. Jake envied him.

"I feel like I joined a club and no one'll tell me the rules," he told Greg.

"I've been lucky, what with Mum and Dad and Kitty. Mebbe when you've made contact with Annie it'll clear things up in your head. Do you want me to come with you?"

"No thanks, mate." Jake shrugged. "I'll work through it like everyone else has had to."

He caught an early morning train out of Marylebone that rattled and hissed through the drab sprawl of suburbia and eventually into the lowland countryside that would lift into the soft folds of the Cotswolds borders. And so to Mrs. Benson's b. and b. According to Greg's in-laws, Annie had left the cottage she shared with Holy Pete to live with her parents in The Trumpet pub in the middle of Daerley Green. Apparently some guy had moved in with her at the cottage – presumably the one Jake had seen her with – and after a while started beating her up. He turned nasty in drink, the story went, and he was more often in drink than not. The police had been called in and there had been talk of taking little Matt into care, a threat which galvanised Annie into her decision to move.

Jake packed his knapsack, paid Mrs Benson who clearly regretted he was not returning so she could learn the next instalment of the story. But when he boarded the bus, he still had no idea how he would approach the girl, any more than he had when they drew to a stop in the market place of Daerley Green.

The Trumpet was a plain square building, whitewashed brick, overlooking the green. Jake recognised it and the chestnut tree from Pete's photos.

So what now?

Jake pushed open the door marked Public Bar, and was greeted by a combination of stale smoke and the sweet tang of beer. Behind the bar, a woman was washing glasses. Her hair was covered by a turban of reds and greens. Most of her was concealed by the bar, but she was thin and had a slouched defeated look. After a few moments Jake said "Can you manage half a bitter for a thirsty man, love?"

She glanced up, nodded, took a glass to one of the pumps.

It was a shock to recognise Annie. Dark shadows under her eyes accentuated the thinness of her face and there was a fading scar over one cheekbone.

"Annie?" It came out involuntarily.

Her startled expression was followed by one of deep apprehension and she glanced quickly over her shoulder as if for a way of escape.

He said gently, "It's all right, Annie. I'm a friend. Jake. A friend of Pete's."

"Pete's dead," she said flatly. "Died in the war."

"I know, I know Annie. I was with him."

There was a silence that seemed to go on for a long time, though it could only have been seconds. From upstairs a small boy's voice shouted something incomprehensible in a cross tone. Annie glanced instinctively upwards and then back at Jake, pushing the glass towards him.

"They never told me how he died."

Oh God, he hadn't reckoned on this.

She went on "There was a telegram saying he was reported killed." She put a hand up to her head as though dredging out a memory. "They said any further information would be immediately communicated to me. But it wasn't.

Communicated, I mean." Her gaze did not flicker. "So what happened?"

"There was … was an accident." He couldn't tell this woman, the love of Pete's life, that he'd only died because of a ghastly mistake.

"A road accident?" Annie laughed without humour. "He could've had one of them here, and I could've looked after him." Suddenly she turned and shouted "Ma! Pa! Come quick. There's a friend of Pete's visiting."

The moment for truth had gone. Best let it go.

Her father was the first to push noisily into the bar. "So what do you want with my girl?" he demanded, weathered face belligerent.

Annie grabbed his arm. "No, Pa. I said a friend of Pete's, not Billy."

The man stopped dead in astonishment, came round the bar, clasped Jake's hand. There were tears in his eyes. "How did it happen, son?"

Thankfully Annie answered for him. "He was with Pete when he died. A road accident. Isn't that …" She fumbled for words. "Isn't that *stupid* to die in a road accident at the end of a war?"

A small round woman bustled in and there were repeated introductions and explanations. Eventually the round woman went to "get dinner – you'll stay of course" and when the pub closed and they went through to the big, cosy kitchen Annie's father said "You'll stay a few days", as a statement, not a question, and her mother said "I've made up the spare room."

In the end he stayed weeks and it was certainly as cathartic for him as it clearly was for them. Stan, Annie's father, ran an early morning milk round and Jake soon joined him so they were back for a mammoth late breakfast before the pub opened at eleven. Beth, Annie's mother, worked on an allotment at the back of the pub which provided most of their fresh produce needs.

Jake revelled in this newly structured life. Now there was a reason to get up in the morning, and after lunch he spent several hours a day on the allotment completely re-organising it, building a small shed in which to keep the tools and to provide shelter. The news of the presence of Pete's Aussie mate Jake in Daerley soon spread and for the first time in civvy street he found himself accosted wherever he went. In the evenings, when the bar wasn't busy they spoke of Pete. Jake was surprised how much they already knew about him, and now he was able to tell them about their p.o.w. life and the companionship they shared. Sometimes he would take Annie out to the pictures or to a local dance. In a curious way, he no longer thought of her as Pete's wife, certainly not the self-centred young woman that came over in her wartime letters to him. However much the result of her own mistakes, her suffering had softened her and her vulnerability had its own attraction. He went to bed physically tired and mentally fulfilled in a way he had not since the war.

The story of Billy gradually came out. "I never thought a daughter of mine could be so stupid," Stan said. "But she was lonely, and he was a good looking lad and he turned her head."

Initially little Matt alternated between sulks and tantrums. But gradually he took to turning up while Jake worked on the allotment. They found a small spade for him and he would nudge at the earth with it. Then Jake prepared a small corner for him which became known as Matt's patch. They sowed some seeds, planted a few carrots, and every day Matt would go to see how much they had grown.

"That child will miss you when you go," Beth said one evening when Jake returned from reading Matt a bedtime story.

"We'll all miss him," Stan said. "But we can't expect him to live on board and lodging and fresh air for the rest of his life." He looked at Jake hopefully.

"'Fraid not," Jake agreed. "Though I've been happier here than I can remember."

"And your parents will want you back, too."

Jake visualised briefly his parents. As far as you could ever tell what Dad thought, he guessed his absence did not affect him greatly. But his mother, that was something different. And then there was Harriet whose recent letters had become probing. "*In case you're interested your new niece has her first tooth, and your nephew is now at play school. I miss you, Jake. Even three thousand miles seems quite close compared with the present twelve thousand. I'm glad the trip's worked out well for you, but if it's difficult to tear yourself away from Annie, why not bring her here?*"

Harriet had an uncanny knack of crystallising his thoughts almost before they came into his head. Against all expectations he had become very fond of Annie. Not in the sense of a great passion, but in the sense of being deeply concerned for her. Of course he found her physically attractive, and knew it was mutual. In the weeks since he arrived she acquired a sparkle that he guessed was in no small measure due to him.

"You've brought her back to life," Beth said. "That Billy creature beat it all out of her. And yet…" She shook her head in disbelief. "And yet Annie couldn't seem to stop loving the wretched man. Until the last time when he knocked her unconscious and she came round to find Matt screaming and clinging to her."

"So what happened to Billy then?"

"He was going off with some of his good-for-nothing friends. To Ireland, I think. Annie said she was leaving him for good. He just laughed and said he'd find her wherever she was."

Jake put his face in his hands. It was then the germ of a thought had taken root in that layer that was just beyond consciousness. Suppose he took Annie back to Australia. She might not be his absolute ideal, but he had become very fond of her. The Australian Government were keenly encouraging new immigrants. She and Matt would be safe. Better still they could settle in W.A. where Harriet would help her find work, make a circle of friends.

He let the idea mature for a few days and then mentioned it tentatively to Stan and Beth. Stan said "Even Billy might baulk at chasing them that far."

Beth said sadly "It's such a long way,". And then she brightened. "But we'd save up and come out to see you all. When Father has retired."

It was time to ask Annie herself. One evening in the little living room behind the bar, after Stan and Beth had gone to bed, Jake did just that. Her radiant smile was response enough. She capped it with "There's nothing in the world I'd rather do, except have Pete back. But given the circumstances, I reckon he'd think it was a great idea."

"How about Matt?"

"It's the best thing that could possibly happen. You've washed Billy right out of his head. I could love you for that alone; but of course there's more to it than that."

Jake put his arms round her. Yes, Pete would certainly have approved, and may be for the moment that was the best justification he would find. "Maybe Matt will come back one day and find the truth. Or his progeny if he has any." He found he liked that idea.

"I guess he might do that. For the moment I think he's beginning to look on you as his Dad."

There was a brief strange moment as Jake contemplated the idea of himself as the father of Pete's kid. "Best leave it that way for the moment." Then he tightened his hold round Annie's slender frame, determined that they would make it work.

Email exchange, Perth, Western Australia and Daerley Green, May 2002 and March 2003

May 12, 2002 – to the Webmaster of daerleygreen.org.uk,

Could you help me trace a connection between one of my distant relatives and Daerley Green? His name was Joseph Wytham-Smith and he came to New South Wales in the mid-19th century. Are there any Wytham-Smiths still in your town? Thank you very much for any leads you can give.
Rowena Johnson.

May 23, 2002

Dear Rowena Johnson,
Your email to the Webmaster has been forwarded to me. How interesting. It seems our family harbours a criminal streak! I have been able to trace the fact that Joseph Wytham-Smith was transported to Australia in the 1840s for the heinous crime of stealing a loaf of bread, not once but on several occasions. I wonder what happened to him.

Justin Wytham-Smith, no doubt related to him, lived here in Daerley Green – it is a village rather than a town – but alas he died very recently. Perhaps he came here because of that distant connection. I am his great nephew, but have changed my name to plain 'Smith' as I eschew pretention.
Sincerely, Luke Smith.

May 30, 2002 Rowena Johnson to Luke Smith

Dear Luke,
How absolutely amazing. I understand Joseph married my great

great grandmother (not sure how many 'greats'), but it didn't work out too well so they parted and she reverted to her maiden name of Johnson.

Now I hope you can help me further. I'm really keen to visit England, and especially Daerley Green, to find out more. Could you suggest somewhere I might stay? I'm thinking of this in terms of spring 2003.,
Sincerely, Rowena.

June 3rd 2002, Luke to Rowena

Dear Rowena,
Great Uncle Justin was the twin brother of my grandfather and, for reasons I need not go into, we were estranged and I had not met him since childhood. So it was a great surprise to find he had left me his property – a cottage in Daerley Green. The tenants of the cottage will be moving out towards the end of the year and I plan a lot of renovation work in 2003, but it should be completed by the time of your visit, so you would be welcome to occupy it, say, for the month of April. I live elsewhere in the village so we would not inconvenience each other.
Sincerely, Luke.

June 5, 2002, Rowena to Luke

Dear Luke,
You are a star. I'll keep you posted. – Rowena.

January 4, 2003, Luke to Rowena

Dear Rowena,
I imagine you will be finalising your plans soon. This is to let you know that I shall be away from Darley Green from the end of

March to April 20. If you arrive during that time, please get in touch with Mike and Sara Hennessey at Hennesseys@abelsyard.com with whom I shall leave the keys. – Luke

January 15, 2003, Rowena to the Hennesseys

Luke Smith gave me your email address. I hope he has got you up to speed as to who I am and why I'm coming to Daerley – to research my family background. I discovered Luke was a distant cousin, probably several times removed, through the Wytham-Smiths. So now I'm coming to the UK to find out more and especially to visit the places where they lived. You can't imagine how excited I am about it all. Cousin Luke says he'll be away when I arrive on April 12th and that he will leave the keys of the cottage with you.. I hope that's OK. If my flight is on time, I should arrive around midday. I can't wait to meet you and become a temporary resident of Daerley Green.
Sincerely,
Rowena Johnson.

January 17, 2003

We shall be delighted to help you in any way we can. Please come straight to Abel's Yard – our cottage is just round the corner from the Market Place.
Good wishes,
Mike and Sara Hennessey

Sarajevo– January 2002/Minkie

Sarajevo, January 2, 2002

Dear Mike and Sara, *Happy New Year!*

Everything's great, but the weather isn't and I'm really missing Daerley, and especially you. What with this being the time for New Year Resolutions, I keep thinking of something Mike used to say : be careful what you wish for. I remember back in England how I used to long for a proper winter with snow and all that I associated with it. Well, now I'm sick to death of the sight of it. We haven't seen the sun for a century. The clouds sit on the mountain and press down on the city as if they would like to stifle us, and out of them the snow falls, steadily, non-stop, silent, so it's hard work getting anywhere and really difficult to keep warm. Mother is worried all the time about keeping them comfortable in that old people's home she's in charge of.

I've moved into a tiny flat in the market, so I can buy fresh veg almost by opening my bedroom window and leaning out. It's just round the corner from where Bozo lives. He's been very helpful but gets very cross when I moan about the weather. He says I'd know what cold really was if I had been here during the siege, when sometimes they didn't have heating for days. In fact, not having been in the siege is a bit lonely-making, because of course nearly everyone else has been and it's a shared experience which is always cropping up. I don't dare talk about my time in Daerley because I realise more and more how lucky I was and what a chasm there is between my experiences and other people's. The only person I can really talk to about it is a woman who spent the war with relatives in Sweden, but she's ten years older and into dressmaking in a big way, so we don't have too much in common.

Reading the letter to Mike over breakfast in Daerley Green, Sara Hennessey paused and laughed at this point.

"No they wouldn't have much in common. Sewing a button on was a major drama for Minkie."

"Still, otherwise she sounds fine," Mike said.

"You think so?"

"Don't you?"

Sara skimmed through the letter quickly to the end. There was an enthusiastic paragraph about a few days she had spent in Novi Sad with their friends Marija and Bogdan, and she was looking forward to going skiing with Bozo and his friends the following month. And then a string of people to whom she sent her love, topped by Justin. But no, on the whole Sara didn't think she sounded fine.

She passed the letter to Mike and said "I thought that opening with *Everything's great* was a tad over the top. She sounds lonely to me. I'm glad she's had a few days of fun in Novi Sad."

Mike folded the letter and put in his pocket. "I guess you're right. You always were more intuitive than I am. Poor Princess."

"Franko said she probably wouldn't find it as easy as she imagined, settling back there. Well she knows she can always come back here." Sara poured herself another coffee. "You know, I miss her far more than I thought I would. We became quite close those last couple of years."

"Yes, I didn't realise until much later how much I was asking of you: dumping an almost-teenager waif straight from a civil war in your lap when you were already half running the village."

"It wasn't just that. We were living terribly separate lives at the time: you jetting round war zones and I involved in every nook and cranny of Daerley life. But it was also the way you both seemed to have something going that I wasn't part of. Of course you could tune into her background in a way I couldn't." She reached over for the sugar. "Seriously, there was a time when I thought Minkie really became the daughter you'd always wanted and we couldn't have. And I confess to feeling … well, just a bit jealous for a while."

"Which was the last thing intended."

"Of course, I know that – even knew it at the time, with my head, but not with my heart. Something to do with self worth, and not even being able to produce a kid like everyone else. Still that's water under bridges and all that." She leaned over to pour him a coffee. "What are you doing today?"

"Research session in the Bodleian. Why don't you come into Oxford with me? We could meet for lunch."

"Can't do. I've promised to produce an outline scheme for a new website for Pippa."

"Do you think we'll ever mutually retire into a quiet old age."

"At forty-something I think we can put that off for a bit longer."

Oxfordshire - Spring 2002/Sara

In the end Justin Wytham-Smith died, as he would have wished, in his own bed in the Fieldings Nursing Home. Sara Hennessey, who visited him two or three times a week, was at first amazed that someone once so bulky, now so shrunken and frail, could dodder on for so long. "Preserved in aspic, dear girl," he joked, and there was probably lot of truth in it, for the Fieldings was renowned for its cosseting and Justin was a popular inmate.

In time Sara took Justin's new persona for granted, slotting her visits in to her busy Daerley Green life as she had always slotted commitments large or small. Indeed he survived another six months after the events around 9/11 which had changed the world and sent major tremors through the Hennesseys' lives. In the end, she took Justin's on-going presence so for granted that when the call finally came, it was a great shock.

"He looks very peaceful," the warden Janet said when she telephoned. "One of the night staff answered his buzzer at around 4 a.m., but he'd gone by the time she arrived."

Sara went to see him straight away, before he was removed to the Chapel of Rest. On the way she nipped a sprig of forsythia from the bush by the front door of the cottage. It was one of his favourites. "Pure gold," he used to say. "Like you, dear girl."

Her throat tightened. The sadness was not for him – he had become impatient to go; but for herself and the void left.

Justin did indeed look peaceful, propped up on his pillows, hands resting over his chest on the counterpane. She placed the sprig of forsythia on them. They didn't look like his hands but like waxwork impressions, as did his head resting against the pillows, the lines and wrinkles that had made it exclusively Justin's face smoothed out in death. She wanted to kiss his forehead, but was afraid of its coldness. *God speed, dear friend,* she thought.

He had probably known as much about her as anyone, apart from Mike. Indeed, more than Mike, for in recent months she had shared with him things that she had shared with no one else; and he had reciprocated. For the first time, she had learned that he had a twin brother James with whom he had an exceptionally close relationship. Then James had been badly traumatised by his experiences on the Somme in the First World War. Justin had made it his mission to extricate him from the deep black hole into which he had sunk; but he failed. And then… At this point Justin had paused and finally said "Well, maybe that's for another time," and she had never discovered what he had been about to say.

The funeral was arranged for the following Wednesday at the Crematorium: a private service for the family. No flowers by request.

"It feels all wrong," Sara protested to Mike as they worked in the garden that week-end. "As though he's being excised from my life without trace."

"Well, it's the family's right."

"Which, according to Janet, means one great nephew by name of Luke who's making all the decisions. I don't even remember Justin mentioning his name. Anyway I don't see that it is their right to deprive the village of the opportunity to celebrate Justin's life. I shall arrange a gathering here after the funeral for any of the family who wants to come and anyone from Daerley who feels like remembering him."

Mike watched thoughtfully as she jabbed at a recalcitrant weed. He had always been the gardener and it was rare for Sara to join him. He suspected this was about a lot more than Justin's death. A whole chapter of their life ended following the departure a few months earlier of Minkie, their Bosnian foster daughter.

"Minkie burst into tears when I rang Sarajevo," Sara said, confirming his suspicions. "But of course there's no way she can come over." Her voice trembled. She tugged at the weed viciously. "Bloody, bloody thing."

Mike put down his spade, went over to pull Sara gently to her feet and put his arms round her. "Hey," he said. "No one could have done more for Justin these last months. And yes, we'll have a small party here and give him a good send-off."

Sara issued her invitation to 'Justin's party' to a dozen of their mutual friends, and left the details with Janet to convey to Justin's relatives. In the end she decided to make a bouquet combining flowers from Abel's Yard with some from The Fieldings' garden and make sure they got to the Crematorium in time for the service. There was a particularly fine early gardenia that Justin had been able to admire from his sitting room window. It was just coming into bud as he pointed out when she last visited him the previous week.

On the day before the funeral she slipped over to The Fieldings to complete her bouquet. The garden was quiet in the Spring sun. A blackbird foraged for worms in a newly turned bed watched intently by a robin from the branch of a nearby prunus. How Justin would have enjoyed watching them, Sara thought, and was briefly startled by a movement from the direction of his sitting room window overlooking the garden. Of course, the infamous Luke.

She made a snap decision. It was absurd to harbour ill feeling towards a man she had not even met. Without further thought she went through the garden door into the building, along the familiar, overheated corridor to Justin's door. In answer to her knock it was opened by a slim young man. Thirtyish, dark hair and dark eyes that gave nothing away. Nothing even remotely to remind her of Justin.

"I'm Sara Hennessey," she said. "An old friend of your uncle."

"Great uncle," he corrected, standing aside to let her in.

Justin's flat was in orderly chaos, furniture moved against walls, books in piles, pictures stacked. He observed her dismay.

"I'm Luke Smith," and when she looked surprised added "I don't hold with this double-barrelled crap. Thank you by the way for your letter. I will reply."

"There's no need." Sara felt growing discomfiture under this unflickering inspection. She went on briskly "I adored your great uncle. Lots of people in Daerley were very fond of him. Of course we respect your wish for a private ceremony, but some of us would like to meet and commemorate his life. Hence the small gathering Mike and I are arranging at our place, Abel's Yard, tomorrow evening. I imagine Janet passed on my invitation to you?"

"She did, and you are very kind. I'm afraid it's unlikely the family will be represented, though of course I can't speak for all the others. None of us is really into playing happy families." He paused and appeared to make an effort, adding more warmly "I'm glad the old boy found so much friendship in his last years. I always thought of him as a bit of an old curmudgeon. Or perhaps 'boring old fart' would be a better description of my memories." Luke became cool again. "But I mustn't keep you. I'll pass on your invitation."

Back in the kitchen of Abel's Yard arranging the flowers, Sara re-ran her first encounter with Luke Smith. A cold fish if ever there were one. She shrugged. None of her business. She'd probably never see him again.

She was wrong. The next afternoon Abel's Yard was crowded with Justin's local friends, twice as many as anticipated. Several had moved out into the garden, stood among the clumps of tulips or under the cloud of cherry blossom half way down towards the old oak tree. Over the years Mike had turned their little patch into one of Daerley's horticultural gems.

Sara felt herself watched, looked up to see Luke's dark gaze upon her. She went over to him, surprised and pleased. "Oh, you've come."

"The only one I'm afraid. All the others have hurried

back to their various points of the UK compass. But I suppose it's an advantage of being self-employed. Anyway there are still things to sort out here."

"Are you staying at The Fieldings?"

His nose wrinkled in distaste. "No, I've checked in at the local hostelry. The Trumpet?"

"It used to be a favourite of Justin's. Mine, too, when I could manage to join him – usually when we'd put the village mag to bed." Sara stopped. Why on earth was she gabbling away like that? She added "That was a while ago when I edited the thing."

"Yes, I'd gathered that you're one of Daerley's luminaries. And your husband a foreign correspondent?"

"Was. He's moved into contemporary history."

"Oh? So he and great uncle Justin had quite a lot in common?"

"Not really." Sara paused, remembering when Mike, too, had more than once referred to Justin as a boring old fart. "Anyway come and meet him and some of Justin's friends."

She noticed that he made a real effort to be pleasant with them, and that his lean ascetic face quite changed when he smiled.

"How on earth did the Wytham-Smith genes produce such a cold fish!" Mike commented as they restored order that evening.

"I though he rather improved on a second encounter." Sara said. "Odd that Justin never talked about him, especially as I gather he's inherited the lot – cottage, goods and chattels. I imagine he'll sell. Didn't strike me as country gent potential."

Gradually the news filtered through the Daerley grapevine. Luke Smith was keeping the cottage, which would have been difficult to sell anyway with a sitting tenant, and had moved into a two-bedroom semi-detached on the outskirts of Daerley Green. Apparently he did something clever with computers.

But Sara had more immediate concerns. An email had arrived from the Bosnian Serb couple that Mike had befriended while reporting on the break-up of Yugoslavia. They had made a life for themselves in the Serbian city of Novi Sad where the wife, Marija, taught and was in demand as an interpreter at international seminars. Now she emailed to say she was coming to a conference in Oxford. Was there any possibility ….?

As she prepared Minkie's old room for Marija, Sara thought back to a general exchange of confessions when Mike had told her that long ago, as a student doing Europe, he'd had a brief affair with Marija. It was long before he and Sara had met and she genuinely believed that he had not resumed it when their paths had finally crossed again during the Bosnian war. By then Marija had in any case teamed up with Bogdan. Both had lost their partners and Marija her two children in the war, and now they had come together to bring up Bogdan's surviving daughter Snežka.

Mike met Marija off the Flights bus in Banbury. They were already well into the 'do-you-remembers' by the time they arrived in Daerley.

It was Marija's first visit to England and she was child-like in her curiosity further boosted by the fact the Queen's Jubilee was only a month away. Daerley Green planned a packed week-end of events and, as usual, Sara was in the thick of it. She would return from some committee meeting to report on the latest spat or agreement and, in return, they drew her into their discussions, mainly about Marjia's concerns for Snežka's and, even more, Serbia's future. Sometimes watching them, Sara tried to imagine them together all those years ago. And couldn't.

"Bogdan thinks it would be good if Snežka came to England. To improve her English, perhaps work with a family. She is not an easy child."

"That's teenagers for you."

"That is not main problem. With her story, growing up has not been easy."

"I'm sure we could find a family for her. And keep an eye on her. I always thought she was a great kid," Mike said. He had a swift memory of her earnest little face and angry words "Why you bomb my country." Minkie had never been so spikey. But then Minkie had always been different.

It was a good opportunity to ask how Marija had found Minkie when she visited them in Novi Sad some months earlier. Marija hesitated, then said "She seemed happy enough when she was with us, but I don't think her return home has been as she expected. Her experiences of these last years have been so different from those of other young people. She is – how you say? - the odd one out."

Marija's visit also coincided with a series of television documentaries spawned by the Jubilee.

"You think she wanted to be queen?" Marija wondered aloud as they watched a very young Princess Elizabeth playing with Corgis on a lawn and later visiting bomb sites in London.

"Poor girl didn't have much choice."

"I think I would have chosen to run away."

And later still, "Oh, but she is beautiful," as newsreels showed the Princess returning to England from Africa a few years later, following George VI's death.

A week after Marija's arrival, Sara was sitting on the bench in Whirling Wood, a mile out of the village. It was a place she came to when she wanted a different space in which to think. The wood was at its best at this time of year: the soft silvery growth of willow and the fresh green of ash contrasting with the still semi-dormant state of the young oaks. In a patch of meadow there was promise of a good showing of ragged robin and oxeye daisy.

A figure approached.

"Good morning Sara Hennessey," Luke Smith said. "May I?" He dropped on to the seat beside her.

"This was another of Justin's favourite places."

Luke grimaced. "My venerable great uncle haunts this

village. I see everyone scrutinising me and marvelling at the complete lack of family resemblance."

Sara laughed. "Oh dear. But I suspect you're very much your own person and it won't worry you unduly. How are you otherwise settling in to Daerley life?"

"Quite surprisingly. It creeps up on you in a curious way. You meet someone who knows someone who knows someone and suddenly you're 'in'. The fact I'm a golf enthusiast probably helps."

"Ah, you've met the Tremaynes."

"A fine specimen is Amanda. Not so smitten by Beresford."

"They're old friends of mine."

"Oh." Luke grimaced. "That's the trouble with the incestuousness of village life. You have to be very careful what you say and to whom. And you … I hear you have a Balkan guest."

"My goodness, you *are* in the loop aren't you! It's an old friend of Mike's attending a conference in Oxford."

"Funny how the past comes back and grabs you at times, isn't it?" And funny how she had been thinking the very same thing. "One of my great-greats was something diplomatic in Yugoslavia before it existed, as it were."

"Justin's father. Yes, he had splendid stories about childhood holidays there. It was one of the things that drew Minkie to him, of course."

"Hm. I can't get away from the old boy can I? And now I have just discovered that through him I have a remote connection in Australia. A young thing called Rowena who plans to come to Daerley next year and research family history." After a moment he went on "Did you know that my grandfather was Justin's twin brother? Now, there really was a gem of a man."

"As a matter of fact I did," Sara said, but once again she thought how extraordinary it was that he had not mentioned him until he was almost on his deathbed. Still, it was quite pleasing to be able to take the wind out of the sails of this arrogant great nephew of his.

Luke was undoubtedly surprised, but nodded, then rose to go. "By the way, one unexpected discovery among his things was a diary. Perhaps you didn't know about that. Reams of it, all in minuscule writing. And immense detail."

And that did make Sara faintly uneasy, as she watched Luke's slim figure recede through the trees.

Oxfordshsire :Spring-Summer 2002/Luke

He had found it buried in the middle of a pile of old magazines and newspaper cuttings. Sitting on the floor in the spare room surrounded by paper, it took Luke a while to recognise the diary for what it was. Then he debated whether his great uncle had been deliberately concealing it or whether his Civil Service training had won out in the end and Justin was about to consign the lot to a shredder. Well, he would never know.

On closer examination the other piles of papers proved to be, not scrap, but selected pages and clippings, each neatly identified and dated. Then he recalled Justin's passion for collecting press references to his particular interests, most of them boringly associated with events in the Balkans and the Middle East. It was clear that at one time the cuttings had been filed according to subject matter, and no doubt somewhere there existed a card index methodically cross-referencing them. Probably he had uncharacteristically shoved them into a heap when obliged to down-size for his move from the cottage to The Fieldings.

The diary was written on sheets of A5, each year kept in a separate transparent folder. The first surprise was the minute writing, compared with his normal sprawling scrawl; cultivated presumably to save space and perhaps to make it less tempting to read. Luke saw that the diary only covered the years Justin had spent in Daerley Green and his next instinct was to chuck the lot out. But as he flipped idly through some pages his attention was caught by references to names now already familiar to Luke himself: Sara, Mike, the Tremaynes, especially Beresford. And, above all, the ubiquitous Minkie.

Given Luke's own lack of interest in humanity, it was ironic that he came from a line of travellers with a predilection for going native, or at least trying to understand how the natives ticked. Well, not all of them. Not his grandfather, but then he'd been the odd one out in more ways than one.

"*No!*" Luke said sharply, and snapped his mind shut against further proceeding down that particular road of betrayal. The sound of his own voice, so vehement in the otherwise empty house, came as a small shock. He swallowed, looked round at the eau de nil walls of the spare room which he had made his overflow office. It could still surprise him how, after so many years, those feelings which he had so deliberately buried would stir in their grave. Like some dormant Frankenstein. But then it was hardly surprising, given how inseparable his grandfather and great uncle had once been that the association with the latter should trigger bitter-sweet memories of the former.

Impatiently, he pulled the first sheets out of the first plastic folder and began to read.

April, 1991

The removals men have left. The woman next door has invited me for a soupçon to eat and I have declined. She is an occasional weekender from London so should not encumber me with too many intrusions. Patronising old fart, Luke thought, and began to feel better.

There are boxes everywhere: of linen, of tableware, of kitchen utensils, of books. Especially books. I told the man called Kev to dump them anywhere as long as it left me a clear passage through to the downstairs lavatory, the kitchen and the stairs. Their dominating presence gives me the illusion of purposes for my life stretching into an indefinite future.

It is, or will be, a pleasing cottage. Correction, cottages. Three benighted families lived in what I will learn to call home, no doubt each blessed with much progeny, and all at the beck and call of the lord of one of three manors who once ruled the community and many surrounding square miles.

Dear me, even now I cannot resist recalling the past before contemplating even the first thoughts of the present, let alone the immediate future. How it used to bore everyone, especially the younger members of the clan. And especially poor young Luke who will probably inherit all this one day."

The last thing Luke had expected was to see his own name. And why the hell 'poor Luke'. He felt a surge of resentment at the thought of Justin's pity. He turned the pages quickly. Nothing more. Justin had rambled into some kind of timetable for what he needed to do in the coming days, and whether and how he would insinuate himself into the Daerley Green social scene.

Luke sat back on his heels. For the best part of a quarter of a century, he had had virtually no contact with Justin. All he knew was that he was something respected and fairly high up in the Civil Service, travelled a lot, had a bachelor pad in Westminster, wrote articles and a couple of books, was occasionally on current affairs programmes, retired and disappeared into the sticks of northern Oxfordshire. His death had been a bolt from the blue. Even more so that solicitor's letter announcing his inheritance.

The jangle of his mobile made him jump.

"Luke? Amanda here. Amanda Tremayne." He pictured her lively face, fly-away haircut, full mouth. "Beresford and I wondered if you'd like to join us for a round of golf tomorrow? May be lunch at the Club afterwards?"

"I'd be delighted."

"Good. Nine o'clock not too early? Obviously the round will be with Beresford. As you known my golf is something you wouldn't want to know about." The laughter bubbled in her voice.

Luke smiled at the receiver. No, but there were a few other things about Amanda Tremayne he would very much like to explore further. "I look forward to it," he said.

The day was fading. He got up to switch on the light, surveyed the papers strewn over the wall-to-wall bland beige carpet. Wouldn't old Justin be surprised to learn how well he was integrating into the peasant lands of Middle England?

Though perhaps not. He had never got to know Luke, the adult. Luke himself had made bloody sure of that.

He switched the light off, went downstairs to the small living room with sliding door on to conservatory and patio. A bottle of Scotch stood on a corner dresser where he'd left it after inviting a neighbour in for a nightcap a week, ten days ago. Luke was no great drinker, loathed the idea of any loss of control, but a celebratory drink, now that was something different.

He poured himself a generous one, added a dash of tap water and took it into the conservatory, still warm from the day's infusion of spring sunshine. He noted the lawn needed cutting, but otherwise the agents had maintained the garden well, it had to be said. Dead boring of course: a strip of lawn surrounded by straight beds full of perennials and some low-maintenance spiraea, mallow, potentilla Maybe he'd add a risqué statue or two, and get that Hennessey woman to advise him on some more interesting plants. All depended on how long he stayed. He sipped his whiskey. It was quite odd but he had a feeling he might be here quite a long time.

And yet a prolonged visit had been the last thing on his mind as he drove to Daerley Green a few days before Justin's funeral. Get it over with, put everything in storage, and get out, that was the original plan. So what changed? Certainly it was nothing to do with the brief re-encounter with an assortment of cousins; or the soulless service at the Crematorium led by someone who knew nothing about Justin. Well, that had been his, Luke's decision. It was never his intention to give the old devil a great send off.

But that Hennessey female had done that, in spite of him. Luke had paused to read the message on the only bouquet of fresh flowers placed on the grass by Justin's name outside the chapel. *Thanks for all the gleams of brightness you brought to grey days. I guess no one could read me as well as you - SH.* Well, that was open to a lot of interpretations. What in God's name had she seen in the old boy?

Intrigued, he had gone to that party of hers and found the sort of cosy set-up he would normally disdain; and a bunch of people who were intelligent and indisputably nice, a galaxy away from his usual small circle of friends who all spoke as though they had swallowed computer users' guides and shared 'in' jokes that pigeon-holed the rest of the world as accordingly 'out'.

He still had not meant to stay, but there were a lot of papers to sort out. And he owed himself a breather. Since he had left Uni-Comp Inc and set up his consultancy, he had worked his socks off. The fact that quite a few of Uni-Comp's clients had come with him had ensured him enough security to establish a firm base from which to plan future expansion. To what degree he had poached them from Uni-Comp's global network would be very hard to prove. The fact remained that he'd been stepping on and off international flights ever since, the hours between spent either working out the next software programme or applying it to some spanking new conglomerate almost anywhere in the so-called developing world.

The act of stopping imposed by Justin's death had left him with an unprecedented sense of limbo.

It was the handling of people that he couldn't seem to get the hang of. In all his life there had only been two human beings that he had loved unconditionally: his grandfather and a fellow university student with mousy hair and grey eyes you could wish to drown in. Both had betrayed him. So, people had become instruments to feed his requirements: expand his business, improve his environment, satisfy his appetites. The latter were ascetic enough. Only occasionally did he allow himself the indulgence of sexual gratification and that only with a partner he could be sure would not be unwise enough to make emotional demands.

He thought of Amanda and smiled.

He had first met her and Beresford on his second evening staying at The Trumpet. Amanda's maturity – she must be at least ten years his senior – had a ripeness that was deeply attractive. Within a couple of hours he'd accepted an invitation to join them at the Golf Club for dinner next day. Which had led him into a foursome at golf from which Amanda was sadly absent, but awaiting them with sparkling eye and moist lip at the 13th hole. He had absolutely no doubt the attraction was mutual.

A local estate agent found him this dreary little semi-detached to rent. He liked its lack of personality. Within a couple of days, Justin's furniture was in storage and all his papers transferred to the eau de nil spare room. There was no reason why he could not operate as well out of Daerley Green as out of his Islington flat. He arranged for a friend to keep an eye on the latter, and for mail to be forwarded.

He joined a Leisure Club a few miles from the village and when Amanda suddenly appeared at the pool in a stunning electric blue swim suit felt no surprise; only a sense of the pre-ordained. They were soon meeting there three evenings a week, with a couple of drinks and stimulating banter in the bar afterwards. Swimming wasn't Beresford's sort of thing, Amanda said. No, it wouldn't be,

But Luke was in no hurry. He was beginning to feel the cocoon of Daerly Green enfolding him: a new, strange but not unpleasant experience. A full blown affair with Amanda would finish it. A flirtation could be kept going for quite a while. It made sense. And, in the long run, it was more exciting.

He poured himself another Scotch, smaller this time, and returned to the spare room. He did not recall noting Amanda's name in his quick riffle through Justin's diary, but Beresford's had been frequent. It did not take him long to find the earliest references: a couple of meetings in the ubiquitous Trumpet. "*...... interesting fellow. With a name like that I might have wagered his career had featured the F.O. But no, he began as a reluctant financier and is now something to do with golf courses.*"

A little later Justin recorded his decision to have a small soirée, introduce the Tremayne fellow to some of the great and good of Daerley Green. About the same time he was expressing concern for Sara who seemed very 'down in the mouth'.

But it was the entry on the morrow of the famous soirée that was really rivetting. The soirée itself was dismissed as a modest success, but in Justin's eyes it was clearly dominated by one event.

"*How truly amazing. It seems that Beresford Tremayne and Sara were at school together. The dear girl did not appear entirely delighted to see him, was quite cool with him. But he was obviously bowled over and, indeed, she looked quite ravishing in great contrast to the rather drawn look of recent months. Not for the first time I wished I were several decades younger myself. On the other hand, I suspect Sara and Mike may be experiencing something of a crisis of confidence in their relationship. A very small crisis I trust, but one that will certainly not benefit from any external complications.*"

Luke re-read the entry before returning the sheet to its folder.

Well, well. Daerley Green was getting more interesting by the minute.

Western Australia – October 1982/Jake

Odd how even after all these years he still spoke to Pete on a regular basis. Usually in his head, of course. Sometimes the conversation would begin with a jocular "*See what a fine mess you've got me into, mate.*" But more often it was a quiet chew-over of events as you do with an old friend, even an invisible one.

Later, when he worried about Matt, he would share this with Pete, but Pete would only tell him not to worry as it would always come good in the end. Of course, Jake wasn't stupid enough not to realise Pete was merely verbalising his own wishful thinking.

Occasionally Annie overheard these one-sided conversations and pulled his leg. When he asked her if she didn't think of Pete she said quietly "You're better'n Pete for me, Jake. He was too nice, too soft."

He'd tried to lighten the mood by joking "You mean I'm not nice? Hard?"

"You saved me and Matt," she replied, staying serious. "I wanted things easy and found out the hard way life ain't like that. To answer your question – no, I don't think much of Pete. That was another life, and I was another person."

Pete's fair hair would have turned grey, Jake supposed, just as his own dark mop had done. He took it for granted that Pete would have retained his wiry build, unlike Jake who, to put it kindly, had developed into a sturdy middle age. Annie was always on at him about diet and exercise, but he'd had a sweet tooth too long to be able to overcome it for anything other than a medical imperative, and he kept well clear of doctors. As for exercise, since his retirement he did the several-mile trail that linked the two shores of the Swan River by two main bridges several times a week. It was towards the end of this circuit that he stopped a while in the paperbark swamp in Sir James Mitchell Park in South Perth to converse with Pete.

This would usually cause a flurry of alarm among the magpie larks but if he were quiet for long enough and there weren't too many others passing through, he would usually glimpse the stealthy movement of night heron or straw-necked ibis. And then he'd come out from the gloom under the paperbark trees and find a bench by the river, looking out across to the silhouette of the city. The central cluster of high rise buildings created a focus for the eye, but wisely the city fathers had vetoed any further upward expansion. It remained a pleasing sight.

And heaven knows they had enough space. How Pete would have loved those massive skies and spaces. But that was a pointless line of thought. Had he lived, would Pete's marriage even have survived the discovery of Annie's affair? Jake reckoned it would have destroyed him. But he had no regrets at his decision to bring Annie and Matt back to Australia with him, to marry her and bring the boy up as his own. He thought it had worked out well, at least for Annie, though they rarely spoke of it. The traumas of her life with Billy seemed to have reshaped her. It was true that she and Jake had little in common, but their sex life was fine if unfruitful, and if there wasn't much intellectual communion, well so be it. Jake's parents had accepted her, even his father had welcomed her with more monosyllables than usual, no doubt relieved that his strange son had found someone to settle down with. But it was probably a good thing they had chosen to make their lives the other side of the continent in W.A., where Harriet had been a gem, helping Annie to settle, find a school for the boy, encouraging Annie to do a course and make some kind of career for herself, while Jake pursued his chosen path as history teacher. She had decided on hairdressing. What a good thing so many women found an insatiable need to change their hair styles. Later Annie had added manicuring to her skills and was happily employed by a small beautician's whose Italian owner was pleased to give her as much work as she wanted.

It helped that this part of South Perth was almost a Little Europe. Annie had fitted easily in among the ever widening range of accents as the new immigrants flooded in, not least the so-called Ten Pound Poms who arrived in droves in search of new prospects and a new life away from the austerity of post-war Britain. She was a good listener and, on many an occasion, Jake came home to find Annie consoling or advising some recently arrived young waif, struggling with the strangeness of tin roofs, outdoor lavatories and huge spiders.

And she had coped admirably with Matt. It had become clear early on that he had more of Billy than of his father in him, both in looks and in temperament. There had been a time back in Daerley Green when, as a very small boy, Matt had followed Jake everywhere, his way perhaps of compensating for the loss of the only role model he had ever known, fickle and volatile though it had been. In their earliest days in Perth, Jake and Matt had explored together, at one point chancing upon a derelict building that had become Matt's favourite haunt. How strange children could be. It was no more than one of the abandoned barracks used for housing immigrants from England if they had nowhere else to go, now neglected and increasingly derelict, like the buildings of an abandoned wartime airfield back in England. How he wished he could live there, Matt said. Whatever the reason, Jake was glad enough to take him there and spend time only a short walk from the river where they would swim and in the evening trawl for prawns in the shallows.

And then suddenly Matt had begun to prefer the company of his peers: tough kids mostly a little older than himself who knew all the secluded places where they could experiment with the contents of an array of bottles, usually nicked from shops in a neighbourhood other than their own. And Matt discovered wonderful new sensations that made him feel as strong and daring as a lion and everything else seem childish. And when occasionally he was very sick the others would laugh at him and say, "Good on you, kid. Now you're all set to start again." And miraculously so it was.

He was only eleven when Jake first found him sleeping off a drinking spree behind the shed at the bottom of the garden. Annie was unsurprised. The macho beer culture of a section of Australian society was heaven-sent for a child of Matt's temperament. After that Matt's progression from headstrong child to tearaway teenager seemed to follow a pre-written script.

Jake had made the mistake of trying to appeal to his better nature. "You're a disgrace to your Dad," he shouted at him once.

"Well, since you're not him, you can get off my back," Matt had shouted back.

Stan and Beth came over for a visit from England. Stan had given up his tenancy of The Trumpet, but they'd bought a cottage just outside Daerley Green.

Thankfully, when Stan and Beth came, Matt was away in Queensland with some of his mates, leading pretty much a beachcomber's existence as far as Jake could make out. But he was grateful for the young man's absence. It was hard to think what he might have found in common with this quiet ageing couple from middle England. Instead they met Harriet and her personable pair, both well launched respectively into careers in engineering and human resources, and if Stan and Beth assumed Matt was in a similar mould, well all to the good.

"You wouldn't recognise Daerley," Stan reported. "Shops closing, big new housing estates bringing incomers from all over the country. Some of them are nice enough, but they seem intent on livening the place up with amateur dramatics and history societies and such like. Some of the older folk aren't too keen, but a big new community centre has been built with all sorts of sports facilities and that's helping to keep some of the youngsters in the village instead of getting up to no good around Banbury."

It was a bit of a relief that Matt did not erupt home as he was wont to do. Stan and Beth returned to the UK after extracting a promise from Jake that he would send Annie home for a visit while "we still have most of our marbles." He had kept his promise and Annie had gone home for a month to Daerley Green a couple of years later. It was during her absence that Matt had made one of his eruptions, this time in the middle of a summer of work experience on a wine farm near Margaret River. With him was a pretty, waif-like creature he introduced as Tracey. "We're having a baby," Matt announced, "so I guess we'll get married."

Jake was surprised that he showed that much responsibility, though in practise it meant that he and Annie were funding both and, eventually, all three of them. It was a good thing that Annie took so thoroughly to Tracey, caring for her as though she were a daughter. Briefly after Rowena's birth, and perhaps because he was present at it, Matt was quite besotted with his tiny daughter. In a few months, though, the novelty wore off and he resumed his nomadic life style, disappearing for long periods and living on goodness-knows-what, but at least it made for a much calmer life for the rest of them. Occasionally they heard echoes of Matt from an unexpected quarter – Jake's parents, now well into their eighties and living in a suburb of Sydney.

"Your Matt called to see us," Jake's mother wrote one day. "He doesn't sound a bit like his Dad, but your father has quite taken to him." Jake almost detected her surprise through her writing and decided that human relationships would never cease to amaze him.

Meanwhile, Tracey did a computer course and began advertising a word processing service from home. She was a meticulous worker and soon built up a steady clientele base. When Rowena was two, Matt came back to Perth and settled for six months. He got a small apartment a few minutes walk away, moved Tracey and Rowena into it, and took a job in a d.i.y. store. It was their first and last taste of family life, but it also provided an opportunity for bonding between father and daughter that left disturbing repercussions when one Saturday he left home and didn't come back. Rowena screamed for him for a week, eventually subsiding into a sullenness that became her hallmark mood. She and her mother returned to live with Jake and Annie and life went on much as before. By now Annie had acquired such a network of friends there was never a problem to find someone to child-sit for Rowena while her mother was working. And it was one of her friends Emma who began a kindergarten where Rowena first faced that essential life skill of interacting with her peers. And did not take to it very well, her interaction with her peers usually taking the form of confrontation rather than collaboration.

"She can be a little horror when she doesn't get her own way," Emma told Annie after the first week. "I guess she'll grow out of it – or hopefully learn to put it to good use. And we've found one unfailing way to distract her. She's turning out to be a real nature buff. When we go for a walk in the park, it's a job to tear her away from the lakes and all the bird life going on."

"She'll have got that from her grandfather."

Tracey became busier than ever with her computing. It was a help when Rowena progressed from kindergarten to pre-School which at least kept her occupied for four afternoons a week, though she remained an exceptionally solitary child. Jake managed her the best, simply ignoring her moods and taking for granted her interest in whatever they might be doing together until the assumption translated itself into fact. With her fairness and blue eyes and tendency to deep contemplation, she was indisputably Pete's grandchild and Jake rejoiced in her. Rowena took to calling him Grumps.

He started taking her to the paperbark swamp. He'd check the bird books so he could tell her about the seasonal movements of the different species, though sometimes he felt as if he were telling Pete as much as Rowena. He also realised that Rowena was taking the place of the child he and Annie had never had. They started keeping a record book, he and Rowena, pasting in pictures of the species they saw, with some comments on the circumstances in which each was seen. Rowena had a surprisingly good vocabulary for her age and became very cross if Jake tried to change her little texts.

"When she's older I'll tell her how we listened to the nightingale and watched the geese fly over the camp," he told Pete in his head

He had become ever more solitary since retirement. While he was teaching, the kids had kept him from atrophying, the dull ones constantly triggering his urge to kick-start their curiosity, and the bright ones challenging the very value of history since 'nobody ever seems to learn from it, do they?' Were they right? Was it all a hideous delusion that an understanding of the past might make an iota of difference to the future? Then one of his pupils would do something unexpected, like produce an essay of great insight, or he would learn some of them had become involved in some movement or charity as a clear consequence of something recently discussed in class.

"I guess in the end," he told Pete, "what it comes down to is you can choose to be part of the problem or try to be part of the solution."

Once Rowena started at pre-School, it became Jake's job to collect her. They would walk home via the paperbark swamp, pause on the quayside to watch the ferry crossing to or from the city centre, then stop for ice cream or hot chocolate, according to season, at one of the coffee shops in South Perth. On these occasions she was a different child, chatting about a day whose events clearly existed in her head rather than in reality, producing drawings which he suspected her teachers never saw.

Then came the day when the pre-School teacher greeted him with "But she's already gone, Jake."

His heart plummeted. "Gone? What do you mean gone?"

"Matt collected her after lunch. He'd just arrived back – from Brisbane I think …."

Jake had gone before she finished the sentence, racing as far as he was capable of racing back across the park, then along two blocks left, one block, right and finally bursting into the bungalow on Angelo Street. Annie was not back. No sign of Rowena. Tracey was at the computer.

"Has Matt been here?" Jake fought for breath to get the words out,.

"Matt? Matt's in Brisbane, Jake."

"He collected Rowena from pre-School three hours ago."

Tracey screamed "No!", stood up abruptly, tipping a glass of juice over her jeans and the text she was copying.

Over the following hours, Jake racked his brains trying to work out where Matt might have gone with the child. Irresponsible though he could be, he was far too devoted to her to risk any harm coming to her. And with W.A. so difficult of access from the other States he would certainly not have attempted to take her beyond its borders. And then he suddenly remembered the derelict barracks that had played such a prominent part in Matt's childhood.

He reached them at dusk which, here in W.A., was a much more short-lived affair than he learned to expect of it in Europe. It was a huge relief to see a glow of light from one of the windows and recognise Matt's ancient four-by-four parked at the side. He noted that this end of the building looked in a good deal better condition than he remembered, and certainly much better than the rest of it. Someone had recently painted the door green and there were even curtains at the windows.

Matt opened the door to his knock and uttered an unsurprised "Oh."

As Jake followed him into the main room, he was astonished to see that it was quite well furnished.

"Does whoever this bclongs to know you're here?"

"Well, I'm not exactly trying to hide the fact."

"No."

"A mate of mine – his dad is in charge of keeping an eye on the place until it's pulled down. Says it's OK as long as I keep it in good nick."

"Which I see you do."

"Yeah, well I do odd jobs every time I'm in the area. And I pick things up cheap at garage sales. It soon mounts up." With the two of them standing in the small room it felt almost crowded. "Sit down," Matt said.

He sat down himself, reached for the glass on the table by the stove. He had clearly been drinking, but not enough to be aggressive or uncomprehending. As far as Jake knew, he was a binge drinker going for quite long dry periods, though he suspected the binges were closing up on each other. Matt went on now "I guessed you'd work out where we'd gone." "We"? Thankfully Jake now spotted Rowena curled up on one of the bunk beds fast asleep.

"You wanted to be found?"

"I suppose." Matt shrugged. "I can hardly be on the run with…" He jerked his head in Rowena's direction.

"No, you can't, son."

Matt lifted his glass, looked at Jake over the top of it, and tossed back its contents. "That's part of the trouble, I'm not, am I? Your son."

"No." Jake held his gaze steadily. "No, you're not, though I've always tried to bring you up as though you were."

"Carrying the torch for your dead pal?"

"Cut it out, Matt," Jake snapped and Matt said straight away "Sorry, booze isn't best mates with good sense. What I really mean is I envy you that kind of friend. Mine have never come anywhere near."

That reminded Jake of something. "Have you ever thought of going back? To where your Dad was born and grew up?"

Matt shook his head. "Guess I prefer easy options. Life suits me here. Why look back? Maybe I did inherit some things from Billy. You know, nurture not nature. His 'live for the day'. His taste for booze. P'raps Rowena will do it for me, go back to Dad's place."

They were both silent, then into the silence a small sleepy voice said "Grumps – are you really there?"

Jake went over to stroke her head. "Yes, I'm here, sweetheart. Daddy forgot to tell Mummy where you were going, but I guessed because this is where Daddy and I used to come a lot when he was little."

"Clever Grumps," Rowena muttered, and went to sleep again.

"So what now?"

"You take her home to her mother. I just wanted a bit of time with her. And I'll make my way east, find my pals on the Sunshine Coast and see if I can work out what to do with the rest of my life."

"I'm always here for you."

"Yeah."

Matt found a tin of stew, heated it over the stove and they ate, mainly in a silence that now seemed companionable. When Rowena woke again, she allowed herself to be transferred to Jake's car without protest. Matt kissed her, but his farewell was thankfully restrained.

Father and son faced each other. "'Bye Dad," Matt said. "And thanks."

Jake raised his arms a little, half in acknowledgment, half in helplessness. Then he got into the car. Rowena was fast asleep again long before they reached the main road.

Sarajevo: Spring 2002/Minkie

On the lower slopes of Jahorina, Minkie sat on a wall looking down on the jumble of minarets, domes, spires, towers of Sarajevo. It was one of her favourite views and one of her favourite thinking places, but she surveyed it now with unusual detachment triggered by the letter she held in her hand and which she had just re-read for the fourth time.

"*Dearest Princess,*" Mike had written. *"Don't be sad that you couldn't come to Justin's funeral. It was arranged by his great nephew Luke, who clearly didn't want anyone from Daerley involved. Funny Justin never mentioned him. Anyway Sara and I both thought he was a cold fish, so it was quite a surprise when he turned up at the little party we had at Abel's Yard as a sort of farewell to the old boy. About twelve people said they were coming and twice that number turned up. The place was ringing with 'do-you-remembers' and your name cropped up more than once. Remember Polly who used to work in Sara's shop? Well, she was there with the oldest of her brood...."*

Minkie looked up from the letter, smiling, remembering, no longer seeing the rooftops of her wounded city but the market place in Daerley Green and overlooking it Sara's shop with its tasteful collectibles, presided over by Polly. Minkie, just thirteen, homesick, afraid, bewildered, for the first time in her weeks in England had felt at ease with the young woman, then extremely pregnant, not so very many years older than herself. Polly, who had barely heard of Sarajevo and certainly had no idea of where it was.

"*... Sara said you'd be sad if I told you, but I know my Princess likes to have the facts as they are. Anyway, nobody from Daerley went to the funeral, but Sara made sure there were some flowers there, a mixture of Justin's favourites from Abel's Yard* *and the Fieldings. And that made me think it would be nice to have a bush in our garden to remind us of him, so I'm planting one of those gardenias he liked so much, in that small bed on the house side of the old oak. Sara thinks I'm a sentimental old thing, but you know that already."*

She could picture the spot exactly where the gardenia would be. For years, once she'd grown up just a bit and begun to feel at ease with Mike and Sara, but especially Mike, Minkie had got into the habit of joining him when he was at home on what he called a tour of the estate, a pre-breakfast potter round the garden to check what was what. She'd learned a lot about plants and garden birds that way, and even more over the years about what made Mike tick. She'd come to realise that the marriage hadn't always been easy. There'd been Sara's affair – at the time she would have furiously denied it, but with the hindsight of maturity there really wasn't much doubt.

"*Now we have Marija staying with us for a few days. She thinks it would be a good idea if Bogdan's daughter Snežka could come to England for a while, perhaps as an au pair. Remember how she chatters constantly – so different from when you first came. Still, I shouldn't make comparisons.*

"We were quite surprised to get a letter from Franko recently. As you know I never quite trusted that cousin of yours – was rather glad to see the back of him when he decided to take his nefarious activities off to Germany. But it seems he's planning on coming back here and opening an agency in Banbury. Completely legit according to him. That'll be a first!

"Do you ever hear from Jesse? Or perhaps I shouldn't ask...."

No she didn't hear from Jesse, or hadn't now for two months. It had stopped hurting. Maybe they had just outgrown each other. Sometimes it was difficult to think of herself as that person who had worked and lived and loved with a young American called Jesse for a whole year in Oxford. They'd been so sure they would make their lives together, but she had insisted that first she must return at least once to Sarajevo. Her return here with Jesse had coincided with the seminal events of 9/11. Jesse had suddenly remembered who he was, where he came from and that terrible event had triggered in him an imperative need to go home. Minkie had felt the equally imperative pull of her roots and decided to stay in Sarajevo. They had exchanged emails frenetically for a while, but the tone of his – and presumably hers – had gradually changed. He sounded ever more American, ever more accepting that he had made the right decision. She visualised his world, clean, fresh, air conditioned, homogenised, and knew hers had been the right decision, too.

It was only recently that there had begun to be time to feel alone, uncertain, afraid.

"*....But then you know I always thought Jesse lacked your maturity.*

"So what else is there to tell you. Oh, cold fish Luke has suddenly discovered an Australian connection: a remote cousin called Rowena who's coming to Daerley to research her family past. Probably next year some time. All these comings and goings. And you know how unsociable I am. You'd better come back and help me cope!"

If only, if only.... Minkie looked up as the muezzin's call to prayer was taken up by one mosque after another across the city. Between the buildings, she picked out the green patches of the cemeteries – Christian, Jewish, Moslem - which marked it as a place that had welcomed all comers over the centuries. Only time would tell if that would become true again. For the moment an increasing number of her Bosniak female contemporaries were covering their hair with the *hijab*. Their lives had been so different – hers in comfortable middle England, theirs in the hellhole of besieged Sarajevo – that she had little in common to discuss with them. When she expressed her surprise to one of her young cousins, she was told "Wearing it gives me a great sense of freedom, that's why." This seemed very odd to Minkie until she remembered that quite a few of her Serb Orthodox friends had suddenly become devout church attenders. It was as if that terrible divisive conflict had pushed them each deeper into their corners. Could any believable God really care what the inhabitants in this remote part of His creation wore or said? It hadn't stopped many of them dying messily at each other's hands.

From the distance, it was difficult to identify the scars of mortar blast and sniper fire on individual buildings. Already a huge programme of reconstruction had filled gaps and restored the damaged neo-classsical facades of Habsburg times. In her view, *baščaršija*, the even older bazaar quarter, had been too prettified. It could have done with a bit of the scruffiness she remembered from her childhood, when most of the items on sale were hammered or carved or spun in cramped workshops at the back of the little boutiques. She suspected a lot of the wares nowadays came from a good deal further afield, but the tourists all thought the bazaar was quaint and probably didn't read the labels. They probably didn't either notice or care that the new mosques rebuilt with foreign money had two or more minarets compared with the single one of the traditional Bosnian mosque. It was Mother who had pointed that out.

Mother didn't often comment on anything that might be deemed politically incorrect. In fact, she didn't comment much on anything outside the day to day problems of running the Old People's Home where she was director, or on matters relating to Minkie's return to her birthplace. Minkie found it a little unnerving. She had become so used to open discussions with Sara and, especially, Mike that she found this reticence in expressing opinion on things that really mattered irritating, at times angering. Gradually she came to realise it was a deeply ingrained part of the mechanism with which her mother had learned to cope with loss, anxiety, fear and deprivation. Even Minkie's prodigal return – a snotty-nosed just-teenager now a confident, attractive 22-year-old – had required a process of assimilation.

Sometimes Minkie caught her mother's look of dismay or bafflement as Minkie came out with an expression contrary to what might be expected from a well-brought up young woman from Sarajevo. She also asked remarkably little detail of her daughter's life in England. After the initial euphoria of reunion, Minkie found this apparent lack of interest hurtful, then just another of the imponderables in re-finding her place in her native city. Heaven knows her cousin Franko had warned her that her return might not match her expectations. She gave a wry smile remembering her visions of cosy outings with her mother revisiting favourite childhood places. For a start many of them were in the surrounding mountains where visits were strongly discouraged as they were still peppered with unexploded shells and mines. And when they had visited Father's grave it had been like standing at the grave of a stranger. Beneath it lay the remains of the man whose hand she had been holding when he was hit by sniper fire. She had torn her hand free and run screaming into the house. If she had come in when she had first been called, he would not have come to get her, might still be alive …. But she had already lived through those arguments a million times in far away Daerley Green.

Now a new factor had come into the equation. Mother was clearly unwell. She denied it vehemently and rejected any suggestion that she should see a doctor, but Minkie had registered that the weariness she showed was more than just the result of her dedication to the job, though this undoubtedly didn't help. She seemed incapable of relaxing, like a clockwork toy that had to keep going until it had run down. But more recently Minkie had noticed how sometimes she winced in pain, dismissing it as nothing when challenged and becoming angrily impatient if Minkie persisted.

She talked to Bozo about it sometimes. He had lost a leg during the siege and was still running the multi-ethnic horticultural enterprise where she had first come upon him soon after her return to Sarajevo. Now she worked with him, or rather the charity that financed the enterprise.

Bozo said she just had to get on with life as they all did. After all, she had chosen to come back and most people didn't have that kind of choice. He could sound quite hard but she knew that in recent weeks he had become rather fond of her. Once he'd suggested she might move in with him, and she'd laughed before seeing from his expression that he wasn't joking. But for heaven's sake, Bozo must be older than Mike!

Mother said she could do a lot worse and that reaction had alarmed Minkie more than anything, as though a trap were closing in. She thought back to her long-ago hopes of recreating the city of her childhood - thoughts that Franko had shared, too, only he'd been obliged to face the reality much sooner. What an irony that her once-suspect cousin had ended up with an agency in Banbury, completely legit, according to Mike's letter.

Minkie folded the letter, slipped it into her pocket, stood up and took a deep breath. It had been her decision to return to Sarajevo; there was nothing to stop her reversing it. Mother would be sad, but not that sad. She might even visit Daerley Green. A bit of courage, a few emails and telephone calls. Thoughtfully she made her way down the steep dirt track back to the city.

Western Australia : 1995/Rowena

Matt's brief abduction of Rowena marked a watershed in her childhood development. She became withdrawn at home, disruptive at kindergarten. Suddenly, the paperbark swamp bored her, and so did Jake.

"It'll be better when she gets into the bigger school," Tracey said hopefully.

But it wasn't. Because she was naturally bright she did well in class, but never showed an inclination to join any group activities. When Tracey suggested she might invite friends home, her answer was a huge shrug and a muttered "they're all boring." Team games were anathema to her, but happily she proved to be a good swimmer, eventually representing the school. Keeping up her training provided her with the ideal and acceptable excuse not to participate in all the sports she hated.

And then, aged fourteen, she met the ill-christened Grace. Grace was sixteen coming on 25: a well built girl, skilful in drawing attention to her physical attributes and with an ability to be extremely charming when it suited her. And Rowena suited her nicely. Grace thrived on her devoted admiration and soon found satisfaction in moulding her admirer in her own image. She also drank, could hold her liquor well, and was clever at concealing both the bottles and the effects of their contents. She was a good teacher in these skills, their practice taking place in a hideaway she had found a mile or so from home on some derelict land: an isolated place where Rowena's first clumsy experimentation with alcohol could occur without witnesses. Dependent as Grace became on Rowena's admiration, she had no intention of allowing her to spoil what had become a very enjoyable fantasy life style. And once she had been on the receiving end of Grace's sharp tongue for losing control after a few beers, Rowena soon learned her own limitations.

Tracey thought it was great that an older girl should take such an interest in Rowena. Jake saw through her straight away. And if Rowena, with the aid of liberal splashing of cheap perfume and much sucking of peppermints could deceive her mother, she did not fool Jake.

"You've been drinking Ro," he challenged her frequently, stating not asking. Always she denied it vehemently and began to avoid him more and more. She had long opted out of walks with him, pleading more urgent demands on her time – homework, school activities, a rendez vous with a friend – usually Grace.

It was Tracey who found her sleeping it off one Sunday at the bottom of the garden, more or less where Jake had come upon Matt in a similar condition so many years earlier. When she at last realised from her behaviour and smell that her daughter was crawling out of inebriation, Tracey said sadly "So Grumps was right all along."

"I wish you'd all get off my case," Rowena shouted. "I'm *four*teen for heavens sake."

Jake had not discussed Rowena's behaviour with Matt since there seemed little to be gained from it. Matt was still eking out some kind of existence on Queensland's Sunshine Coast and began to telephone quite regularly. It was when Jake saw the effect that Rowena's behaviour was having on Tracey that he finally decided it was time to involve her father, blurting it rather more baldly than intended and before he had time to notice that Matt was uncharacteristically subdued. He was silent for so long that Jake said "Are you still there?" just as Matt was saying "Christ, you don't want to be lumbered with a female version of me."

"I love that girl, Matt. It breaks my heart."

Another silence, then "Leave it to me. I'll call her around nine this evening. Try and make sure she's there."

It was then Jake registered there was something different about Matt. "And you? Are you OK?"

"Yeah… No. No, I guess I'm not OK. Two of my best

mates topped themselves yesterday in a motorboat accident."

"Oh Matt…."

"They were fooling about. It needn't have happened." His voice cracked. "Didn't you always tell me you get out of life what you put into it? They were drunk."

"Things aren't always that black and white."

"Yeah, and sometimes they are."

When the phone rang just after nine that evening, Jake let Rowena pick it up. He heard her delighted "Dad? Hi!" and quietly went out of the room.

From the kitchen he heard "Great" repeated several times, interspersed with a quieter murmur and quite long silences as she listened. At last he heard "Yeah, absolutely wicked. See you," and a final clunk of the receiver replaced before the door was flung open.

"Grumps, Dad has had a simply magic idea. He's gonna arrange for me to stay with Greatgrumps and…"

"Greatgrumps?"

"Your *father*," Rowena said impatiently. "…and Greatgran. And Dad'll come down from Brisbane and show me the bright lights of Sydney and…"

"And has – er – Greatgrumps been consulted?"

"Of course." Rowena's impatience grew. "They think it's a wicked idea too."

And how wicked, in all its senses, they may well learn the hard way, Jake thought. And his next thought was how very surprising that Matt could turn deviousness to such a positive purpose.

Greatgrumps and Greatgran lived in a terraced house in a quiet suburb of Sydney. Rowena could hardly remember them from an early childhood visit from which she retained a vague picture of a silent old man and a white-haired old lady. It was a disconcertingly accurate picture, she discovered, though she had not remembered how discomfiting Greatgrumps' pale blue gaze could be.

Still, she wasn't too worried since the main purpose of the adventure was to see the bright lights of Sydney with Dad. And Greatgran made a real fuss of her without asking the boring questions that old people usually did, like what did she want to do when she was grown up? But the days passed and there was still no sign of Dad.

"What's keeping you?" she asked him crossly when he rang at the end of the first week.

"Sorry, sweetheart. Something's come up. Let me have a word with Granddad."

Next day, Rowena was sitting on the porch, unpicking a knitted jumper for Greatgran without much good grace. Greatgrumps was in his rocking chair in the open door into the living room, seemingly reading. Suddenly he asked "So why did you do it?"

Rowena frowned at him "Do what?"

"Your father says you get drunk, are sick all over the place."

Wait till she got hold of Dad. "Oh, that. I was bored wasn't I?"

"So it was exciting was it, throwing up in the flower beds? Being sent home from school. Worrying your mother to death."

Rowena shrugged. "Not my fault if life is boring."

Greatgrumps took off his little half-moon spectacles, placed them on the small table by his chair, closed his eyes. Rowena thought he had fallen asleep and was about to creep away when, still with his eyes closed, he said "If you were eating a bowl of some sort of soup and someone's eye landed in the middle of it, would that be exciting? Or you put your hand out and felt another hand, only it was just lying there, not attached even to an arm let alone a body, would that be exciting?" He opened his eyes and met Rowena's horrified disbelieving stare. "Well, would it?"

"That's disgusting."

"So is throwing up in flower beds. The guy who lost his eye, and the one without a hand, they didn't have a choice."

He closed his eyes again, leaned his head back. Rowena didn't like silence, so she said "We're doing Gallipoli next term. You know, war stuff."

Eyes still closed, he nodded. "Odd to think my life is your school history." The thin old face cracked into a small smile and Greatgrumps opened his eyes. "I don't suppose you can imagine me then, not so many years older than you are now."

It was a challenge. Rowena took on challenges. She put down the old sweater she was unravelling, leaned forward and looked intently into his face. With age it had lost flesh so that the nose seemed sharply pointed. The eyes were faded blue above sunken cheeks. Impossible to turn any of them into youthful features.

Greatgrumps made an impatient "Tschuk!", reached back on to the window ledge behind him, brought down a framed picture. As far as Rowena knew, it had been there forever, but she had never looked at it before. Not really looked.

It was of Greatgrumps and Greatgran on their honeymoon. Greatgran had a funny old fashioned hair style which flopped forward hiding much of her face. But Greatgrumps was open faced, laughing, handsome, with a little moustache. Rowena looked at it for a long time, then back at the old man, and then the photograph again.

"You look really cool," she said at last, and he knew enough to recognise it as a compliment.

"She was very beautiful, your great grandmother," he said. "We were so young, only eighteen, but we were very much in love and the only answer seemed to be to get married before I went to war. By the time I got home your Grumps was two years old."

Rowena went on holding the framed picture, looking at it. "Tell me about your war," she said.

So he began and went on telling her, talking for hours

over the coming days as if a dam had burst, not only about the fear and the tiredness and the hunger and the smell and the lice, but about the comradeship and the laughter; and about the humanity they had found in the most unexpected places. Once, after a big battle, there had been so many dead and wounded that the smell and the cries were terrible; and someone arranged for a truce long enough to collect the wounded and bury the dead.

Greatgran interrupted. "You'll give the child nightmares."

"No he won't," Rowena said, because these were the most amazing things she had ever heard, and she couldn't wait to tell Grace all about them.

So Greatgrumps described how the Anzacs had climbed out of their trenches, and the Turks out of theirs and, side by side, they had set about tending their comrades, burying the dead ones, carrying the living ones to safety. It was then, Greatgrumps said, we began to see they were suffering just as much and were just as afraid as we were. Sometimes their trenches were so close to each other they could clearly hear other's conversations, even if they could not understand the words. They began lobbing tins of bully beef into the enemy trenches, and got chocolate and grapes in return. "The grapes were especially good," Greatgrumps said, his gaze and his mind far, far away. But it hadn't stopped the carnage from continuing.

It was all so vivid that the sounds and pictures stayed in Rowena's head, sometimes seeming more real than the sights and sounds of Sydney, when Dad eventually turned up. He stayed a few days and listened to Greatgrumps' stories and they seemed new to him, too.

"We're doing Gallipoli at school," Rowena told her father. "All battles and dates and numbers of casualties. Boring. They ought to have a Greatgrumps in every classroom to turn those casualties into real people."

"You're a bit of ghoul, aren't you," Matt teased.

"No, I'm not. But it makes you wonder why we keep

having wars. You'd think someone might have worked out how pointless they are. What about Grumps – presumably he was in the next war?"

"Yeah." Matt was silent for a long moment, and then added something very puzzling. "It changed my life. And yours come to that. Ask him to tell you about it some time."

On her return to Perth, Rowena was so absorbed in telling Jake all she could remember that she forgot to ask him about his war. He listened quietly, marvelling at this new insight he was getting of his father, sad that he had not asked the right questions at the right time himself. Grace, in contrast, was quick to discourage Rowena from talking about all that boring stuff she had already had rammed down her throat at school. So Rowena lost interest in Grace and started hanging out with a mixed group of teenagers. Some of them were into sex but after her first few experiences of clumsy fumblings, Rowena decided either she was getting it wrong or it was highly overrated. When challenged by a worried Jake she vehemently asserted "I don't do drugs". But she certainly continued to do alcohol.

She really looked forward to those trips east to stay with Greatgrumps and Greatgran for part of the summer holidays. But a year later, Greatgran died and Greatgrumps was finally obliged to give up his unit and move into Great Ends, a residential home. Fortunately the couple who ran it happily took in Rowena for bed and board for modest rates. Jake assumed the arrangement might be disastrous. But no. In addition to Greatgrumps, Rowena discovered a whole community of ageing men and women with whom she found a surprising affinity and whose amazing tales she now began to inscribe in a small stiff-backed book so that she could tell Jake all about them on her return to W.A. Sometimes she felt she was leading two lives: the carefree, let-it-all-hang-out one with her peers in W.A., and the briefer but in some ways more intense periods of sharing in Greatgrumps' life.

Then one evening the two became confused. Rowena had gone for a stroll in the neighbourhood, found a neat bistro she hadn't noticed before, gone in for a coffee, met a group of the local young, stayed for a bottle of wine. And another. And another. The full effects didn't hit her until she was half way back to Great Ends. She was mad at herself at first, and then felt a deep resentment that it wasn't all right to be a carefree teenager like all the others. Then she went behind a wall to vomit and crouch there until several groups of people had passed, hearing their snatches of conversation, wondering if ever in her life she would be able to sound as they did, so at ease with thc world.

By the time she reached Great Ends, she was full of self-loathing and resentment. She had never been so late and the doors to the entrance lobby were bolted.. When there was no reply to her fourth or fifth ring, Rowena began knocking on the door, quietly at first and then with increasing urgency, accompanied by appeals that became insistent demands.

She was finally heard by two of the night staff who had been attending to a minor emergency at the back of the building: a male nurse and a porter. They were not gentle with her, bundling her in and towards her accommodation with an unbroken commentary on her lack of control, her ego, and the effect it might have on the residents who had done more in their lives to earn their rest than she was ever likely to do. Back in her room, Rowena was sick again and fell into bed where she must have crashed out for she awoke some hours later fully clothed. She forced herself to undress, take a shower, dress, and went down to Greatgrumps' room feeling like death.

He was reading the paper with the magnifying glass that he now needed. Without looking up he said "So why do you do it?"

"I don't. You know I don't. That's the first time that's ever happened here…."

"That's not what we were discussing."

So why did she? "It just makes me feel so good. So powerful. As if I could do anything in the world."

"Mmmm. And then there's the not remembering what'll

happen if you don't stop."

"But there's no need to remember, is there? Not when you absolutely *know* that this time's going to be different?"

"But it never is, is it? I guess that's why they knew it would always work, that stiff tot they gave us before they sent us over the top. God, it made us feel powerful, too. Powerful enough to get out of those trenches and get killed."

The ill feeling filled her like the end of all hope, and the sense of shame was the worst of all. "Sorry, Greatgrumps."

"Don't feel sorry for me. *I* don't feel like you're feeling. But you've got it all to come – all those wonderful years of exploring who you are and what you will do with that knowledge. I put my life on hold somewhere in 1916 and no one showed me how to take up the threads again, though heaven knows your Greatgran tried." Suddenly he turned the focus of his pale blue eyes on her. "Rowena, Rowena. These summers with your visits have been some of the best of my life. I think you've got something out of them too. Just remember this one basic thing about alcohol – it's not the effect it has that matters in the long run, it's the illusion you allow yourself that you are the one still in control."

"Sorry, Greatgrumps," she said again. "Maybe it's just in the genes, and I've inherited it from Dad; though I wonder where he got it from."

"Not from his Dad, according to your Grumps."

Rowena looked at him in bewilderment. "What are you talking about? You know he didn't inherit any such thing from Grumps."

"Precisely." As he noticed her deepening puzzlement, the old man put a hand up to his head, began to say something, changed his mind. "I had no idea you didn't realise. You'd better talk to Jake when you get home."

Rowena did not waste any time. On her first evening back in Perth, supper over, the washing up done, Tracey back at her computer on some rush job, she challenged Jake.

"Grumps."

"Mmm?"

"You are my Grandad, aren't you?"

"What a funny question to spring on me. Your Grandad? What makes you ask?"

"Something Greatgrumps said. And then there was something Dad said about what you did in the war having affected his life, and mine."

Jake began to speak, changed his mind and sat deep in thought, dredging through layers of memory that stretched across half a century and half way round the world.

After a while Rowena said impatiently "For heaven's sake say something." There was a tremor of anxiety in her tone."

"Sorry sweetheart," Jake said at last. "I can quite see how you came to be confused. After all it's something I suppose has never really cropped up: the fact that your Dad couldn't remember – God, never even saw his real father."

Now, the following silence was broken by a small muffled sound and looking across at Jake, Rowena was shaken to see the tears streaming down his cheeks. She bounded over to put her arms round him, rocking him as sometimes he had rocked her when she was sad. "Don't Grumps. I don't know why you're sad, and I'm sorry, sorry, if it's my fault."

Jake stroked her head, sniffed, fumbled for a handkerchief, blew his nose. Then slowly, quietly, he told her about Pete, how they had met, about the camps, and the march, and the friendly fire, and how he had lost his best friend in the world.

When at last he stopped Rowena said "I can't believe you haven't told me all that before?

Jake shook his head. "In some way, though a day never passes when I don't think of Pete, it's a part of my life that was quite separate from everything that happened before and since. Our life as a family here has always seemed so separate, so self-contained .... And then when your Gran died a couple of years ago …" He looked at her helplessly. "I don't know, Sweetheart, I just don't know."

Rowena went on staring at him, this new amazing knowledge slowly filtering into her comprehension. "So," she said at last. "Some trigger-happy moron took some pot shots at a column of men thousands of feet below on the ground without checking out who they were, and completely re-wrote my life for me."

Her anger took him by surprise. "Well, it wouldn't have been like that. Everyone wanted the war over. Try and imagine, Europe was exhausted by five years of fighting, millions had suffered unspeakably …"

"So was that a reason to kill a few more, for no more reason than they happened to be in the wrong place at the right time? And no, I can't imagine. I don't begin to have any idea what it was like, so maybe that's what I have to do - go to Europe to learn what it was like," Rowena stormed, "and find the bastard who murdered my grandfather."

"And what good will that do?"

"I'd have thought you of all people would understand. It seems I've been living some massive lie for the whole of my life in a country – a continent - that might have just been some far away place I might one day visit if some toerag hadn't picked off my grandad because he was feeling trigger happy one day over Germany." She burst into tears.

Jake said quietly "Has it been so bad, living here with us?"

Rowena wailed. "No of course not. It's just that I'm not sure who I am any more, or of the bits of the jigsaw that make me tick. May be I never have and that's why I've been in such a muddle. Now I want to know everything about this place whose name I can't remember and that I'd never heard of until a few days ago."

"Daerley Green."

Jake went over to his desk and, after shuffling around in a

drawer for a few moments, he brought out an envelope and riffled through a small pack of photographs.

"I found these among your Gran's things after she died. There should be more somewhere, but it's a start."

He spread them out on the table. There was the pub run by Gran's parents in Daerley Green; the farm where Granddad Pete had worked; the thatched cottage with Gran, young, fair, fluffy-haired, standing at the gate; a sequence of snaps of Matt at various ages, scowling out from under a mop of thick black hair.

Rowena went on staring at the photographs. "What was he like, your friend Pete?"

"I think you would have been very satisfied with him as a Granddad," Jake said.

Oxfordshire – April 2003/Rowena

"Perhaps we should've offered to meet her at the airport," Mike said at breakfast on April 12th. "Not much fun arriving unwelcomed the other side of the world."

"Well, it's too late now," Sara observed, "Anyway, we can take her under our wing once she's here. Though in the first instance it will have to be your wing."

A telephone call the previous evening had summoned her to an urgent job at the publishing firm in Banbury for which she freelanced. After a stint at his desk, and a sandwich and beer at The Trumpet round the corner, Mike settled for an afternoon's gardening. The garden had always provided his place of therapy for dealing with pre-occupying thoughts and they were particularly preoccupying during this time of the escalating shock and awe bombardment of Baghdad. 'Shock and awe' had become the mantra of the politicians and journalists most of whom had probably never been anywhere near a bomb, never mind an onslaught on this scale. All he could think of was the poor devils on the receiving end.

"It'll provide the best recruiting agent for the suicide bomber brigade you could wish for," he said bitterly, watching the orange and black spumes billow above the city skyline.

"But we had to do something," Sara countered. "We couldn't let that awful man flout international law indefinitely."

She couldn't seem to see that this was precisely what the Coalition had done itself.

He was dead-heading the tulips in the front when the taxi drew up. As he helped Rowena with her luggage, he noted appreciatively the elfin face framed in long bouncy fair hair. "Who would have thought Luke could have such a pretty cousin."

"Is he not pretty himself? Well, it's a pretty distant cousinship." Rowena turned back to pay the taxi driver, reached in to hump out a rucksack almost as large herself with a large stuffed koala bear sitting on the top. "Hello, I'm Rowena Johnson, and you have to be Mike Hennessey." She saw a tall man, dark hair touched with grey, early-forties, squarish face with lines that told of both worry and good humour.

"Definitely, not," Mike said. "Luke pretty, I mean. And yes, I'm Mike, and Sara is very sorry not to be here to greet you. I thought we might have a traditional English cuppa and go through Luke's notes before I take you across to the cottage. It's only a short step."

He left her in the living room with a sheaf of typed sheets while he went off to make tea. She spent a few moments absorbing the room's feel, book-lined walls, ornaments and pictures that told of distant travels. The room had a comfortable self-contained silence and, through the window, there were glimpses of a well kept garden. Luke's notes were prodigious but well organised with sub-heads and sub-sub-heads and cross references covering every imaginable question and contingency.

"Phew!" Rowena said, as Mike returned with the tray. "Information overload you might say."

"Yes, Luke tends towards precision. In that if in nothing else he takes after his great uncle."

"You don't sound very taken with my distant cousin."

Mike shrugged. "I hardly know him. Truth is Luke does not make himself readily knowable. And that is in direct contrast to his great uncle. Justin was a great friend – well, especially of Sara, and even more …."

Rowena followed his glance to the photograph on the windowsill and went over to look at it. Large dark eyes above high cheekbones, framed by long black hair returned her gaze. "Your daughter? She's lovely."

"Foster daughter. She's gone back to her roots in Bosnia. She was just a kid when she came to live here and became our daughter so to speak. Yes, she's lovely. Then a couple of years ago she went back, and decided to stay."

"That was a great thing you did." Rowena put the picture back on the windowsill. "You must miss her."

"It was right she should go back." Mike avoided a direct answer. "And she keeps in touch."

Rowena stayed by the window looking out, "What a beautiful garden."

"My pride and joy," Mike came over to join her. "You're good at saying the right things, aren't you?"

"My family would be amazed to hear that. Especially Grumps. That's my grandfather. At least I thought he was until a few months ago. That's one of the reasons I'm here, to research the family."

Mike nodded, assuming it was not necessary for him to be privy to her conundrums. Heaven knows his own past had been fraught with enough imponderables. "Next time you come I'll give you a conducted tour of the garden. And you can tell me more about the grandfather who isn't. If you want to."

"I'd like that."

They were collecting up her luggage in the hall when the doorbell rang. With an impatient exclamation Mike flung it open to a young man, thirty-ish, good looking, well-dressed.

"Oh, Franko," Mike said discouragingly. "It's you."

"Yes it is. Good afternoon Mike. I hope you received my message."

"Yes, I did, but you forgot to mention when you might arrive. I'm afraid this really is not a good time."

"That is clear." The young man's glance slid from Mike to Rowena, and paused appraisingly. "Perhaps tomorrow morning?"

"Yes, yes. Come at ten o'clock and Sara will be here too." Mike almost nudged him out of the way with Rowena's large suitcase. She followed, the rucksack on her back, pulling the smaller vanity case by its handle on wheels.

It took Rowena about three days to get on top of the jetlag. She used the time to make Luke's cottage her own, installing her large Koala bear by name of Bunbury on the fireplace in the living room; buying enough flowers to bring colour and freshness to rooms that had been lifeless for too long; pinning up some of her own sketches of home in the kitchen and tiny hallway. Luke rang her from London on the second day to announce his return at the end of the week.

She also used the time to try and get in touch with Granddad Pete's world. She couldn't yet think of him as her grandfather: Jake had taken that role for too long – all her life in fact. Pete was still just a smudge of a young man on some old dog-eared black and white photographs that Jake had found after much rummaging. And Annie, her grandmother, just a smudge of a young woman with fair fluffy hair standing at a cottage gate.

Rowena found the cottage after much probing down by-ways, on the edge of the village. Clearly off-comers had bought it and spent a great deal on modernising it. It was a picture postcard cottage with roses round the door, a big swinging seat on the patio at the back and solar panels let into the roof. Clearly environmentally friendly people. It was also obviously only used at week-ends and empty, so she had plenty of time to poke around.

The Trumpet, which Annie's parents had run for years, had been completely refurbished too. Going in for a coffee one morning, Rowena found not the smallest echo of familiarity to tell her that she had ever had the remotest connection with it. The present owners had only been in residence a couple of years and knew little of its history, let alone its previous occupants.

It was then she suffered her first attack of homesickness. The depth of it took her by surprise. Heaven knows she had travelled enough through the length and breadth of Australia, New Zealand, the nearer parts of Asia. But this England where people looked much as they did at home, and more or less spoke the same: this was something different. Daerley Green was enchanting, just what any Aussie would expect an old-world village to be, and she thought she might get to like it a lot. But these people were so buttoned up. Friendly smiles, curious glances, but don't-get-too-close-please-before-we-know-you-better. Sara had made contact and come round for a coffee, admiring her drawings and Bunbury, but clearly preoccupied with many involvements and commitments.

Oh well.

By now familiar with the by-ways and alleys of Daerley Green, Rowena headed for The Trumpet on her fourth evening. Whatever else, it had a reputation for good English cooking, a phenomenon that she had yet to experience. She settled for roast beef, Yorkshire pudding, roast potatoes and parsnips, carrots, and couldn't fault any of it. She was awaiting apple pie and custard when she became aware of a familiar figure approaching: thirty-ish, well-dressed, good looking. Outrageously good looking. Mike's unwelcome visitor Franko.

"We were not introduced," he said.

"Well, clearly you are not a Pom."

"What is Pom."

"Do sit down. Short for Pommie. It's what Australians call the British when we want to be less than complimentary. But don't ask me why."

Franko looked puzzled, then smiled making him even more good looking. "Not Pommie. I am Franko from wherever I happen to be. But I was Franko from Bosnia."

"Oh, the same place as Mike's foster daughter?"

"So you know already about Minkie? I am her cousin. Mike thinks I am bad influence for her. He is perhaps right. Or was. Some things I did were as you say dodgy. But now I am business man and good boy." He glanced at Rowena in way that made her doubt it.

"Anyway, your Minkie is a long way away now."

Franko sighed. "Too far. But I hope to change things. I hear life is not perfect for her in Sarajevo these days."

The apple pie arrived. Franko ordered coffee for them

both.

Rowena said "I never did understand all that terrible civil war business."

"How can you understand when we do not understand it? But we must do the best we can with new situation. It is more easy for me, I am Bosniak, that is from the Moslem community, at least in theory, though in practice I only believe in what I can do for myself. Minkie is half Serb." He smiled at Rowena's patent incomprehension. "It is long story. I tell you when we become friends. I hope it is so we become friends. But now you tell me why you come so far to be with the Pommies in Daerley Green."

So Rowena, aware that she was enjoying the appraising looks of this attractive man, told Franko about Jake and how he had been with her grandfather when he died and how he had then befriended her grandmother, brought them to Australia and helped to raise her father.

She grinned. "I see that not surprisingly you are confused.

Franko grinned back. "I see your family relationships are as complicated as mine. And how about this Luke whose house you are living in. Are you sleeping with him?"

Rowena gave a grunt of shock. "You don't mince your words do you?"

"Mince…?"

"Oh never mind. Not only have I not slept with him, I have not even met him. He is a distant cousin of my grandparents."

Franko put a hand to his head in mock despair. "Please no more relatives. I have not met Luke either, but Sara tells me he is cold fish."

"Funny, personally I found Sara a bit on the cold-fish side herself. I preferred Mike."

He shook his head sadly. "Mike does not understand me. Sara has woman understanding. I go to see her when Mike is not there and tell her I am worried about Minkie because I love her like a sister, and I know it is not right for her to stay in Sarajevo. After war everything different there. She wants to make things the same as before, but not possible. I learn this long time ago.

"So what was this dodgy thing you were doing? If you feel you can tell me."

"Oh yes, I feel. It was smuggling things, people. Now I'm completely legit, squeaky clean. I have office in Banbury to help the new Europeans find jobs here. This is good place for them. English people not like some jobs, but Poles, Czechs, Slovaks, they are very happy to do any jobs and be here. Send money home and still have enough to live. I am thinking perhaps it would be better if Minkie come back here now and work with me. She is very good with people, probably even better now her American boy friend go home."

"You didn't like him?"

"He take Minkie's attention away from me." Franko gave his big disarming grin. There was no denying his great attraction. "You have boy friend?"

"No, and I'm not looking for one."

"OK, I just be your friend, though I cannot stop being boy."

Rowena laughed. "Time I got some shut-eye. Can't think why it's taking so long to crack the jet lag."

"Perhaps you must also crack the culture differences," Franko suggested shrewdly. "I find it so every time I come back. It is so with some English, they speak one thing and mean another. Please tell me I can be your friend, and that you will come and see my fine office in Banbury very soon." He handed her a business card.

"Yes, and yes again," Rowena said as she tucked it away in her wallet and fished out a credit card to pay the bill.

In bed that night, she extracted Franko's card from her wallet. *Matchmakers*, she read, *linking the right skills to the right jobs*. A line of pegs of different shapes culminated with a square peg about to drop into a square hole. Simple, clever, saying and meaning the same thing.

She snuggled back into the pillows. Would an affair with Franko be a good idea? She thought of his dark appraising look across the table and knew that the attraction was mutual. She'd be the first to admit that she didn't know much about love, but she did know quite a bit about sex. It was a while since she'd had a relationship.

She reached across to switch the bedside light off, and lay staring up into the darkness, alleviated by a light patch where street lights filtered through the curtains. On the whole probably not a good idea, she thought, as she drifted into sleep.

Two evenings later, she opened the door to a slim young man, ascetic narrow face lit briefly by a smile.

"You'll be Rowena Johnson. I'm Luke Smith. I do apologise for not calling in advance, but there are some papers I need from the gloryhole."

Rowena stepped aside to let him in. "It is your house," she pointed out. "Can I get you something while you're looking?"

"Coffee would be good, thank you."

By the time he returned to the living room with a file of papers, Rowena had a tray, jug of coffee and plate of biscuits set on the small table by the fireplace.

"I see you brought a friend," Luke commented nodding at Bunbury lolling on the firplace. He sat in the armchair opposite her. "And added a few nice touches around the place."

"Thanks."

"Settled in all right? Got to know the Great and the Good."

"I don't know about that. The Hennesseys have been helpful, and I've met Franko whatever his other name might be."

"Oh the foster daughter's sultry cousin. Not sure I'd trust him too far." Luke sipped his coffee. "But then I'm not a generally very trusting person."

Why didn't that surprise her? "Anyway, I'm eternally grateful for your offer of a roof to an unknown distant cousin – distant in all senses of the word."

"It was your first email that intrigued me. You referred to a mystery about your grandfather who originated from Daerley. And I have a grandfather mystery too, though it was a great uncle who actually lived here."

"Tell me more."

"Not a great deal to tell. Apparently Grandpapa took a shine to me and completely took the family by surprise by emerging from behind a wall of silence that dated back to his time on the Somme in the first World War. It was mutual. I adored him back. Than suddenly, from one day to the next, I was told he was moving to somewhere in the west country and I never heard from him again. Not a dickie-bird. He died soon after."

"That's terrible."

"It was pretty awful for a nine-year-old." Luke drank his coffee in silence for a few moments, then said "You're staring at me."

"Sorry. I was trying to visualise you aged nine."

Again that smile, briefly illuminating the ascetic face. "I don't think I was a very prepossessing child – clearly Great Uncle Justin didn't regard me as such for I never heard from him either. Which was why it was so gob-smacking when I found I had inherited this little lot." He put his mug down. "Now it's your turn."

So Rowena told him the little she knew about Grandfather Pete and his deep friendship with Jake who had eventually married his widow and brought up her child as his own. "Somehow no one ever got around to explaining this until a few weeks ago. I just assumed Jake was Matt's Dad and therefore my Granddad. That we were a quite boring conventional family apart from a brief fling that Gran had with a traveller or gipsy or whatever the politically correct term is."

Luke leaned back in the armchair. "I don't do politically correct. I don't do predictable either. Seems to me it's the unpredictability of almost everything that makes life bearable. Take that boring great uncle of mine. Who would have guessed that in his old age he would find a sudden urge to commit to paper not only his experiences of rural life but some of the undercurrents that he has unearthed. If you can unearth an undercurrent. Anyway, he hints at some pretty rum goings-on." Luke stood up. "We must talk more, but for the moment I have some deadlines to meet. Call me if you need anything. And don't get up – I know the way out."

Rowena heard the front door close behind him and sat for a while reviewing their first encounter. And came to the conclusion she wasn't sure she terribly took to cousin Luke.

Then she remembered Franko's question as to whether she was sleeping with this Luke. "No, Franko," she said aloud. "And I can't see it happening. Absolutely not."

Oxfordshire : spring 2003/ Rowena

"I suppose some people would think I've gone a bit over the top?" Rowena said. It was as much a question as a statement.

"In what way?"

"Travelling half way round the world to check out something that happened in the middle of the last century."

It was a week later and she had returned to Abel's Yard at Sara's invitation to report on how she was settling in and to 'let us get to know you better'. Sara was making lunch while Mike gave a tour of the garden. They had passed the gardenia planted in Justin's memory and reached the old oak where Mike assured her there were carpets of crocuses in due season. Rowena had explained about Jake and Pete and the friendly fire.

"Something that affected your whole life," Mike pointed out.

Rowena smiled at him. What a nice man he was. "Were your parents in the war?"

"Oh yes. Father especially had a hard time, part of the liberating army, one of the first to go into places like Belsen." He added "Concentration camp."

"Yes, I know what it was," Rowena said testily. "It was our war, too, remember?"

"Sorry. Anyway, I don't think Father ever got over the things he saw, though I don't think I've fully appreciated that until quite recent years. He just couldn't settle, so when the Sixties happened…" Mike paused questioningly.

"Yes, yes. Flower power and free love."

"Well, something like that. Father –and even more surprisingly Mother – took to it as to the manor born." He stopped.

After a moment Rowena prompted "And?"

"And I absolutely loathed it. All that unstructured living

for today. And the worst of it was that all the other kids loved it. Well; most kids would, wouldn't they?" He stopped again. "You're good at making people talk aren't you?"

"Am I?"

"Lunch," called Sara from the kitchen door.

Over home-made country vegetable soup and hot garlic bread, Rowena told them of her initial contact with the Commonwealth War Graves Commission. And of her encounter with Franko. Mike grimaced. "Don't trust that young man too far."

"Oh come on Mike," Sara put in. "At least give him credit for identifying a gap in the market, and then filling it. Agreed some of his earlier methods were questionable but ... Well, have you seen his office at the back of the market place? He's got a really business-like set up. And he's doing well."

"People like Franko always do well."

"Don't be so unforgiving. It's unattractive, as well as out of character." Sara went to retrieve the soup tureen for seconds, saying over her shoulder. "We don't squabble much."

"On the contrary, I was thinking that's just the kind of banter I missed in my teenage years. Dad was hardly ever there, and Mum too busy playing both parents ever to really chill out. Your Minkie was lucky. You must have been great parents." Too late she saw something raw and hurting flicker across Sara's face, quickly overlayed by a laconic "I suppose other people's parents often seem more enviable than one's own."

"You can say that again," Mike said ruefully. "But it didn't stop her going back. I mean Minkie to Sarajevo."

"And Luke – how are you getting on with him?"

"He's only been over once so far. Not exactly cuddly is he?" Rowena glanced slyly at Mike. "On the whole, I think I prefer Franko."

Sara said "Yes I think I share your preference, though I don't truthfully fancy cuddling either."

"Come to think of it, it's a while since I've cuddled

anyone," Rowena informed Bunbury on her return as she settled down to read the local paper before going to bed. Normally she relished the chit chat of small town news: - the blast at week-end binge drinkers, this school or that which had won some environmental award, the grief of a family whose son had made the ultimate sacrifice in Iraq, an ex-addict who had made good. But that evening she couldn't settle. *What on earth am I doing here?* became an entrenched mantra in her head. Suddenly she missed Jake dreadfully, and even more funny old Greatgrumps who, after all, had triggered off this whole adventure.

Restless, she wandered out through the back lobby. As his health deteriorated, Justin had sold the quite substantial parcel of garden to his neighbours and just kept a square patch which he had turned into a patio with tubs and raised beds, and built an outhouse for tools, with a small desk and lamp to which he would retire if he wanted to escape the telephone and front door bell. Rowena had already pottered about in it several times, but this was the first time she had poked around in an old cupboard and found, stuffed at the back of it, an old plastic bag: one of those black plastic bin bags with something very bulky inside.

Easing the opening loose, she put in a tentative hand, felt the edge of a cardboard box. With a bit of shuffling and manoeuvring, she edged the box out. An exceedingly full box, stuffed with small red notebooks of the kind you could buy at any stationers. She opened one and then another. Every page crammed with small writing, so small it would have been hard to read if its neatness had not made it almost as clear as print.

April 12, 1922 Swiss Cottage: Is James at last showing signs of improvement, or is that wishful thinking ...?

Rowena put the notebook back exactly where she had found it. These must be Justin's diaries, and he had kept them in meticulous order.

But hadn't Luke said he had the diaries at his house? She took out another of the little red books – 1933; and another – 1958. Luke had said the diaries were all dated from the time

Justin had moved to Daerley Green. Clearly these were of a much earlier period or his life, and somehow Luke had missed them.

Well, for once she'd have one up on him

Or how about having much more than one thing up on him? How about reading them and getting insights Luke had never had?

. She could almost hear Jake's voice say *It's not done to read other people's diaries*. Ah yes, but that was living people. Dead people's diaries were always being published. Once they were dead, their diaries became history.

Didn't they?

She took the little red notebooks out and checked their dates. They were already in chronological order: from 1920 to 1975.

Rowena took the first half dozen, made herself a cup of coffee and went to curl up in the big armchair in the living room. Most of it was boring stuff, verbal shorthand for the kind of days he was having at this early stage of his civil service career. But there were brief sorrowful references to his brother James, Luke's grandfather. He had survived the horrors of the Battle of the Somme a broken man. In those early days of psychiatric treatment, he had been shuffled from one hospital to another, eventually a long-stay institution in the north where Justin visited him occasionally and even thought he saw signs of improvement.

As she read on, flipping quickly through the less interesting stuff, slowing down as she came to the encounters between the two brothers, Rowena had a curious sense of déjà-vu. She leaned her head back against the embracing headrest of the armchair. But how? And then she remembered those conversations with Jake, his sadness at the lack of rapport he had with his own father, locked behind the wall of his unspeakable experiences in Gallipolli. It was like some kind of survivor's guilt, Jake had described. As though he felt he had had no right to survive the horrors that had destroyed so many.

Reading Justin's diary, it was not always clear whose survivor's guilt was in question. James' for coming out of hell alive if not whole, or Justin's for escaping the hell in the first place. Bedridden with rheumatic fever at the outbreak of war, Justin had been left with a weak heart in addition to eyesight that had never been good. He clearly didn't do emotion on paper, but minded terribly that, for all practical purposes, he had lost the brother who had been his soul mate through childhood and adolescence, and now felt some responsibility for guiding him back to normality. Or as near normality as possible. There was a hint of impatience, too, that James could not confide in the one person he should have been able to trust.

By 1922, James had moved into Justin's flat in Swiss Cottage. But, once out of hospital, he sank into a deeper black hole. Justin's efforts to bring him into social life failed totally. James would make his excuses early in the evening and disappear into his room.

"You're not even trying," Justin snapped once.

"To do what?"

"Live."

"What for?"

This was one of the few conversation recorded in the little red books. Then one Sunday James suddenly returned from church with someone called Mary. Ah, Mary - Luke's grandmother. Quite soon James and Mary married and moved into a small house in Hampstead. Mary Robyns, according to Justin, was a gentle, God-fearing young woman who made it her mission to give James a normal family life. She had two miscarriages before bearing him a son Gilpin in whom James took no interest at all. He seemed a pallid boy in all senses of the word and Justin didn't seem to take to him much either, but tried at least to provide him with a role model. Gilpin became a teacher and surprisingly fell in love with and married a beautiful and bubbly fellow teacher who in due course presented him with a son Luke. And then the unexpected happened. James formed an attachment for his grandson that he had never shown for his son. And Luke adored him back.

How very, very surprising, Rowena thought, suddenly catapulted back to the present by a backfiring car nearby. And how odd that she was once again being plunged back into 20th century history. And, good God, it was two o'clock in the morning and her eyes felt as though they had been rubbed with sandpaper.

"I could do with some light relief," she informed Bunbury as she headed for bed, and decided to visit Franko's new office sooner rather than later.

There was no mistaking Franko's delight at seeing her next morning. He was casual in a very smart denim suit, and his office was small but exuded efficient busy-ness. Two desks supported the latest computer models each operated by a young lady. Both attractive.

Franko introduced them. "Not Pommies," he said. "Lisa is from Czech Republic, Nada from Poland. And this," he told them, "is my very good Aussie friend Rowena."

Lisa immediately set about making extremely good coffee, and there was an exchange of backgrounds punctuated by phone calls answered in English or a variety of languages unrecognisable to Rowena.

"Next year we will be more and more busy," Franko said happily. "There will be new EU members and many more waiting to work here."

"Unless they make regulations to stop them."

"They not make," Franko said. "Here are not enough nurses, or bus drivers, or water people."

"Plumbers."

"Yes, plumbers, and many many other jobs for which I will find people. Very good people."

It was enormously refreshing to be with someone who was so optimistic and confident that he was doing the right thing. After a couple of hours, Rowena headed for the Spiceball Leisure

Centre for an hour in the gym and wasted two more window shopping in the Castle Centre before returning to Franko's office.

"Now I take you to dinner," he said as he closed up and headed for the stairs leading to the small flat above the premises.

The first surprise was how comfortable he had made it. Futons covered half the floor of the living space with a colourful scattering of cushions. Shelves with books, CDs, DVDs, hi-fi equipment filled two of the walls. A small TV crouched in a corner. There was a shower room and a tiny kitchen from which in due course Franko produced an amazingly good goulash. They ate it from a low table, sitting on the futons, with a heavy red wine from Istria. And they talked far into the night, not clever or funny talk, but from the heart. Franko listened to the story of Rowena's troubled teens, her discovery of Greatgrumps. And she learned something of the dreams he had shared with Minkie as a child, how they would recreate their Sarajevo into its earlier image, and how his dreams had been destroyed and, along with them, much of his idealism.

"But now you have it back?"

"No, that one is dead. But perhaps a new different one comes for this new different world." He sat watching her for a moment, then reached out a hand to touch her cheek. "You are very beautiful, my Aussie friend," he said. "I would like to live with you a bit. I think you like, too?"

When she didn't answer, he went on "Perhaps it is too soon, too big commitment. I not like too big commitments either. Perhaps we stay sometimes together, sometimes not. Have free arrangement."

"I like free arrangements," Rowena said.

Franko nodded, leaned forward, kissed her lightly on the lips. "You call me when you want to come."

"And you tell me if you already have arrangements."

"I do not make multiple arrangements," he said, and looked so shocked Rowena almost laughed.

She felt light, carefree. Here, she instinctively knew, was

the right, uncomplicated person who would look out for her without wanting to possess her. A thought struck her and she gave a rueful grin. “I can think of someone who won’t approve of such an arrangement,” she said.

“Me too,” Franko said. “If he finds out.”

Oxfordshire : spring 2003 – Luke

"So what did you have against that great uncle of yours? He always struck me as harmless enough, if a tad tedious. Sara, of course, adored him."

Amanda and Luke were in bed in his drab little house on the edge of Daerley Green. Luke put down the book he was reading and considered the question. Beresford Tremayne was away looking at golf courses in France, but it was already some months since Luke's flirtation with Amanda had burgeoned into an affair. Beresford, now running his own consultancy, was quite often away, so Amanda was quite often with Luke. They were good together: not only in bed, but temperamentally ideally matched. Amanda no more wanted the inconvenience of leaving Beresford than Luke wanted a long term commitment. He had already surprised himself how long the relationship had lasted. He also found it hard to believe that Beresford could be so self-centredly complacent that he was unaware of Amanda's roving interests. But that, after all, was Beresford's problem and he undoubtedly had roving interests of his own. That much had been spelt out clearly in Justin's diary.

Now, Luke countered Amanda's question with another. "Have you ever loved anyone completely and unconditionally?"

"Mmm… I guess not."

"Well, I did my grandfather. I was obviously a huge disappointment to Pa. And Ma was beautiful and adored by all, and hadn't the faintest idea of what it was like to be an introverted mess."

"Is that what you are? You could have fooled me."

"Was. I've learned coping mechanisms. Anyway, Granddad was another lost soul – had been since as a teenager he saw things no teenager should ever see in the trenches of the Somme. He was lost for many years, and then a year or two after

I was born, we found each other across the great divide of generations and experience: the embittered and the innocent."

"Yes, I can see it was a major thing for both of you."

"When Ma and Pa divorced and Ma re-married, I spent a lot of my early childhood with my grandparents. Grandmum was an angel, though a bit too pious for my taste. But Granddad spent hours with me, telling me stories, taking me for walks, playing games. Then, because they lived quite close, it became routine that he would walk me to play school and later primary school." Luke thought for a moment. "And it wasn't just that we had a great time together. I overheard Ma say one day that it was a miracle how I'd brought Granddad back to life, and I really believed that I had some kind of special power. For the first time in my life I felt that I mattered."

"So what's all this got to do with Justin? And where was he all this time?"

"Officially he'd retired, but in fact he was co-opted on to some think-tank. Something to do with the Cold War. He was in the Soviet Union a lot – even China I believe. I've never been that interested. Anyway he wasn't around much. Then Ma got pregnant and produced a little half sister. Apparently I didn't react too well. It was about that time Justin seemed to be around more and also then that they decided to send me to boarding school. Perhaps it was just a coincidence, but I certainly took it for granted that Great Uncle had a big say in it." Luke paused. "I think that was without doubt the unhappiest time of my life. Granddad tried to change their minds but my Stepfather had never liked him and Ma was far too enchanted with new motherhood to take my part. She really was a selfish woman. Probably still is."

"That's a hard thing to say about your Mum."

"Oh Mandy, Mandy, haven't you learned yet that's just what I am. Hard. It's one of the reasons we get on so well."

"I'm not hard."

"Yes you are. Well, maybe opportunist would be a better

description. You're not at all bothered about cheating on Beresford."

"He cheats on me."

"So that makes it all right?"

"Oh, you...." She pouted at him. "So what about boarding school?"

"I was bullied until Granddad taught me some really great army holds that depended on agility and guile rather than brute strength. After that I was mostly ignored. It was a lonely time."

"Oh. Poor little boy."

"And then one Christmas – the second Christmas I think – I came home and found Granddad had moved to Cornwall, about as far as you can go without falling into the sea. I was devastated at first, and then I thought, well, may be it could be a really good thing. I could go there in my holidays and have him all to myself. Mother took me once, just for the day, and for the first time Granddad seemed a really old man. But I still thought I'd be able to go and stay. The invitation never came. Of course I thought it was my fault, that I must have done something terrible, so I wrote a long rambling letter to Granddad apologising for whatever it was I'd done. He didn't reply but Great Uncle Justin came to visit. Though he was Granddad's twin, he always seemed much bigger. Overpowering. Even when he tried to be gentle and reassuring, he was scary. He told me that Granddad wasn't very well and needed to have a quiet life for a while. Of course, I couldn't understand why he couldn't have a quiet life *and* see me, so I became more convinced than ever that I'd done something wrong. And then..." Luke stopped and gave a little shudder. "...and then a few months later the Headmaster called me in and said Granddad had died. And clearly that was my fault too, since I'd helped to bring him back to life in the first place."

"Poor little boy," Amanda said again quietly, and rolled over to wrap herself round him.

Next morning, Luke was in the kitchen turning bacon slices in a pan when Amanda said from the doorway "Smells heavenly. I'm ravenous."

He paused to put the oven on, check the bread was in the toaster and glanced round. She was leaning against the doorjamb, her full figure barely concealed by the flimsy arrangement she called a housecoat. He thought of switching off the gas, pulling the flimsy arrangement off her shoulders and steering her back up the stairs or into the living room. And decided against it.

"You'd better cover yourself up if you want to be sure of breakfast in the foreseeable future," he said.

She flicked the flimsy thing at him provocatively. "I keep forgetting about this amazing stamina of younger men," she said and went off to dress.

Luke grinned. It was one of the great things about Amanda that she could stop him from taking himself so seriously. In return he'd managed at least to temper her dreadful snobby streak. Yes, they were good for each other.

"Whatever possessed you to buy this miserable place?" she had asked on her first visit.

"Thank you. It has already been pointed out to me that I'm on the wrong side of the traffic lights. You really are an appalling snob, Mandy."

Nobody else was allowed to shorten her name and he had noticed Sara's raised eyebrow the first time she overheard it. It gave him a pleasing sense of possession, just as it amused him to oblige her to move down market to share his bed.

"Anyway," he told her more than once. "Over here I don't keep tripping over people I know."

"It won't stop them knowing your business," Amanda said. "You're irrevocably part of the village now, my friend. For instance everyone was agog when that Aussie wench moved in to you place recently. Including me, I might add. But after a bit of judicious spying I decided she wasn't your type."

"No, brash young things fresh from Down Under and doing their Europe thing are absolutely not my type."

"What did surprise me though was Sara's reaction to us: surprised, but uncharacteristically non-judgemental. I mean there are times when she can be a bit prim."

"Can she now?"

The fact that she was non-judgemental, though, was hardly surprising, mused Luke, scooping the bacon slices on to a plate and sliding it into the oven. He drifted into the tiny dining room that gave on to the small conservatory and went to sit in the shafts of sun that penetrated it briefly at this season and time of day.

It was a while since he'd browsed through his great uncle's diary, but it had given him invaluable insights into the undercurrents of Daerley Green life. Though as a boy and young man he had come to detest Justin, blaming him for the destruction of the only meaningful relationship in his life, he recognised his intelligence and intuition. In his diary Justin had expressed conviction and concern that Sara and Beresford were having an affair at a time when Mike was frequently away covering the Bosnian and Kosovo conflicts. Sara Hennessey and Beresford Tremayne – now there was an unlikely coupling. What did these women see in the wretched man?

Luke was sure that Amanda had no knowledge of that particular adventure of Beresford's; she had been working in the U.S. at the time. And Luke had no intention of telling her, at least not for the moment. He revelled in the power of knowledge, but felt no urgent need to exercise it, any more than he felt a need to make any one place his own. Indeed, it was altogether amazing how his days, weeks, months in Daerley were now on the brink of stretching into over a year, and he could think of no good reason for ending them. Apart from the occasional trip to London or overseas, he could conduct his consultancy work as easily from here as from anywhere. He had acquired an acceptable circle of acquaintances which included Beresford against whom he greatly enjoyed testing his golfing skills in the knowledge that he was matching him at his own game in other areas of his life. Occasionally the Hennesseys invited him round, as much in posthumous regard to Justin as for any other reason, he suspected, but he enjoyed their intelligent company and the puzzlement he was clearly causing Sara. Mike did not try hard to disguise his indifference. These social occasions and a weekly session in The Trumpet kept him well abreast of the main goings-on in the parish.

"So that's where you're hiding." Amanda joined him in the conservatory, now fully dressed, her russet hair caught up in a scarf of old gold chiffon that was a perfect foil for her moleskin pants and moss green shirt.

"Not hiding, thinking."

"You're not going to become all thoughtful and interesting, are you? That would spoil everything. I suppose it was all that introspection last night."

"Don't worry, Rabbit. It's all out of my system now. I'm right back to my usual self-absorbed, self-contained egotism, without a thought for others."

"Well, try and keep a thought for me just for a moment – like giving me a lift into Banbury this morning. Thought I'd look into that agency run by that good looking cousin of young Minkie and see if he can find me an *au pair.*"

"What on earth do you need an *au pair* for?"

"Oh, I probably haven't mentioned our imminent entry into the international golfing scene? Beresford's chairing a new consortium of the best courses in Europe with interchangeable booking facilities and organised touring groups. We're going in for entertaining big time this summer, and I need help."

""Then better make sure she's not young and pretty. The *au pair,* I mean."

"Not sure if ugliness features on many people's CVs. And come on will you, I'm starving."

In the end Luke went with her to Franko's small but smart enterprise near Banbury market place, and he came up with the perfect solution. "You like girl or boy *au pair*?" he asked. It seemed young male students from eastern Europe were proving very popular as home helps at the dawn of the 21st century. "Many come from big families," Franko explained. "They know how to take care of young children, keep house clean, and if the house is a bit lonely in the country, then housewife like to have strong young man like protection…"

"And may be for other purposes," murmured Luke.

Franko looked at him sharply. "Hanky-panky not allowed."

"I'm not sure I'm keen on the idea of you with a strapping young man," Luke said.

"Don't tell me I'm listening to a hint of jealousy."

Franko looked from one to the other with interest. "My young men have girls or wives back home. Not play the field. While you think about this, Lisa will make coffee. Please, Lisa."

A pretty girl with high cheek bones and a pony tail went to a corner of the small office and busied herself with a kettle and cups. From there she said "My boy friend Marek make very good house help. He is arriving soon. And I make sure absolutely no hanky panky."

And so it was settled. Marek would be the first candidate as Amanda's assistant in her new hostessing calendar, and she would send him over at a mutually agreeable time to help Luke with the garden and general maintenance.

"That's what I call a really cosy arrangement," Amanda said, sipping thick black coffee. "Now Franko, do you have any recent news of that charming cousin of yours?"

"Yes, have news. But I worry for Minkie. I think it was big disappointment that she could not change everything back to how it was before the war. When we were children we had such plans. I become realist. Minkie stay idealist. Now there is a man in love with her, but I know him and he is too old. And her mother is very ill so she must stay and look after her." He shrugged. "It is my want that she come here, help me with my business."

"Well, that would make Mike one very happy man to have her back here."

"Though perhaps not working with me!"

"And how about young Rowena? Are you going to enlist her on the staff too?" Amanda asked.

"Rowena she has other plans. She is making research. But yes, we are very good friends."

"So I hear," murmured Luke

Beresford was due back that evening. Luke drove Amanda home, resisting the temptation to linger. On his return to Daerley Green for the first time in a long time he went into the spare room and retrieved the box of folders containing Justin's diary. Riffling through the sheets of paper covered with great uncle's tiny, clear writing, he found himself re-reading his entry describing Beresford's arrival in the village and his first encounter with Sara Hennessey at Justin's party. There was firstly the amazing discovery that the two had been at school together and secondly Sara's patent displeasure that he had suddenly re-entered her life. Clearly Justin had come to the conclusion that it had been more than a casual acquaintance in the playground.

A few months later, Justin was expressing disquiet. *It appears that Sara has quite forgotten her antipathy towards Beresford. I saw them sharing a joke in The Trumpet this lunch time. Indeed it is a long time since I have seen her look so relaxed.* For a while the old boy seemed pleased that there was someone to help Sara get a bit of fun out of life, though a proviso cautioned *I sometimes wonder whether Mike realises how much of a strain his long absences put on their relationship.*

There were several references to the time they spent together, including a day on a canal boat which Beresford had arranged for Sara, Minkie and one of her friends. Sara had apparently begun to talk of him in a quite different way. So had Minkie. Once a huge fan of Beresford's she began to find him a bit invasive. Because she adored Justin, she probably said more to him than to her foster parents. And then a few months later still an entry in Justin's diary read: *I truly hope that Sara's and Beresford's simultaneous absence from Daerley last week-end is no more than a coincidence. I'm not usually a bad judge of character, but I think I may have been quite wrong about Beresford. I suspect the attraction of a woman like Sara will far outweigh any considerations as to whether or not she has other commitments. And when I saw Sara in the Co-op this morning, she was uncharacteristically short with me.*"

Not only a boring old fart, Luke thought, but an interfering one, too. The affair – if affair it were – seemed to have trailed on for a considerable period, before Justin recorded his relief that Beresford had moved out of the village and Sara become very involved in a small electronic publishing enterprise in Banbury. So that, he seemed to imply, should be that. There was a reference to Amanda's return from America. Apparently she had transformed from a rather prissy school teacher at a small public school to a smart jet-setting career woman, a fact that was not to go unnoticed by Beresford for long. Amanda prissy? She must indeed have changed. Clearly Justin did not approve of the transformation, except inasfar as it drew Beresford's attention away from Sara. It provided Luke with another source of pleasure that their tastes in people were so diametrically opposed.

Or was that really true? Sara and Mike were pleasant enough. He would have to reserve judgement regarding Minkie. By all accounts she was a paragon of all the virtues, not a quality that usually rated high in Luke's book. But by the sound of things he might have the opportunity to judge for himself before that much longer.

Sarajevo : autumn 2003/Minkie

The first snows were powdering the highest tops encircling Sarajevo. Lower down, the forests ravaged by mortar fire and felling during the siege were now showing signs of re-growth. Yes, forests grew again, buildings could be repaired and rebuilt; but the soul of a city developed over centuries, even millennia, was another matter.

"You're far too introspective," Bozo told Minkie on a regular basis. He had given up trying to persuade her to move in with him, perhaps assuming she would do so eventually because she had nowhere else to go. He was right about the introspection. Her mother said much the same. Most of those who had lived through the hell and the uncertainties of the siege had acquired a layer of acceptance that still evaded Minkie.

"You think life wasn't full of uncertainties for me living in England away from you all?"

"But at least you had the certainty of knowing your house would be standing in the morning, Jasminka, and your …. and Mike and Sara would most likely still be alive." Mother had never really taken to the name Minkie had adopted for herself in England.

It became pointless to discuss. She had been lucky beyond belief, of course she had, and Minkie knew that however hard she tried she would never have the gut-level understanding to forge here the kind of friendships of her growing-up years in Daerley Green.

She still worked in the office for the charity that was trying to create bridges across the ethnic divide, but most of their efforts were concentrated now outside the city in smaller rural communities where the need to make a living was obliging people to communicate. Even in the city Minkie marvelled at the conversations people from different ethnic backgrounds could have with each other without as much as mentioning the war.

Emails from Daerley Green sometimes gave her a greater sense of reality than what was going on around her. Most of them were from Mike, occasionally from Sara, and then suddenly they started coming from Franko. Between them she pieced together the changing scene in north Oxfordshire. Rowena, the Australian girl, was now settled in Luke's cottage, though Minkie still thought of it as Justin's. Mike judged her to be a pleasant young woman, though it was a pity she seemed to have become excessively friendly with Franko. According to Franko himself it meant they saw a lot of each other, and she sometimes stayed over at his place. Well, well. As for Justin's great nephew Luke she only had the Hennesseys' rather negative assessment by which to judge him.

But most amazing news of all was that Amanda Tremayne was having an affair with the very same Luke. Amanda had become Minkie's teacher soon after she came to Daerley. Then she, Amanda, had disappeared to America and returned transformed into a surprisingly eye-catching media executive. In the meantime, Beresford, whom Minkie had once adored, had almost certainly had an affair with Sara while Mike was abroad, and Minkie had quite gone off him. He had probably met his match with Amanda.

All in all it was a bit depressing how people changed – or how your view of them changed. OK, it was part of the growing up process, but it would be nice if just someone stayed as you expected. Justin surely would have done, only now there would never be a chance to find out. She remembered a conversation she'd had with Jesse, her American boyfriend, bemoaning the fact that all the people who formed the fabric of her life were disappearing from it. Well, he wasn't going anywhere, he'd said. And then he had. As soon as the horrors of 9/11 had registered, he'd rediscovered his roots and hot-footed back to the States.

Just as she had never forgotten her roots and chosen to retrace them. She'd been thinking about him a lot more recently, especially as the extent of Mother's illness became agonisingly clear; and wondered if he had found things as changed as she had. Of course it wasn't comparable. Jesse had only been away a few years with frequent visits back. She had been away from Sarajevo nearly half her short life.

The character of the city had changed so much. Most of her Serb friends and their families had moved either into Serbia or areas of Bosnia that were predominantly Serb. Her father's Bosniak side of the family had never approved of him marrying her Serb mother in the first place, so there was a tight-lipped civility in response to Minkie's return, but precious little warmth. Even her childhood friends from all ethnic walks clearly found the gulf in their teenage experiences more or less unbridgeable.

"You have to understand," Bozo tried to explain to her. "They lost their childhood and indeed a lot of their friends and, as far as they were concerned, the rest of the world didn't give a damn." He paused and touched her cheek gently. "And you are a little unusual Jasminka. Most young people would have made a new life and waited until they were successfully established and then come back to show how clever they were."

"That's cynical."

"I am cynical and with good reason." He glanced at her slyly. "If we were together I would certainly become less cynical."

Ignoring that Minkie said "And then there is my mother."

It was only after the initial euphoria had worn off and Mike and Sara had returned to Daerley Green in September 2001 that Minkie realised how unwell Branka was. Stubbornly she refused to see a doctor until she collapsed one evening a few months ago, and Minkie bundled her into a taxi and took her to the hospital. There were a lot of tests. It was cancer, a woman doctor said. It was in several places. There could be some surgery, some therapy, but long term the prognosis was not good. Branka had not looked after herself and was not strong to fight the cancer. There had been a war, Minkie pointed out, and it had not been easy to look after oneself. Yes, she was aware, the doctor replied. And looked very tired.

"Poor Jasminka," Branka said. "You found your mother too late."

Branka had her thyroid removed and when she regained some strength submitted to a combined course of radio and chemotherapy on an inoperable growth on her liver. She was very sick and her hair fell out. The old people's home, of course, had to replace her as director, but they let her stay in a small dilapidated flat in an annexe. Minkie and Bozo redecorated it. There was a large bed-sittingroom, a shower, a smaller room. No kitchen, but Branka wasn't eating anyway. Minkie gave up her job with the charity and moved into the smaller room, and ate in the home's canteen, helping out with the care of the elderly residents when she could. It was particularly at these time that she thought back the many years to the war, when this same building had been a children's home and Minkie had lived here some months following her father's death. It was here that Mike, a journalist covering the war, had first seen her, and from here that she had started the long and difficult journey to Daerley Green.

After she had teamed up with Jesse to run the travel agency in Oxford, she had managed to save quite a bit of money. Now she transferred most of it to Sarajevo. During one of Branka's periods of remission, Minkie took her to a small hotel on the Adriatic coast, north of Split, and for three weeks mother and daughter got to know each other, not so much as mother and daughter but as friends. In far away Daerley Green, Minkie had dreamed of such a circumstance even after she was told news of her mother's death, clinging stubbornly to the thought that if you wanted something badly enough it would happen. It was not at all as she had dreamed, for she had imagined herself showing her mother the soft Cotswold countryside, the crowded streets and well-regulated colleges of Oxford, the mellow-stoned villages, just as Mike had shown them to her in those first terrible bewildering weeks away from home. Instead Minkie pushed Branka in a wheelchair beneath the rugged, stark grey karst of the Dinaric Alps or sat with her under aromatic pines by the amazing colourscapes of the sea. They differed in their opinions on almost everything, but explored their differences with interest and affection.

"Your father would have been so proud of you."

"If he had lived I would have stayed here," Minkie said. "And probably died instead."

"What will you do when I have gone?" There was no point in either of them pretending it wasn't going to happen.

"I'd rather think about what I'll do while you are still here."

Once Branka exclaimed starkly "If you had married Jesse and gone to live in America…"

It seemed inconceivable now. "You were right, he was too young."

"I'm glad you agree that I can be right."

"Just as I am right that Bozo is too old."

Branka was silent for a moment. "I don't like to think of you alone."

No, neither did Minkie in her darker times. But for the moment there was only one way to live and that was within the day. And in a way these were some of the most fulfilling days of her life, justifying her stubborn belief in her mother's survival against all the odds. Now at last Branka asked her about her life in England down to the smallest detail. It was as though a physical barrier had been removed; perhaps a barrier behind which she had once put Minkie beyond reach and therefore beyond grieving.

It was late September and the weather was perfect. Branka began to eat a little, get some colour back in her cheeks, and a soft fuzz of hair covered the bald patches on her head. It didn't last. Soon after their return to Sarajevo, she relapsed, setting a pattern that was to dominate the next few months, the remission periods gradually shortening, the relapses worsening.

During the better times Minkie helped Bozo at the charity; during the worst times, he would take time off to stay with Branka to give Minkie some free time. They became very close, and the thought that they might make a life together no longer seemed so strange. Minkie sensed that this gave comfort to her mother. In her free hours, she would take a bus into the mountains and find the places where she and Franko had roamed as children, making a tree house here or seeking out wild strawberries or bilberries or mushrooms there. It was a strange limbo time between past and present into which the mails from Daerley Green increasingly felt as though they came from another planet. Mike emailed almost daily, anguished that he was not there to help, yet always lightening his messages with some local gossip that would at least briefly take her mind off the present darkness.

As they headed into another autumn, Branka was clearly increasingly exhausted and losing the will to live. At times her whole being was twisted with pain and as the level of pain relief necessary to make each day tenable increased, she agreed to move into a small annexe of a care home outside the city.

"It is a good place," she said. "Here you can die with dignity."

Minkie's days became totally directed towards spending her time with her mother, though Branka's awareness of her presence and where she was varied from hour to hour. In due course she was aware of very little, but there were flickers of recognition and pleasure that justified the hours of waiting. Bozo came when he could but the hospital was some distance from the city.

Branka died early one Thursday morning. Minkie had sat with her all night and finally plunged into the sleep of exhaustion in a chair by her bed. She awoke as a nurse came in, checked her mother and said quietly "I'm sorry, she has gone Jasminka."

"She didn't say goodbye," Minkie protested. But knew

that's just what they had been saying to each other over the last weeks and months.

As they had agreed, the funeral service was held in a small church in a nearby village. Everyone from the old people's home came, even the oldest and most disabled. And Bozo, of course. Afterwards they accompanied the coffin to the cemetery where Minkie's father was buried and she stood watching as they were at last reunited.

During the last difficult weeks, Minkie had almost persuaded herself that the anticipation of grief would alleviate the reality of it when it came. It was not so. It was a grief quite outside anything of her experience, for it was not so much for the loss of a mother as for the loss of all that might have been and that she could now never know. Back at the old people's home as she put her mother's few belongings together, the finality of all that unknowing finally consumed her and she began to weep uncontrollably. Bozo found her hunched on the bed, clutching one of her mother's dresses, her body heaving with sobs, her face contorted with pain.

Gently he raised her to her feet, put his arms round her, rocking her like a child, not saying anything while she sobbed and mumbled in a mixture of English and Serbo-Croat into his chest. Now when he suggested quietly that she should move in with him for a while, she raised no objection.

His small flat overlooked a courtyard in the old part of the city. He put her to bed in his bed and made her a glass of herbal tea, sitting beside her while she drank it, still there when she awoke several hours later. The next day they went back to the old people's home to remove Branka's things. There were pathetically few, filling a couple of suitcases, plus a box of ornaments and trinkets. Bozo took a few days off work. He cooked simple meals for them, only going out to shop in the nearby market, otherwise always there to listen as Minkie talked and talked as she had not talked before about the loneliness of her childhood and the hopes that survived through it all of finding her mother again and the remembered idyll of pre-war Sarajevo.

At last he said "I'm not sure if there ever was such a place outside your head Jasminka. But we have the possibility to rebuild it at least partly in our own image. To be part of the solution rather than part of the problem. You and I. But you will have to start eating again, or you will not have the strength to be part of anything."

Was that where her destiny lay? Instinctively she knew that it was not a good idea to make life-changing decisions at a time of such emotional turmoil. She longed to speak to Mike but could not find the words to begin to express her feelings in an email. Her head ached with uncertainty and confusion; she felt sick with hunger but could not eat.

One afternoon, as she left the flat Bozo asked "Where are you going?"

"For a walk. Does it matter?"

"You're not well. I like to know where you are."

"Oh, I'll follow the river, if you must know…" She was impatient to be off.

She must have walked further than she realised, following the river one side, crossing one of the bridges and back along the other. They had made good progress with the reconstruction of the National Library, but the Museum to Young Bosnia was still closed and the footprints marking the spot from which the student Gavrilo Princip had shot the Archduke Franz Ferdinand in 1914 had not been reinstated.

She leaned over the bridge rail looking down at the river, shallow swift, tinged red brown from the silt brought down from the mountains. Like a river of blood. So much blood shed over so many centuries.

"Minkie!"

She was hallucinating. No one here called her by her old name. She looked round. A man was coming towards her. A familiar man.

It couldn't be. Those sorts of miracles didn't happen.

Mike said. "Princess, I'm so, so sorry I wasn't here for you."

Minkie looked at him uncomprehending, put out a hand felt the roughness of his coat. The words wouldn't come.

"Bozo called me a couple of days ago. He was worried." He held out his arms and Minkie crept into them. "Come home, Princess. Come home."

Oxfordshire : January-April 2004/ Minkie

The tracks through Whirling Wood were thick with mud after heavy rain. Minkie sat on the bench by the wildflower meadow, bereft of any colour on this early January afternoon. How often she had sat on this bench with Justin, sharing with him the imponderables of her teenage years. How often, indeed, had she come to this spot looking for balm for her sorrows or space for her overcrowded head.

A robin landed on a nearby branch, bobbed a few times and then treated her to its mournful little winter song.

"Thanks," Minkie said. "You sound a bit like I feel."

"Surely not," a voice said and she looked round to see a slim man with dark eyes and thin face. He went on "You have to be Minkie, though you have cut your hair since the picture in the Hennesseys' living room."

She hesitated. "And you must be Luke Wytham Smith."

"Luke Smith," he corrected. "I don't go in for pretentious double barrels."

"Justin wasn't the slightest pretentious." Minkie said indignantly. "I expect it was a generation thing.

"May I?" Luke joined her on the bench. "You may be right. But in any case I'm delighted to meet the paragon of so many virtues in the flesh, though I would have expected you to be in a lighter frame of mind."

"I have just lost my mother. In effect, for the second time."

He bowed his head in acknowledgement. "Sorry, I'm not usually so clumsy."

"Yes, but it's not only that. Sarajevo had changed more than I could believe. Of course I expected the city to be different after so much devastation, but not the people. Not so much anyway." She paused, wondering why she was babbling away to this stranger.

"Circumstances change people. I guess you will have changed too."

"You sound like Justin."

That seemed to startle him., "Heaven forbid."

Minkie glanced at him curiously. "Why are you so against him?"

"Did you know he had a twin brother, James?"

It was Minkie's turn to be startled. "No. No, I didn't. I wonder why he never mentioned him."

"I wonder. James was my grandfather. I adored him. And then he vanished completely from my life a few years before he died."

"What did that have to do with Justin?"

"That's what I'd like to know. But I do know he was very much around when I was suddenly bundled off to boarding school."

"What possible motive could he have had?"

"Who's to know anyone else's motives in any given circumstances? For instance, what decided Justin to keep a diary of his life in Daerley Green? There's lots about you incidentally. All of it glowing."

He was making her feel uncomfortable. "Should you be reading someone else's diaries?"

"I can't think of anyone more entitled." After a moment he went on, "I gather you're staying with the Hennesseys. If you ever feel like more space there are a couple of rooms to spare at my cottage. I'm sure Rowena would welcome some congenial female company."

"I don't think she's short of company," Minkie said.

He glanced at her. "Oh, of course, your handsome cousin. From all accounts it's a rather on-off affair."

To his surprise Minkie burst out laughing. "You can't imagine how funny it is to be catapulted back into the seething gossip of Daerley after a couple of years in Sarajevo where everyone keeps everything so close to their chest you have no idea what anyone thinks about anything." She suddenly looked brighter. "You've quite cheered me up. And thanks for the offer. I may well take you up on it, especially once I've got a job and can pay my way. I think Mike and Sara need their own space too."

Luke nodded, got to his feet. "Well, I'm sure the Daerley grapevine will tell you where I am at any given moment."

Minkie knew that her greyness of mood was not entirely to do with her mother's death and the changes in Sarajevo. It was also to do with the changes in Daerley Green. After the joy and relief of Mike's unexpected presence in Sarajevo, they had talked for hours back at Bozo's flat. They all agreed it made sense that she should return to Daerley for a spell.

"You can always come back here," Bozo said, but didn't sound very hopeful.

"Or you could come to Daerley."

"I do not think a one-legged Bosnian Serb would be very welcome to your immigration people. Besides what would I do there. I am used to how things work or don't work here."

And that summed it up, Minkie thought. You got used to how things worked or didn't work in a place. At one time she had known precisely how that would apply to Daerley Green and now she didn't.

Mike had reminded her that things would be different. Her best friend Azzie had emigrated to the U.S.; her American boyfriend Jesse had returned to his roots. And, of course, there was no more Justin.

"But Franko is there," Minkie said, refusing to be dismayed. "And even if you don't think much of him, you said yourself he's making a real success."

"Yes," Mike admitted. "Which means he's quite preoccupied with it when he's not preoccupied with his new girl friend."

"Oh yes, that Australian woman."

Yet, despite all that she had expected a different reception from Franko, though it began warmly enough. Jumping to his feet as he saw her come through the door, he held out his arms and shouted "All the church bells must ring and all the people celebrate."

She laughed, delighted at his absurd extravagance, and allowed him to waltz her through the narrow spaces between desks as he exorted Lisa please to quickly make some coffee. After the introductions and the coffee, as thick and strong as in Sarajevo, he had taken her up to the flat. She looked round it curiously, noting the odd feminine garment trailing on a chair. He noticed her noticing.

"I told you about Rowena."

"You did. She's not very tidy."

"And you are a bit cross with me, my Jasminka."

"Not cross, but I suppose I like to have you to myself."

"Last time you did not want me. You were too busy with your Jesse and you sent me away."

"Last time you were doing some very dodgy things," she reminded him.

"Not dodgy now. But it is true that my business takes a lot of me, and Rowena must have something too; but there is still much for you, my darling cousin."

"Oh, so take me out to dinner tonight."

His face crumpled with disappointment and Minkie noted wryly that he was still a marvellous actor. "This evening I meet director from big office in Northampton who wants workers."

"Tomorrow evening then."

"Tomorrow I see Rowena. First time in ten days."

And so it went on.

At Abel's Yard, Mike was busy on a new book relating the Balkan conflicts to the worsening situation in the Middle East, though from time to time he took her for a pub lunch somewhere in the neighbourhood. Somehow, though, the total sense of ease she had once felt in his company just wasn't there. Sara was grappling with deadlines for a project for Cyber Inc's expanding publishing programme.

But the one she missed most was Justin. He had been amazingly intuitive and had seemed to know her mood before she even opened her mouth. Now, she got into the habit of strolling down to Whirling Wood most days. Occasionally she would meet Luke on his regular constitutional.

"Still communing with my late great uncle?" he asked her once.

"As a matter of fact, I am."

"What a strange young woman you are." But after that he rarely exchanged more than a casual "Good morning."

"*You have far too much time on your hands young woman. Remember, when you were here before you were fully occupied, either at school or at work. And you had Azzie and Jesse. And me.*" If she didn't actually hear Justin's voice, she could recreate his precise intonations in her head. "*Why don't you go and explore some pastures new?*"

"But how? You've all gone and everyone else is so busy and wrapped up in themselves."

There was a measurable pause before the thought – Justin's or her own? – came "*And what about that extraordinary bucket on four wheels you called a car!*"

"Robbo! Robbo! Of course." Minkie had shouted the words, then looked round self consciously thankfully to find there was no one there, before turning her concentration on her once faithful companion.

Mike had presented her with the Robin Reliant when she started her first job. It had been parked – bright red and looking slightly absurd - amongst the usual collection of Toyotas and Transits, Vauxhalls and VWs on the market place. Most people – not least Franko – were very rude about it, but she loved it as she would probably never love another car. How could she have forgotten about it?

"I did wonder," Mike said when she rushed home to enquire. "I've given her a run every now and then, and she's in a lock-up just round the corner. Let's go and look."

"She's even more beautiful than I remember," exclaimed Minkie as Mike lifted the door and Robbo's gleaming red greeted them. Mike smiled as her enthusiasm; for a moment it was like old times.

"Feel like a run?" she asked.

"Sorry Princess. I'm fighting a deadline. But soon, soon."

For the moment it didn't matter. Minkie got into the driving seat, switched on the engine, felt the throb of power and, with it, a new promise of independence. Instead of going down to Whirling Wood each day, she now nosed Robbo out of the lock-up and headed for nowhere in particular. It became a kind of game. Sometimes she would decide on turning alternately first left then first right; sometimes following the whim of the moment at every cross roads. She found herself in villages with peculiarly English names like Lower and Upper Slaughter, or creeping down narrow tracks that came to a dead end in a farmyard.

"Why don't you take a map with you?" Mike asked when once again she could give them no idea of where she had been.

Couldn't he see that it if she could pinpoint her routes, they would no longer be entirely hers?

She did check the map though when she got home on the day she met Jiff. It had been one of her follow-the-moment's-whim days which brought her to a village somewhere in the triangle between Burford, Stow on the Wold and Chipping Norton. It had a wide treeless green laced with little channels of clear flowing water and a lot of ducks that hustled hither and thither on some mystical mission of their own. The pub overlooking this scene was old and low-ceilinged and thatched. Inside it was empty except for an extremely dishy young man behind the bar.

"G'Morning." His intonation immediately revealed him as Antipodean. "Well, you're a treat for tired eyes."

"You're not so bad a sight yourself."

Raised eyebrows. "Hey, you're pretty chilled out for a Brit."

"Perhaps that's because I'm not a Brit."

"Ah. So where from?"

"Bosnia, if you know where that is."

"Oh I know all right. It's where people were killing each other like crazy a few years ago. How come you stayed so pretty and fresh and serene?"

"I spent the war here in Daerley Green with some of those buttoned-up Brits."

He looked momentarily shamefaced. "That's cool. I met an Aussie Sheila from that place a few days ago."

"That'll be Rowena."

"She came in with a rather sinister kind of guy."

"That would be my cousin Franko."

He grimaced. "Not doing very well am I? Perhaps I'd better stick to my job and ask what I can get for you.."

"Something with cranberry in it. And the avocado and prawns sound good."

"With white or wholemeal bread, or *pitta*."

"*Pitta*."

She sat the bar while he served her. He was after all the first dishy young man who had shown an interest in her for a while. In fact, with his floppy fair hair and broad build, he reminded her a little of Jesse. But she didn't mean to say so aloud.

"It's the long hair. Ma always said I was beginning to look like a girl."

"Jesse, spelt J-e-s-s-e. He was my boy friend, an American."

"The Americans tend to go in for weird names don't they."

"What's yours then?"

"Jiff." He laughed. "I guess that's pretty weird too. It's short for Julian Ivan Forsyth. I think the Ivan bit is an echo of Slav ancestry."

"Perhaps we're related."

"The way I'm feeling, I hope not. Say, does the fact I remind you of this Jesse mean you might say yes if I ask you out? I could pick you up in Daerley Green and we could try that new club in Banbury. My nights off are Tuesday and Thursday."

"Thursday would be OK."

"Great. I'll pick you up at seven and we'll have a meal first. This coming Thursday.""

It was sod's law that over breakfast that Thursday Mike said "I've decided to take an evening off. Fancy going for that spin?"

"Oh I wish I'd known – I've made a date for tonight."

"Sorry, I didn't realise you had such a busy schedule." Perhaps it wasn't meant to sound sarcastic, but it did.

It was Minkie's great hope that Mike would be out when Jiff arrived. As luck would have it, both he and Sara were in the front garden of Abel's Yard.

"Mike and Sara, this is Jiff Forsyth from Melbourne. Jiff, Mike and Sara Hennessey who gave me a home during our war."

"Hello Jiff," Sara said.

"Unusual name," Mike muttered.

"She's nice," commented Jiff, as they drove off. "He's as buttoned-up as the Brits come."

"Where on earth did you find him?" asked Mike next morning. "Looks as though you picked him up in some bar."

"As a matter of fact I did. But he's fun and that's what I feel like at the moment: having a bit of a good time."

"And did you?"

It had been OK, but not all that great, though she wasn't going to tell Mike that.. The meal at a pub on Banbury's outskirts had been average, and the night club full of flashing lights and excessive noise. Jiff had suggested they should find somewhere quieter next time, if there was going to be a next time. At that stage Minkie could not see any reason why not.

They went out for a couple of months. Jiff liked walks too and the best times were when they strode across winter fields and through bare-branched woods brushed with hoar frost, arriving, flushed and well exercised, in some pub where they would sit cradling their lagers in front of a crackling fire. He asked her a lot about her life in Sarajevo, how she had come to Daerley, the difficulties of going back to Bosnia. Minkie thought it was great that he really seemed interested. Occasionally they went to a rave, once or twice to a concert in Oxford. Jiff pronounced that he was more earthy than highbrow. Perhaps she expected too much from people, Minkie thought.

Then came the day they returned to the thatched pub on the green quite early and Jiff invited her up to his room. Seeing her expression, he said "It's OK, I'm not going to attack you, much as I should like to."

It was a large, pleasant room with a view over the green. Near the window in an alcove was a computer. Jiff went over to boot it up, flicked through a website, and finally said "Wow, how about that?"

Coming to look over his shoulder out of curiosity, Minkie found herself gazing at a bare pair of the largest breasts she had ever seen. Jiff began to scroll down the screen so they were presented with a curvaceous torso from various angles, gradually moving down to a pair of parted legs.

Minkie leaned over pushed the off switch. "You're filthy!"

Jiff switched the machine on again. "I thought this young woman might help to warm you up a bit. Heaven knows you could do with it!"

Minkie paused only to slap his face before storming out of the room and out of the pub. Thank heavens Jiff's car had been unavailable that evening, so they had used Robbo. Minkie fell gratefully into the driving seat and drove back to Daerley at speeds that were certainly not legal. She felt violated, as though the pictures on the screen had been of her.

Oxfordshire : April-June 2004/Minkie

On the evening that Minkie stormed away from Jiff, Sara was alone in the living room when she dashed into Abel's Yard.

"Good evening Minkie," she called, and Minkie back-tracked down the stairs to stand in the doorway.

"Oh," Sara said. "I gather it wasn't. A good evening I mean. I rather feared that enthusiasm for Jiff might wane in time."

"All I wanted was a bit of fun," wailed Minkie. "Fill in time. I don't feel I fit in as I used to."

"Poor Minkie. Not everyone's idea of fun is the same. As for fitting in, it's not working out as you hoped, is it? Mike and I rather expected Franko to snap you up."

"I don't think there's room even for an extra mouse in that office of his."

"How about Cyber Inc?"

So Sara arranged for Minkie to meet Pippa, the exotic Australian who had launched Cyber Inc a few years ago and stayed on to manage it when its success attracted a buy-out at the turn of the century. They had met long ago.

Characteristically direct, Pippa said "Wow, such a swan out of a modest duckling! You would be an asset to any front office."

"She has a great deal more than decorative value," Sara said firmly. "Don't forget she ran a successful travel office in Oxford for a couple of years with that American boyfriend of hers."

"Yes, and I was thinking of tapping into that very experience to expand into the overseas – or at least European market. Maybe that handsome cousin of yours might have some input, Minkie? Not to mention contacts –for example, printing abroad and cutting costs?"

"Could be. But I've been thinking that I really should do a course to update myself on the ever-changing new technology. I've got a bit rusty. How would that fit?"

"Great. And I'd rather start you off part-time anyway. Find yourself a course and we'll work your hours round it." Pippa paused, looked at her speculatively. "As long as you won't disappear as soon as you're getting useful."

"No way. I've done with wandering for a bit."

"That's good to hear," Sara said.

It was generally agreed that, having decided to stay, Minkie needed space of her own. Mike pointed out that there was plenty of room in Luke's cottage where Rowena was staying. Minkie had a curious feeling that he would be glad to get her out of the house. By now she had met Rowena a couple of time and had not felt particularly drawn to her. Still, Luke's cottage – originally three workers' cottages knocked into one – had space enough for them not to trip over each other too often. Minkie was out much of the time anyway, and Rowena spent a lot of time in libraries or on the internet trying to glean more details of the events that had led to her grandfather's death by friendly fire. Minkie did not frankly understand why it was so important. World War Two was history. It was when death struck someone whose hand you were holding at the very instant that you might justifiably want to know the who and why of it. But she sensed it would not be a good idea to say so.

Most of those on her course were much younger. She settled for three classes: digital photography, image editing, and advanced web page design. Two were on weekday mornings, but web page design was on a Wednesday evening. When it was over she took herself for a drink in the Horton Bar of the Whateley Hall Hotel, partly to unwind, partly as an exercise in nostalgia. It was here that she and Azzie had come in another lifetime after their office-cleaning jobs as Azzie filled in time before emigrating to America, and Minkie became a first-time wage earner saving for that precious return trip to Sarajevo.

It was on the second Wednesday that she became aware of someone watching her and looked across to a man, alone at the bar, eyes crinkling in amusement. When she caught his eye, he came over.

"This isn't a pick-up," he said. "At least not in the usual sense. (a) I know your cousin Franko, and (b) I've been watching the back of your head for the last two Wednesday evenings."

Minkie recognised him then as a figure at the back of the class. "You should have been concentrating on your computer screen," she said sternly. "How do you know Franko?"

"My father runs a small packing factory on the Cherwell Estate and sent me to negotiate workers. I'm Philip Renton, by the way. My friends call me Flip."

Minkie inclined her head. "Well, you know who I am. So why are you into web page design?"

"Trying to persuade Dad to join the 21st century. I thought it might be more persuasive if I came up with a good design."

"You should try Cyber Inc."

"Yes, I know about them, too. But I prefer to do it myself." He smiled. It was a nice smile. "Though I wouldn't discourage any input you care to make."

"So what's with this Flip guy?" Minkie demanded of Franko a few days later. "I can find my own men, you know."

"I think my choice is better. He is good man. And I think my cousin has too serious life. First with Jesse. He was OK but…" Franko gave that shrug that was more expressive of his reservations than any words. "Then that terrible Australian." (How on earth had he found out about Jiff?) And Bozo in Sarajevo – much too old. You must have fun, Minkie, before *you* get old." He hunched himself into such a caricature of an old crone that she had to laugh.

"I think I have a few years yet," she protested. But, in fact, she agreed that life had become far too circumscribed for a nearly-24-year-old, and had made an arrangement to see Flip the following day.

The relationship took off like a runaway train. Flip was on the rebound from being dumped after quite a long partnership with a young Canadian on a post-graduate course in Oxford. Minkie just wanted some fun. They did a few meals, concerts, raves, and then Flip suggested Minkie should move in with him. He had a cottage in Warwickshire only a mile or two from the Tremaynes.

Mike was appalled when the news filtered through the grapevine to Abel's Yard. "I'm not even sure he's an improvement on that Jiff person."

"It's none of our business," Sara said, though she was none too reassured by Flip's playboy reputation.

All the same, Mike tackled Minkie over their next pub lunch.

"You're oozing disapproval," Minkie said.

"He has a reputation, Princess."

"For enjoying himself, which is just what I feel like after too many serious years. Look, Mike, I'm nearly 24. I reckon that's old enough to be responsible for me."

"You can't blame someone who's very fond of you worrying about the company you keep. I appreciate your teenage years were more stressful than most, and that you have a right to want to make up for that…."

Minkie interrupted "You probably don't realise how patronising that sounds."

"Or you how brittle you have become."

"I'm sorry to be such a disappointment."

"I'll never be disappointed in you, Princess. But perhaps sometimes a little afraid for you."

They parted coolly, conscious that a small rift was somehow widening as they met less frequently and in the end not at all. Minkie's life was suddenly packed with her courses, her work at Cyber Inc, and an increasingly full social life with Flip's wide circle of friends. Minkie wasn't keen on a lot of them.

They smoked and drank a lot and quite a few of them took drugs, including the hallucinogenic variety. Flip teased her when she refused to join him on a 'trip out', on what he called a voyage of discovery more memorable than anything she had ever experienced. She had seen too much of the effects of such trips in Sarajevo to be tempted. If he wanted a fellow drug-head, he'd have to look elsewhere she told him. But she did drink more than she usually did to try and match his mood, and found she enjoyed the effects..

It was when they were both at home in Flip's cottage that she was at her most content, gradually transforming its austerity into the welcome of a home. There were flashes of memory of the home she had built out of the tiny flat in Oxford a few years earlier. Not that there was the slightest resemblance between Flip and Jesse, and Minkie was glad of that. She had learned the hard way the pain of over-dependence.

"Proper little nest-maker, aren't you?" Flip teased, but she knew he liked the results of her efforts.

Jesse had teased her, too, when she had brought some knick-knack back from Oxford market for their little flat off the Woodstock Road, or found a new way of re-arranging the furniture. She had thought then, as she did now, that it was something to do with creating her own territory since she did not belong to anyone else's. Sometimes in town she would sit in a café window and observe the criss-crossing paths of so many strangers each on a particular mission which linked them to other unseen strangers in a dizzying extrapolation in the network of belonging. It was odd because she had not been aware earlier of un-belonging. Indeed her attachment to that little Oxford flat had even finally caused her to question the wisdom of that journey to Sarajevo. But she had gone, and there had been the totally unpredictable 9/11, and bit by bit the people who provided the safety net of her growing up dropped away.

Then came the night she became involved in a brawl and ended up in a police cell. She had no memory of the sequence of events but apparently she bit a policewoman's arm. She had somehow become separated from Flip and it was not him whom she asked the police to call; but Mike. He arrived at the police station at 2 a.m. to bail her out and drive her back to Daerley where Sara put her to bed.

He had gone into Oxford when Minkie came down to breakfast next morning, feeling like death.

"Is he livid?" she asked, struggling to chew her way through a piece of toast.

"Disappointed I think would be more accurate. What happened?"

"Flip and I were out with friends in a bar, and someone suggested trying out that new place in the town centre. There was a fight – I don't remember how or why it started, or in fact anything else."

Sara drove her home and Minkie rang Mike that evening, subdued and apologetic. He was really quite good about it, joking about broken beauty sleep. But he wasn't so amenable a couple of weeks later when something similar happened again. This time it wasn't so late and it wasn't the police who called Mike but a pub landlord. She wasn't so drunk either that she couldn't remember his fury.

"Haven't you ever been drunk, you sh-sad thing?" she slurred at him.

"You just listen to your dad," the publican said.

"He'sh not my dad," Minkie spat. "If only he could remember that."

She was to remember the look on Mike's face and the silence that followed long after she had forgotten their words. They'd had a bad fight once before, years ago in which she had shouted at Mike that she wasn't his kid and he'd no right to make decisions for her. Sara had healed the rift that time, but she couldn't now.

Franko wasn't prepared to dish out sympathy either. "This Flip is perhaps not right person for you," he said after listening to her account.

"I thought he was a great buddy of yours."

"Even I can be wrong," Franko said. "Why you don't move back with Rowena? It is a nice place."

It was as though she was caught on a track to some unknown destination and couldn't get off. Most of the time she didn't want to get off. She'd never had so much fun, so much admiration. In Sarajevo no one had taken any notice of her. Except Bozo. Here the rest of the gang called her their 'little Balkan babe' as though she were something special, like a mascot. The more they said it, the more it reinforced her growing sense of having missed out on a big chunk of life which other people took for granted: the chunk that was about growing up, having fun, making mistakes, falling flat on your face, picking yourself up, having more fun. Except, a small voice pointed out somewhere in her head, she seemed to keep repeating the same mistakes.

She never meant to get drunk. There was always that point when life seemed just great, when she persuaded herself that a little, little drink more would make it totally perfect. And from then, it all descended into mayhem. Flip said she shouldn't worry, she was an absolute star when she was out of control, and never better in bed. Which was a pity since Minkie could rarely remember any of it.

Most of the gang were ten, fifteen years older than she was. They tended to have partners rather than spouses, sometimes swapping amongst themselves, "though I'm not swapping mine," Flip said firmly once or twice when it was proposed. Curiously the swapped partners did not seem to mind, and Minkie wondered whether it might be rather interesting to spend some time with one of the others. She was partly intrigued, partly repulsed by the idea, and not sure how she felt about Flip's display of proprietorship.

Then one evening he seemed to have changed his mind. Something had come up, he said, and he'd asked Craig to take her out instead.

"You didn't ask me," Minkie said.

"No, well it's not easy get past the Aussie dragon of Cyber Inc. But if you mind I'll cancel it."

Craig was the most dominant member of the gang. Probably the wealthiest, too, which was no doubt why he attracted the best-looking women though, with his shaven head, nose ring and developing paunch he wouldn't have been Minkie's first choice. She knew he fancied her, probably because she was so different from the others. Well, it could be interesting.

"No, it's OK," she said.

Craig picked her up at Cyber Inc. She noticed he had made an effort with his appearance: smart casual but with more emphasis on the smart than usual.

"Thought we'd try Go West, that new place on the way to Warwick, Babe," he said as they settled in to his BMW

"My name's Minkie, not Babe."

"OK Minkie. I like a girl who knows her own mind."

Go West had had good coverage in the county papers and even a paragraph in one of the lesser Sundays. The décor and the staff got more attention than the food and it was easy to see why. Its theme was the great migration west of the Mississippi. The waitresses were wenches with flouncy skirts and low cut bodices that did nothing to conceal their ample proportions. There were saddles and harnesses, a lot of ancient weaponry, and paintings of covered wagons on the wood-panelled walls, and a background of western music.

Craig ordered a bottle of champagne without consulting Minkie. As the waitress leaned forward to fill the glasses and present them with an impressive cleavage, Minkie put a hand over her glass and said "I'd really appreciate a St. Clement's," adding apologetically. "Been rather overdoing things recently."

She had once confessed to Mike, because she suspected he felt the same, how out of place she felt at social gatherings as she never knew what to say. He'd advised "You don't have to say anything. Just grab someone and ask them about themselves and there'll be no stopping them."

Craig had apparently read the same book of etiquette for he began asking about her childhood in Sarajevo. That really surprised her and she warmed to him. Eventually she said "Now tell me about you" and, once launched, Craig had an inexhaustible series of stories on his escape from middle class turpitude, some of them very funny.

In due course they chewed their way through a fairly ghastly steak which called itself a California Supremo accompanied by Hill Billy French fries and a Mexicana salad.

"Sure you won't change your mind about the bubbly?"

"I think I'm quite high enough on oranges and lemons."

"I better get you another then," Craig said, heading for the bar.

It was half way through an outrageously rich dessert that she began to feel muzzy. Well, it had been a long day. Fighting it, Minkie said "Pity Flip couldn't make it this evening."

"His bad luck, my good fortune," Craig grinned. He added almost to himself "Though it's surprising what a little persuasion can do."

"How do you mean?"

He moved a little closer. "You really are a bit of an innocent aren't you Sweetie? Come on, you know I've fancied you for a long time. Flip certainly knows." He poured himself another glass of champagne. "And I guess he's better looking than me. But influence counts, too. I have a lot of that, know a lot of people that could put business in the right direction."

Minkie frowned, trying to concentrate through the tiredness. "What are you saying?"

"I'm saying that Flip finally appreciated that being so dog in the manger with you wasn't entirely to the advantage of his business expansion."

Minkie felt sick, as much at Flip's duplicity as Craig's clumsy courtship. The tiredness was making it very difficult to think straight, and she reached out for her glass, almost knocking it over.

"You all right, Babe?" Craig leaned towards her. His hand brushed her knee and began a gentle caressing movement.

"Yesh. Yes, I'm fine. Jusht, just tired." She couldn't understand why the words were coming out slurred. "But I think I'd like to go home."

"Just sit quietly and you'll soon be fine," Craig said, his voice soft, coaxing. His hand was slowly working its way up her thigh. With an effort Minkie removed it.

"What's wrong, Sweetie?"

"Not Sweetie. Minkie." Her voice had sunk to a whisper and all she wanted was to sleep, sleep, sleep.

Craig moved away a little and now, his voice concerned, said "You really are off colour, Sweetie, aren't you. Poor Princess."

Mike called her Princess, not anyone else. Suddenly she wanted to get away, stood up, lost her balance and fell back again. "I'll call Mike…" she whispered. If only she'd brought her mobile with her. Then remembered that Mike wasn't interested in her any more.

"Who the hell's Mike?" Craig demanded, but for the moment Minkie couldn't think who he was or why she was there. Only that she wanted to get away.

Craig got to his feet, put his hands under her elbows and helped her to stand. She didn't want to go with him, and began to cry.

"Don't be silly, Sweetie. I'll take care of you." He steered her to the door and out across the car park.

"Don't wanna go…" Minkie whimpered.

"Don't be silly, Sweetie," Craig said again, manoeuvring her more firmly now.

She managed to struggle free as he opened the passenger door, and began to stagger back towards the restaurant. Someone was coming out into the car park in a hurry and she thought perhaps they could help her, but Craig came after her, cross and cursing now. There was a scuffle and she was being pulled back to the car, bundled in, the door slammed behind her.

And then she crashed out.

Oxfordshire : Spring 2004/Rowena

Hey, remember me? Has the country of your forebears so bewitched you that you've forgotten your old Grumps who misses you like hell? Jake refused to have anything to do with modern technology and had scrawled his message on a postcard showing the South Perth riverside parks with a huddle of trees marking the paper bark swamp where they had spent so many hours together.

Rowena glanced at her watch. It was 9 a.m, so 5 p.m. in Perth. As soon as she heard his voice, the Antipodean drawl so much more pronounced now that she hadn't heard it for a while, she felt a wave of nostalgia such as she hadn't felt since her earliest days in Daerley.

"I'm an ungrateful pig," she said.

"You are," agreed Grumps. "You're also twenty-something and enjoying the sort of good time appropriate to twenty-somethings." No point in saying that most of her peers had settled down by now, probably with a couple of sprogs. "How's that young man of yours?"

"Not really mine. Just a good time partner, I suppose. But you'd like him. Why not come over?" She warmed to the idea. "Yes, oh yes, do. Then I could stop feeling guilty."

"Don't think I haven't thought of it. But doc says it wouldn't be fair on the airline."

Rowena's heart did an uncomfortable flip. "What does that mean?"

"Means my ticker needs a quiet life if I'm to get the longest use of it. Which means you'll have to get back here to tell me all you've learned about Pete."

"Not that much yet, though it's not through want of

trying." Though, let's face it, she could have tried a lot harder. "The R.A.F. Museum people say there were seventeen Typhoon squadrons serving on the continent at the time of the friendly fire, and gave me a string of squadron numbers. The only way to find out which was the one involved would be to check their operations records books at the National Archives."

"Sounds daunting."

"I was thinking of taking a trip over. You know, to the actual place where it happened. It would be amazing to be where you and Granddad had been all those years ago."

"I wish…" Jake began, but Rowena interrupted sharply "Don't even go there. A Grumps with a crook ticker is *not* what I need. Nor what Granddad would have wanted."

Jake surrendered. "Just make sure you come back safe" – *and before too long* was implicit. "Oh and by the way, I've just unearthed some old photos to send you which might amuse you."

Life had recently become complicated and was about to become more so. Late that evening Franko telephoned and said tersely he would be arriving shortly with Minkie in tow. It was an apt choice of words for when he turned up soon after midnight, Minkie was draped round his neck and smelling rather strongly of vomit. He lowered her on to the sofa and gave her face a few sharp slaps.

"Hey!" protested Rowena.

Minkie moaned a few times, eventually opened her eyes which were quite unfocussed.

"Better get basin." Franko said, and Rowena did, just in time.

"What the hell happened?"

"A bastard man I thought was a friend try to drug Minkie."

She had never seen him so angry. When Minkie stopped vomiting, they managed to get her upstairs and into bed, and then Franko explained how he had taken a client to Go West and seen Minkie and Craig, and, knowing the latter's reputation, had kept an eye on them, seen Minkie's changing behaviour, followed them out to the car park. Rowena, reckoning that Franko was as practised in recognising rogues as anyone, did not question his judgement.

"I'll call tomorrow to see she is OK," he said.

"I'll take care of her," Rowena said, and found she liked the feeling of sharing the responsibility of Minkie with him.

She was checking her email next morning when Minkie came down, pale and hollow-eyed.

"How did I get here?"

"Franko brought you. I gather he wasn't very happy with your choice of companion last night."

"The bastard put something in my drink." Minkie glared at Rowena. "And if you say anything about people not playing with fire if they won't want to get burnt, I'll, I'll…"

"I'm hardly likely to, having got burnt quite a few times myself."

Minkie looked interested. "Really? I thought you were one of those sensible people who gave trouble a wide berth." She paused to consider. "But then Franko wouldn't have become as smitten as he obviously is."

Not the right moment to explore the implications of this, Rowena decided, and instead said "I'll make you some coffee. Anything to eat?"

Minkie's expression was answer enough. "I'll try some toast to see me through the morning." She glanced at her watch. "Oh God, it's that late. Forget it, I'll grab a sandwich after my course."

"You'll eat some toast on the bus. Come on, push off and get dressed. You've got fifteen minutes."

After Minkie had left, Rowena felt strangely restless. The telephone call to Jake had unsettled her. The gentle reminder that he was not immortal also reminded her that she couldn't loaf around in Daerley Green indefinitely. It was true that she had done quite of lot of research and equally true that it hadn't got her very far. Also that she had got through a fair chunk of her savings. Jake had sent her some money through the bank, but it wasn't on that he should be subsidising her good time which, after all, is what it was for the most part. She had omitted to mention that her researches had been liberally interrupted by trips with Franko, mostly around the UK but also to continental Europe, mainly Poland and the Baltic States. Once or twice she had thought of suggesting a detour to the Luneberg Heath area where Grumps and Granddad Pete had been on that awful march, but they were always in a state of hurry, hurry, hurry. Franko needed to visit agencies in these countries to drum up workers in this or that field. Rowena soon came to the conclusion that he had a stake in the foreign agencies as well as the UK one which, like the spider in the middle of a web, directed its attention to wherever it was needed.

Her glance fell on the plastic bag full of Justin's diaries. It was a while since she had looked at them. There had been a rather boring stretch as he eased his way up the Civil Service ladder, finding he had a liking and a bent for dealing with his foreign contemporaries, which served him well in the Board of Trade and subsequently Foreign Office. This included a year in Amman, Jordan, which could have proved interesting except that he seemed to have been demoted to a rather boring job which kept him desk-bound. He also went through a period of being terribly preoccupied with his own health. Things brightened up a bit when he returned to London but there were still lots of references to places and people she had never heard of and she began to empathise with Luke's assessment of him as a boring old fart. Then suddenly there were fascinating if elliptical references to a love affair he'd had some years earlier with the daughter of an attaché working in the Russian embassy. Their best efforts to keep their relationship secret had finally failed, the attaché and his family were dispatched back to Moscow, Justin sent to Jordan. Ah, so that accounted for the boring desk job. By the time they met again in Moscow some years later she was married, though a few brief moments alone together confirmed that their love had mutually survived.

So not such a boring old fart after all.

Presumably Luke knew nothing of this. Rowena decided to put out a few feelers.

"Didn't your great uncle ever marry?" she asked him soon after.

"Seemingly not." Luke had hesitated before going on "But surprisingly he did have a bit of a fling. Some Russian diplomat's daughter. That must have caused a flurry in the F.O. dovecotes! Enough for him to be dispatched to the Middle East and for her to be bundled back to Moscow. According to his diary, he spilled all this out to young Minkie one day, when she was mooning over her American."

"May be he has other attributes you have yet to discover," Rowena suggested.

"I doubt it," Luke said in a tone that indicated the subject was not up for further discussion.

Now returning to his diaries, Rowena saw that this meeting with his lost love had triggered a period of introspection that thoroughly unsettled Justin's usual equanimity to the extent of affecting his work and provoking some criticism from his superiors. It was at this point that Justin invited himself to James's cottage for a week-end. And where should that cottage be but in the small town of Charlbury, roughly central to the triangle of green uplands between Oxford, Banbury and Cheltenham. The two brothers had spoken on the phone, exchanged Christmas and birthday messages, but had rarely met since Luke's birth three years earlier. Luke's parents Gilpin and Penny were teachers in a local school. It had been a source of astonishment to everyone that inarticulate Gilpin should have turned out to be such a good teacher, let alone attract anyone as vivacious and gregarious as Penny. But Penny proved to have more social than maternal instincts. Luke was clearly a mistake. Penny loathed having to give up her job, was bored out of her mind by babies and baby talk, and got a baby minder at the first opportunity so she could get back to teaching. After one or two baby minder disasters, Gilpin's mother put her foot down and insisted that the infant Luke should be dropped off at the grandparents' cottage each morning. Over the following months, Luke spent more and more time there and it was then that James gradually emerged from the twilight world into which he had retreated after the Battle of the Somme, finding a rapport with this unscarred scrap of humanity that he had never managed with anyone else.

By the time of Justin's visit, Luke was a lively three year old, vaguely disciplined by his grandmother, totally indulged by his grandfather. It was clear from the diaries that it was a huge disappointment to Justin, then teetering on the brink of clinical depression, to find James's attention so absorbed in this mini human.

Reading these passages, Rowena clearly saw how a mutual antipathy had begun. Luke, now thoroughly accustomed to being the main focus of James's attention, recognised, however dimly, that he had a rival competing for it. Justin, who had done everything in his power to pluck his twin from the terrible black abyss in which he had sunk, now found that a precocious toddler was succeeding where he had failed. By thought association, Rowena also began to acquire a new insight into Jake's relationship with Greatgrumps who would have been James's contemporary and likewise suffered from his experiences in the same war, albeit in different theatres of it; and subsequently her own special relationship with Greatgrumps. In fact, she had been to him what Luke was to James. How very weird. And what new vistas of human behaviour were suddenly illuminated by the seemingly haphazard juxtaposition of cause and effect.

Rowena sat holding the pages of Justin's diary for a long time, thinking herself into a situation whereby at that vulnerable time in her life she had been abruptly excluded from seeing

Greatgrumps. And had the first glimmerings of what had happened to the secure cocoon of Luke's life.

But why? Why had James suddenly turned his back on his adored grandson?

The phone rang. "Shit," said Rowena.

"Wondered whether you might like to join us for a light lunch," said Sara's voice. "We haven't seen you for a while. And may be you know more about Minkie than we do these days."

Oh yes, she knew quite a lot about Minkie. But hardly of a nature to be transmitted to anxious ex-foster parents.

"Be with you in half an hour," she told Sara.

It was good to see the Hennesseys again. Mike, taking a breather from his latest opus on Balkan history, was unusually relaxed, and for some reason Sara seemed to find Luke's fling with Amanda highly amusing. They were relieved to learn that Minkie was moving back with Rowena and happily did not enquire too deeply into her erratic life style.

"And you are clearly a stabilising influence on Franko. He's quite the respectable yuppy these days," commented Mike.

Rowena wasn't sure how much she wanted to be regarded as a stabiliser in anyone's life, but if it made for easier relationships, then so be it. She decided to put out a tentative feeler of her own.

"It seems odd that Justin, with all his travels and undoubted charm, never married," she hazarded.

"According to Minkie he had a huge unhappy love affair and never looked at another woman," Sara said. "She winkled that out of him when she was going through some trauma with her own boyfriend, Jesse."

How amazing that half the world seemed to know about Justin's lost Russian love, but no one knew about his twin brother.

Back at the cottage she returned to the diaries. Justin's visit to Charlbury that week-end had not been a success. His conviction that if anyone could understand his sense of isolation and loss then it would be James proved misplaced. But even Rowena, more than half a war-free century later, could see that the loss of a love, however great, could not be compared with the ongoing hell of trench warfare as described by Greatgrumps and presumably comparable to what James had experienced on the Somme.

Could James' lack of empathy, his preoccupation with his grandson, have triggered off a jealousy in Justin that had influenced him for years to come. Surely he could not have been so small minded?

The next day she went to the library and took out a hefty book of edited diaries and letters of those who had taken part in the Somme campaign. She was reading it when Luke called in a couple of evenings later.

"I didn't know you were into 20th century history."

"My grandfather was at Gallipoli. I guess the Somme was a similar kind of hell."

"Hm. My grandfather was there."

Rowena just stopped herself from saying yes, she knew, since there was no reason why she should know. And decided that subterfuge was not her forte.

"Did he ever talk about it?" she asked, remembering too late that James had been excised from Luke's life while he was still very young.

"Never got much of a chance to ask," Luke said, turning away to collect some papers he had dumped on the table.

Some of the diaries on the Somme were heartbreaking, in places because of the harrowing detail they contained, in others because of what was so obviously left out in order not to distress families at home. In contrast, letters from home with their news of every day trivia brought a brief release into the unreality of the world they had left behind before awareness of the there-and-then reality of soggy discomfort and fear took over again. And then Rowena's eye caught the word 'Gallipoli' and she was right back with Greatgrumps in his residential home in a Sydney suburb, watching his every expression as he vocalised his memories perhaps for the first time. It was mind-boggling to realise that survivors of that terrible campaign had then crossed another continent to serve on the Somme. The diaries contained references to how some of them now thought almost with nostalgia of those dry trenches infested with mosquitoes and bugs compared with the glutinous rat-infested quagmire in which they now found themselves. Some of the descriptions of battlefields strewn with dismembered bodies were almost unbearable to read. A corporal describing such a scene berated himself for his lack of feeling and sometimes this acquired detachment turned into black humour; but far more dominant was the fear that was part of every waking moment.

How had they all coped, and then managed to pick up the threads of normality after such experiences? Of course a lot of them hadn't. Greatgrumps hadn't, nor had Luke's Granddad. Nowadays people tended to pooh-pooh the modern trend for counselling, and maybe things had swung too much in the direction of finding excuses for all and any outrageous behaviour in incidents from earlier life. But she guessed the likes of Greatgrumps and his contemporaries might have benefited, not to mention all those around them. Rowena suddenly felt an enormous sadness for all those lives not only broken on the battlefields but by lack of understanding when the men came home.

She slipped on a jacket and went out into the Spring evening, passed the usual group of youngsters hanging around the market place, too young to get into the pub, but defiantly flaunting their right to pollute their lungs with whatever they were pumping into them. Fluctuating sounds of conviviality came from The Trumpet. Almost certainly there would be someone in there ready to buy her a drink, have a chat; but she wasn't in the mood. She walked on turning a corner or two, and saw Mike Hennessey cutting back the tulips in Abel Yard's small patch of front garden.

“It seems such a pity to put an end to such an amazing sight,” Rowena said, pausing at the gate.

Mike smiled. “I guess it wouldn’t be so amazing if it were like that all the year.” He stood up, easing his back, observed her for a moment. “You’re looking bit down. Problems?”

“No, I’ve just been reading diaries from the Battle of the Somme.”

“Good Lord. You’d better come in and have a coffee. It’ll be an excuse to rest my aching back, and enjoy a bit of company – Sara is at one of her innumerable meetings.”

“So why the Somme?” he asked, filling the kettle in Abel Yard’s pleasant kitchen.

Rowena stood at the window looking out over the back garden. “Justin’s gardenia is going to look a treat. Er – yes, the Somme. It was something Luke said. About his grandfather James being in World War I, and Justin not because of health problems. And I started wondering if the reason for James’ being so unapproachable was the same as Greatgrumps…”

“Greatgrumps?”

“Sorry, my great granddad. He was at Gallipoli and it affected the rest of his life. Not least it affected his relationship with his son, my Grumps. In fact, there wasn’t a relationship.”

Mike paused in pouring hot water into the coffee machine. “What a strangely thoughtful young woman you are, Rowena. It never occurred to me to question what the effect of being part of a liberating army might have had on my Dad.” He poured the water and stirred thoughtfully. “May be that’s why he suddenly went all free love and flower power.”

“Your Dad was into free love?”

“Not exactly. At least not as far as I know. But he and Mum did the whole bit – communal living and self sufficiency. And I simply loathed it. So what’s your theory about Luke’s grandfather and the Somme.”

"That he couldn't talk to his own son but was finding the beginning of a relationship with his grandson."

Mike poured coffee into a mug and slid it across the breakfast bar to Rowena. "But didn't he move away when Luke was sent to boarding school?"

"Yes, that's the bit of the mystery I haven't solved yet, along with why Justin kept so shtum about his twin brother. Especially when they were so close as children."

"So it seems, from what Sara managed to get out of Justin just before he died."

"Perhaps people are more ready to talk near the end of their lives."

"Yes, and Sara has a talent for extracting information from people, almost without them knowing it. It seems after he had a horrendous time during the Somme campaign, James spent some time in what was probably one of the country's earliest psychiatric hospital; but it didn't do much good. After that he lived in Justin's flat for a very long time; but Justin couldn't do much with him either. Fortunately around the time Justin was beginning to get postings abroad, James met Mary, and they had a boy called Gilpin."

"Sounds as though Sara should have been a journalist like you."

Mike smiled. "Not nearly pushy enough. Anyway, she doesn't get her information through incisive questioning, but by a process of empathy and absorption. Like a sponge absorbing water. It wouldn't have worked in many cases in the world of hard news."

Rowena sipped her coffee. "You'd have thought that having a child might have given James a new outlook. Though come to think of it, it didn't happen in the case of Grumps and Greatgrumps. Absolutely no meeting ground between the two. And then of course Grumps went off to war, and you know the rest." She wandered back to the window to look out over the garden again. "I wonder.... I wonder if all those years later, after

Luke was born, and James became so fond of him, I wonder if Justin felt resentful that this small kid was succeeding where he had dismally failed."

"That sounds too small minded for the Justin I knew."

"Yes, but you knew the mature version. Perhaps at that particular time he was going through difficulties himself."

"Even then." Mike stood up and stretched. "Oh well, I guess we're not going to solve the mystery quite so easily. How about a tour of the estate and tell me about Minkie, or as much as you feel is transmittable."

As always after visiting the Hennesseys, Rowena returned to the cottage feeling refreshed. It was that evening that in a packet at the bottom of Justin's plastic bag she found some quite different mementoes of his past. There were a couple of photographs: one of two young men posing rather self consciously, the other of one of the young men in army uniform attached to a couple of letters from James addressed to Justin.

Rowena read the letter, skimming through it guiltily as though James himself might catch her reading. It was short and immensely sad telling of the death of his best friend and of the fear and discomfort that were now the only constants in his life.

She looked at the young faces in the photograph, open, guileless, mirror images of each other. Justin in civvies, James in khaki. The last item in the pile was a circular plaque carrying an impression of Britannia holding a laurel wreath and accompanied by a lion. An unfamiliar name was inscribed on it, probably of James' best friend. Round the edge of it were the words *He died for freedom and honour.* She fingered the plaque. It was quite heavy, but it didn't seem much in return for a man's life.

Grumps' photographs arrived next morning. Minkie, looking a whole lot better, came down while Rowena was sifting through them.

"It's like another world isn't it?" she said, passing her a photograph of the High Street with a wide grass verge, empty except for a couple of small cars and a horse-drawn milk float.

"Hey, and look at The Trumpet! And all those old guys standing outside puffing away at their pipes. And what about this one with the thatched cottage?"

There was a young woman standing at the gate. As it was in black and white you couldn't see the colour of her hair but it looked fair and fluffy. Behind her stood a young man, tall, slim, his hands on her shoulders.

"That'll be Grandmum. And …" Rowena looked more closely at the picture and felt an unexpected tightening of the throat. "Granddad Pete, my real grandfather. The one that was killed b-by …." Her voice broke and she stopped.

Minkie took the picture and look at it closely too. "She's pretty, your grannie. And your granddad looks really dishy." She went on looking at them for a while. "I can't imagine having a granddad for so long and then finding out that he wasn't. It was friendly fire that killed your real granddad wasn't it? I couldn't see why that was so important before, but now I think I can."

"Wasn't it the same for your Dad in the Bosnian war? Friendly fire?"

"Well, I'd hardly call it friendly. I was holding his hand at the time."

Rowena gave a cry of shock. "That's unimaginable. How have you managed to stay so sane?"

"Thanks."

"I've never really understood that war of yours."

"Join the club," Minkie said, and unexpectedly and spontaneously leaned over and gave Rowena a hug.

Oxfordshire : Spring 2004 – Luke

About the last person Luke anticipated or wanted to find on his doorstep when he opened the front door that afternoon was Beresford Tremayne, not least because he was expecting Amanda.

"Hello, so what brings you here?" was all he could think of saying.

"I'll come in," Beresford said, putting his words into action. His bulk filled the small hall of Luke's house. As he pushed the door shut behind him he went on "I know you were expecting Amanda, but I thought it was time to express my views on the affair you are having with my wife."

"Oh." Luke led the way into the small sitting room in which Beresford's size seemed marginally less intimidating. "I suppose you could interpret it like that. I think of it rather as a good friendship with ramifications."

"It's the ramifications I object to."

"Well Amanda doesn't seem to," Luke said. By the time he had decided it was not a very clever thing to say it was too late for Beresford had already hit him quite squarely on the jaw. As he stood rubbing it, in surprise as much as in pain, a musical warble began to emanate from Beresford's pocket. He extracted a mobile, listened, said "Yes, I'm with him now," and then handed it to Luke.

"What's going on?" Amanda's voice sounded anxious.

"Beresford just slammed me in the jaw," Luke said. "But I don't think it's broken."

"I'll come round…"

"No, I don't think that's a good idea." Luke held his jaw, feeling the swelling rise.

"Who would have thought he had it in him?" The bubble of laughter in Amanda's voice was both unmistakeable and hurtful; so was the suspicion of admiration it held. Luke handed the mobile back to Beresford and said "I suspect she's quite enjoying being fought over."

Beresford grunted, switched the mobile off without saying anything further and slipped it back into his pocket.

"I take it," Luke said casually, "that she doesn't know about Sara."

"Know what?"

"About the little fling you had with her on and off while Mike was away."

"How the hell…?"

"Great Uncle Justin wasn't exactly discreet in the diary he kept, especially if you are as good at reading between the lines as I am. Or are you saying I got it wrong?" Luke gently ushered his uninvited guest towards the front door and opened it. As Beresford reached the gate, Luke raised his voice slightly. "But my guess is that I didn't. Get it wrong, I mean."

Beresford got into his car and drove off.

"One set all," Luke murmured as he closed the front door.

The ache in his jaw became steadily more persistent and there was a lump like a small egg by the time the doorbell rang again at five o'clock. He swore loudly.

"I heard that," Rowena said as the door opened, then she saw his jaw. "Ouch."

"So what can I do for you?"

"Have you got any peas?"

"What?"

"Frozen peas. For your jaw." She pushed past him to the kitchen, rummaged in the frozen compartment of his fridge, said "Ah" and extracted a small bag of frozen peas. "Go and lie on the sofa," she said.

By the time she rejoined him she had knocked the bag of peas into malleability, wrapped it in a thin towel and now applied it to his jaw as he half lay on the sofa and looking quite sorry for himself.

"Make a cup of tea, find pain killers," Rowena muttered to herself as she placed the towel against his jaw. She was surprisingly gentle. "Just hold it in gently in place."

"Any special reason for your visit?" Luke mumbled. "I assume it wasn't just to check on my supply of frozen peas?"

"Tell you in a minute."

"The painkillers are in the bathroom cabinet."

He heard her run up the stairs, a gentle clatter from the bathroom and then her descent, the sound of the kettle being filled, and in due course Rowena reappeared with a small tray bearing a mug of steaming tea, a glass of water and a small container of aspirin. He took the latter first, wincing a little with the pain of swallowing.

Rowena watched him thoughtfully. "I'll hazard a guess at Beresford Tremayne."

Luke grunted.

"Well you were hardly discreet. My guess is that Beresford was the only person in Daerley who didn't know." She paused. "I wouldn't have thought he had it in him, lashing out like that. It's all right, I'm hardly going to weep for the hurt pride of our village Lothario. Come on, drink your tea."

While he took his first sips, she began rummaging in a plastic bag she had brought with her. After a moment she put a small packet on the sofa beside them and, on top of it, a couple of photographs. Luke picked them up, frowning, studied the smooth young faces, felt long-ago memories stirring.

"Where did you find these?"

"There was an old plastic bag squashed at the back of a cupboard in that little shed place Justin had on his patio."

Luke picked up the top letter, looked at it a long time before opening it. His head was down, one hand still lightly holding the ice pack in place and he was glad she could not see his expression as he read it, or the tears that flowed unchecked.

"I burst into tears when I read them," Rowena said from the other side of the room. She had gone to stand by the window looking out on the tiny patch of back garden. “I hope you don’t mind that I did read them.”

He managed a noncommital grunt.

Rowena went on “Perhaps if everyone was obliged to read letters like that on a regular basis there might be a universal uprising of nausea against war.”

Luke made a show of reading the letters again. He fumbled for a handkerchief, blew his nose, paused to acclimatise to the jabs of pain, cleared his throat, then said “That might have been true fifty years ago. But several wars and as many decades later, precision bombing must have removed any sense of human involvement that combatants might have felt for each other. Even in World War Two, the young pilots of Bomber Command were far removed from the results of opening the bomb doors and the few flashes of explosion thousands of feet below. How much more so now that missiles are directed at targets that are beyond the horizon.”

“Not much hope then for any of us,” Rowena said. She removed the tray, leaving the unfinished mug of tea on a table beside him, and went out into the kitchen. Automatically she did some washing up, wiped over the surfaces, rinsed through a couple of towels. When she returned to the living room, the mug of tea was untouched and Luke was fast asleep. Clearly the aspirin had worked. She stood looking at him for a few moments. He looked quite nice when he was asleep. Even vulnerable. Quietly she removed the photographs, the letters and the plaque and let herself out.

The two photographs were lying on the coffee table in the living room when Minkie returned from work that evening. Rowena was on her mobile saying “… perhaps you ought to get it checked out by the doctor? Call me if you need anything.”

Minkie flung her bag on to the sofa, picked up the photographs and asked “Problems?”

“Luke seems to have walked into a door.”

“Careless.” A pause. “When did you become Luke’s

ministering angel? What's happened to Amanda."

"Seems as though they've split. I happened to call in with those." Rowena nodded at the photos in her hand.

"To think I used to admire that woman. I mean Amanda. And Berry – Beresford. Ah well." Minkie turned her attention to the photos and was quiet for some moments. "They're really cute in another-world sort of way, aren't they? Why do they seem strangely familiar?" She stared at Rowena, then with growing comprehension, went on "Ah, Luke, grandfather James, great uncle Justin, twins. These are Justin and James? Amazing." She sat down, peering closely at the faces. "They are *so* alike. I can't begin to understand why Justin never spoke of James."

"May be when you are that close to someone, you have to cut them out of your memory as well as your life when they've gone," Rowena said, doubtfully. "I dunno. I've never had that close a relationship, except perhaps with Grumps and I would never stop talking about him."

"He's still here," Minkie pointed out. "And I think it would be different with a contemporary. May be like Franko and I when I first came here. I'd spend hours talking to him in my head and even writing to him, but I don't think I talked much *about* him."

Rowena looked at her curiously. "It's funny to think of him and you as kids together."

"We were inseparable. And had such plans to make the world see the error of its ways. It was a terrible shock when we first met up over here and I saw how much he'd changed – had got into some really dodgy things in order to make money. And then he said I'd had it far too easy ever to understand …."

"I gather he wasn't too legal in his early days. And I sometimes wonder how completely legal he is now."

"Anyway, what did Luke have to say about the photographs?"

"He was very quiet. And then he read the letters and was even quieter. They are quite upsetting. Read them."

Minkie took the flimsy sheets from their envelopes and read them slowly. "Very upsetting," she said, without looking up. "Poor Justin, and even more, poor James. And this is just a taste. No wonder it affected him so badly. But it still doesn't explain why Justin never spoke of him, nor why Luke disliked Justin so much."

It was time, Luke decided, to check out his flat in Islington and catch up a little with the London scene that had once been the principal backdrop of his life. A few days should be enough to let his face get back to normal and allow any rumours on the Daerley grapevine to reach their zenith before giving way to the next item of hot gossip. His friends were suitably impressed by his jaw, now an impressive palette of purples, blues and greys. He embroidered a story which was near enough the truth to earn him a touch of admiration. But when the time came to go back to Daerley he felt curiously unreluctant to leave.

On his return the messages on his answering machine included three from Rowena. The first was a breezy enquiry into his state of health; the second, tinged with anxiety requested him to return her call; the third informed him he might was well resurface as no one seemed to have noticed his absence, but he noted the tinge of anxiety was more marked. He called her back and left a message on her answering machine suggesting they might meet up for a drink at The Trumpet some time.

He found himself thinking about that next morning as he strolled down the field track to Whirling Wood. He had not earlier given much thought to Rowena other than as a rather brash Antipodean to whom he had given temporary house space. She certainly was not his type even if she were not already committed to that flash cousin of Minkie's. Not that that would have been any obstacle if he fancied her. But he didn't. He was merely grateful for her ministrations after his run-in with Beresford and touched by her concern.

"'Morning. Seems as if Spring has come at last." A man

with a dog walking in the opposite direction interrupted Luke's thoughts. His climatic observation was clearly rhetorical, but Luke paused to watch his receding back view, and to register that he was doing what countless Daerlians had done before him: strolling down to Whirling Wood to clear his thoughts and – yes, enjoy the quintessential Englishness of this patch of Oxfordshire. Sara had done it. And Minkie. And Justin. His diary had been peppered with references to strolls down to Whirling Wood.

What thoughts had he had to clear?

Luke resumed his walk. It was always muddy at this bottom end of the field track before it reached the narrow private road you crossed to reach the wood. It was a while since he had been down here and he paused at the squeeze gate leading into it to observe the changes. Sara always said this was a great time and he could understand why as he took in the almost explosive visual return to life after the bare-branched winter. True the oaks were still semi dormant, and the ash fronds young and delicate, but the willows shimmered over-all in green so soft it was almost tangible, and glinted with the soft silvery catkins which in due course he reached out to touch and stroke and marvel at their sensuousness. He paused to review his thoughts. At what point had he acquired this talent to distinguish without hesitation between oak, ash and willow? It was not so long ago that his total arborial repertoire had been limited to the London plane.

He noted that the grass rides that wove a figure-of-eight through the small wood were in need of cutting; that the first ox-eye daisies were in bud and that a small clump of ragged robin shivered gently in the breeze. He did not remember learning the appearance let alone the name of ragged robin. Amanda would have made an unlikely teacher? Probably Sara on one of their occasional coincidings in the wood. It pleased him that he had acquired this knowledge so effortlessly.

He moved on to the centre of the wood where a small patch of grass had been transformed into a wildflower meadow. There were signs of leaves and flowers of other plant species he could not name. For some reason he remembered a passage in Justin's diary describing his first encounter with a very young Minkie. It seemed he had come upon her clutching a sad wilting collection of plants with which she planned to make a soup, as they had so often done back home in Sarajevo. And, at a deep, almost impenetrable level, he felt a shaft of sorrow that he had never experienced that compassion which everyone in Daerley attributed to his great uncle. The old boy could surely have told him the name of every plant now contributing anonymously to the wild flower meadow at his feet. Luke took a few paces and sat on the wooden bench which lay in the dappled sunshine. Its surfaces were a maze of carved initials and he found himself running his fingers over them, trying to put names to them.

And then he heard a noise. Not so much a cry as a groan, like someone turning in their sleep. He listened, became aware of the deep sound of silence in a way he had not before. The silence was immediate, all around him, accentuated by the pale thrum of traffic in the distance and the even paler hum of an aircraft. Looking up he could see its white vapour trail as it headed towards London from who-knew-where.

And then he heard the groan again.

He traced its direction and followed it to the bushes thickly gathered on the bank of the stream that provided a boundary for the wood on its gentle meander towards the Cherwell valley. The groan came again. Not a child, nor an animal sound. He stood in the silence waiting for it to be repeated, glancing in every direction. And finally saw on the ground a few yards away a scattering of rags: a human-shaped scattering that suddenly twitched and revealed the human beneath it.

Some subconscious awareness of Luke's presence must have roused this being, for in a flurry of movement it leapt to its feet and faced Luke, fists balled and ready to strike. Luke jumped back more in surprise than in fear for there was little threatening about the slim young man with the pale face.

"Whoa, whoa," Luke exclaimed as if to a restless horse, and held out his hands placatingly.

The young man lowered his fists but stayed poised for attack, breathing heavily. Then he said something fast and incomprehensible.

"'Morning Luke," Both men turned towards Minkie now approaching across the wildflower meadow. "Did you get Rowena's message about … Oh." She broke off, noticing the curious scene before her: Luke facing an angry young man who appeared to have been pulled through a hedge backwards. "What's going on?"

"I'd be glad if someone would tell me," Luke drawled. "This young man clearly has a problem, but I'm not sure what language he has it in."

Minkie approached them more slowly, moved passed Luke towards the young man.

"Careful," warned Luke. But Minkie had started speaking to him, quietly, slowly, but equally incomprehensibly. The young man watched her, began to relax, spoke again briefly.

"He's Polish," Minkie said. "I can only understand a bit of what he says. But I guess he must speak some English."

"Yes, I speak," the young man said. "Not very good, but I speak."

"What's your name."

"It is Stan."

"Shan?"

Unexpectedly the thin, pale face broke into a smile. "Stan. But I think Shan I like better."

"Let's go and sit down Shan," Minkie said, held out a hand which he took and followed her to the bench.

After a moment he stopped staring at his feet and sat looking around, at the wood coming to life, at the patch of meadow, at the tumble of bushes and ancient willows marking the bank of the stream.

"Well done," Luke said.

"I see your jaw is better."

"Rowena told you about that?"

"She mentioned you had walked into a door." Minkie's grin indicated she did not believe a word of this. "And no one has seen the Tremaynes recently."

"Hm. What was Rowena's message about?"

"Oh, we have a leaking washing machine and the door coming off a kitchen cupboard."

"I can mend." They turned to Shan, now sitting up looking a good deal more prepossessing now that he was alert, had straightened his clothing, run a comb through tawny hair. "I can many things."

"Good, good. And so you shall young man. But first tell us why you are sleeping here and why you are so angry."

It was a hesitant, disjointed story, but common enough. He had paid an outrageous amount of money to come to England eighteen months earlier in return for his passage and the promise of a job. The job was with a dubious food processing works in the middle of an agricultural nowhere on the borders of East Anglia and Lincolnshire. The pay was minuscule and the accommodation in drafty sheds with the most basic facilities.

"Our pigs have better," Shan assured them. When he had saved a few pounds he had walked out and discovered the difficulties of finding work without a permanent address and of getting a permanent address without work. He had slept rough in parks, in doorways, been moved on, stayed in a hostel where his last few pounds were stolen. Then a man befriended him and offered him work in a bar in Banbury. Only it seemed the work included some favours.

"Favours?" queried Minkie.

"I think he means sex," Luke said, and Shan nodded. "Well," Luke went on. "I can offer you some work, a roof over your head and no favours."

Shan looked at Minkie, unsure if he was understanding correctly. She explained about Luke's house and the jobs that needed doing, and when they were finished they could always find him odd jobs somewhere in Daerley Green. Shan looked as though he couldn't quite believe his luck.

"It's all right," Minkie said. "Everything will be all right now."

"For first time I think so." Shan looked round the wood. "This is good place."

"Yes, it's been a good place for me, too." Minkie stood up, held out her hand again. "Come on Shan."

They took the field path back up to the village. Shan kept stopping to look back at the expanding view as they climbed the short steep hill.

He said "I can some farming too."

"Your family are farmers?"

"No, my father drink much, do nothing. But I work in fields after school and in holidays, try to make money for family. But father drink everything. I come here for better life."

"Poor Shan," Minkie said.

Luke observed his young companions with amusement. He saw Shan become increasingly infatuated with Minkie while she showed for him the concern of an older sister. He guessed they were much of an age.

When they reached the cottage, Rowena was heating soup from the freezer for lunch. They explained briefly about Shan, and while she got more soup from the freezer showed Shan his new accommodation. It was a small box room, just big enough for a single bed and a small chest of drawers. Minkie stood in the doorway while he arranged his worldly possessions contained in a small rucksack that had once been red but now was mainly a grubby grey. There were some papers, a dictionary, a couple of tee shirts, underwear, a pair of sandals with a strap hanging off. Not much of a total for one young man's life.

"We'll put those through the washing machine," Minkie said, grabbing the clothing.

"Why you so kind?"

She perched on the edge of his bed, trying to find the words that would make sense to him, and in a few sentences told him the history of how she had come to Daerley Green.

He nodded and after a moment said "I will do many things for you and your man."

There would be time enough later to explain that Luke was not her man, to introduce him to Franko who would help him get more work, to the Hennesseys who would take him under their wing because that was the sort of thing they did.

In due course Shan was amazed to learn that, though Luke owned the house, he did not actually live in it and had another house on the edge of the village.

"He very rich," Shan judged. Then, in case this should be regarded as a criticism, added quickly, "But very good man."

And Minkie had to agree that Luke was proving to be good in ways that quite surprised her.

Oxfordshire : summer 2004/ Mike

"I keep forgetting I'm married to a telephone," Mike said.

It was breakfast time. Twice he had begun to say "I think it's time you and I had a talk…" Twice he had been pre-empted by her mobile.

"No, sorry, I can't" Sara said into the receiver. She put it down. "I've switched it off and I'm all yours."

"You actually said 'no' to something," Mike said.

"I quite often do. But you've had your nose buried in the Balkans so long you wouldn't have noticed."

It was something they had come to accept long ago: that work was something they could not easily share. Mike's fascination with the Balkans went back to a book he'd picked up in a second hand shop as a boy. From that his interest had spread into other realms of history, but the Balkans remained his first love. Sara's interests were inextricably bound up with the here and now of middle England.

Sara prompted "So what's on your mind?"

"That we seem to have started inhabiting two different planets again."

"Hasn't it ever been thus: you in your big lake and I in my little pond?"

"But that's the point. I'm not longer in a big lake. I'm here in dear old claustrophobic Daerley."

"Physically maybe, but in every other way you're as inaccessible as ever."

That came as bit of a shock. "Well, it must stop. It has stopped. The book is with the publishers. I'm free as a bird. Let's take a few days … weeks off. Go for a lengthy potter through France…"

"Darling Mike, you're impossible. You may have met your deadlines and be at a loose end, but I have a website to edit and a study to do of brownfield sites in the Cherwell valley."

"You mean why is it our time together always seems to revolve around my timetable?"

"Well, yes, since you put it like that."

"I'm not sure we can change that. My commitments tend to be mega and long term, while yours are numerously small and more immediate."

"Surely there's nothing to stop you fitting some play time into a mega long-term schedule?"

"You're right. *Mea culpa.* May I put in a formal request for dinner out at a pub of my choosing and at a time entirely of yours?"

They settled for a Wednesday the following week at a pub on a village green about 20 miles away. It was not a huge success despite an excellent *coq au vin* and forest fruits mousse. Sara's mobile rang three times during the main course. Then, having switched it off, she discovered on checking it later that she had missed a commission for a rushed job for a travel supplement.

"It's not as if we need the money." Mike tried to be consoling.

"It's nothing to do with money," Sara said crossly. "It's to do with being me in my own right."

He was about to ask her what that meant, but thought better of it.

"One of the problems," Sara said, "Is you don't have a way of relaxing: like a group of mates to help fill in your spare time."

"You mean I ought to join the pub-going fraternity?"

"There are worse ideas. There was a time when you weren't averse to a session in The Trumpet."

"That was usually after a few weeks spent in someone else's civil war. That tends to change your priorities."

"Why not take Minkie out more?"

"Her life seems to be bound up with courses, free lancing

and stray Poles. But at least that's an improvement on the ghastly crowd she got in with that Flip fellow."

Sara nodded. "Yes, I think you were right when you said she was making up for all those lost years."

"Mm. Anyway, to come back to us – I'll try out your pub crawling idea, and hope you can fit me in from time to time into your busy schedule. As long as we never allow ourselves to slide back into that non-communicating limbo of a few years ago."

"I hope we're both older and wiser enough for that not to happen." He hoped so, too.

It was the following week that Mike had an email from Marija saying she was returning to England for a month's course and could she possibly….?

"Great." was Sara's reaction. "She'll keep you happily occupied for a while."

She was well aware of Mike's brief affair with Marija while he was on a student tour of Europe long before he had met Sara, and completely confident that Marija, now partnered with a fellow Serb, was no emotional threat. What she did not know was that she had borne Mike's daughter, and Mike had only discovered this by chance long after the child, Sonja, had been killed by mortar fire along with her step-father and half brother during the siege of Sarajevo. He had come close to telling Sara several times but, knowing that she was herself unable to have children, it had seemed too cruel.

When Mike returned with Marija from the airport it was something of a surprise to find she had become a trim forty-something, her jaunty fly-away hairstyle reverting to the auburn tints of earlier years.

"Doesn't she look great," Mike said, as the two women greeted each other.

"Yes, doesn't she?" both of them chorused and then laughed.

"I guess the comment applies to you both anyway," Mike said, heading upstairs with Marija's suitcase.

"I'm really sorry Marija," Sara said over supper. "But I'm not going to be very sociable for a week or two as I have some rush work. But Mike's just finished a book and will be delighted to have more than his own company." Ouch, that could have been better worded, but no one seemed to notice the implication.

"Do not worry. My course is quite – how you say? – heavy. I shall have much homework and a full head."

"How is Snežka?"

Marija grimaced. "She is not easy girl. Her father worries. She wants to make better world, but alone…"

"Single handed. Yes, Minkie was like that. It was quite hard learning it is easier to say than to do."

"Perhaps I send Snežka here to work for family. She admires Minkie very much and would learn from her."

Marija's course was three mornings and two afternoons a week. They came to an arrangement that Mike would drive her in to Oxford, go to the Bodleian to start research on his next project while she was at her class, then pick her up. Most days he drove her back to Daerley with a mountain of homework, but sometimes they went for lunch and a walk in the surrounding countryside, or visiting one of the gardens for which they both had a particular liking. Mike's best form of relaxation had always been to work in the garden, and the only echo of a link with his dead daughter had been her apparent love for wild flowers.

Once when he was guiding her through some of his favourite narrow alleyways to a pub said to have been the haunt of Oxford's literary grandees, Marija suddenly stopped, laughing. Mike stopped, too, mystified.

She said at last "You remember how that first summer I took you into every nook and cranny of Sarajevo, bombarding you with facts, willing you to love my city. And now, twenty, nearly thirty years later…."

"…. I'm bombarding you." Mike reached out and took

her hand. "You didn't have to will me to love your city. I already did. Or perhaps it was my guide that I loved."

She drew her hand gently away. "We were so young Mike. Innocent. At least I was. And I think you a little, too."

"Not too innocent to have a daughter."

"Exactly: too innocent to avoid having her. Don't go there, Mike. Please. It has been hard to go on with life. Without Bogdan it would have been impossible."

"For me it is not having any memories of her that is hard. Just a photograph of a face that has something of mine, and her hands holding some wild flowers that showed in her there was something, however small, of me. But you are right Marija. We must not go there."

But tricky moments like these were rare. On the whole they were relaxed together as happens between friends who go back a long way. Mike told her of the ups and downs of his relationship with Minkie, how he had alternately worried about her, been angry with her or delighted in watching her grow into the lovely young woman she now was. One of the hardest times, he confessed, was when he realised through Franko that Bozo had fallen for her.

It was Marija who suggested that Minkie should join them on one of their garden visits. It was a small garden in a village tucked into the undulating countryside west of Banbury, and Mike was so enchanted with it he insisted on going round it again. Certainly from a relatively small area the owners had created a little masterpiece, with herbaceous borders, a mini woodland, a lake with an island and a pair of grebes shepherding their fluffy brood into the reeds away from the possible threat of visiting humans, an autumn corner that would be a blaze of colour and produce a rich harvest of berries in due season, and innumerable enchanted corners where a well placed syringea framed an elegant sculpture or a buddleia swarmed with butterflies.

As Mike headed off for his second tour, Marija and

Minkie found a bench by the lake and watched the grebe parents slide cautiously into the open.

"Tell me about Snežka," Minkie said.

Marija was glad to talk. There was probably no one better than Minkie to understand the rebellious behaviour of her step-daughter whose golden memories of early childhood in Sarajevo bore little resemblance to the reality.

"She'll grow out it," Minkie assured her at last. "Only don't tell her that – she'll hate it. Anyway it's not so much growing out of things, but that other things come along and take priority."

"You're so sensible."

"Hm. I'm not sure Mike would agree."

"Well, perhaps we'll send her to England on some work experience and you could share your sense with her."

"I'll do my best."

They were silent for a while watching the grebes. One of the youngsters, bolder than the rest, had headed to the bank and was trying unsuccessfully to scramble up it, repeatedly falling back into the water.

Minkie laughed. "He reminds me of my cousin Franko."

"Let's hope he's as successful."

After a moment Minkie said "Snežka is very lucky to have you. I remember that photograph you sent Mike years ago, with your husband and children. I can't begin to understand how you survived that experience."

"I'm not sure I would have survived without Bogdan. I hope you will meet him one day." Marija rummaged in a zipped side pocket of her handbag, brought out two folded sheets of paper. Unfolded, the first one showed a laughing young man, his hand on the shoulder of a boy who was unmistakably his son.

"He's dishy," approved Minkie.

"Dishy?"

"Good looking."

"Yes, yes. He was. Both. My Nikolaj, senior and

junior." Marija handed her other folded sheet. "And now my Sonja. She would have been a bit older than you by now."

It was a close-up of a girl, about twelve years old, square face, straight dark hair, serious eyes staring back at the camera. Nothing of her father there, nor her mother. And yet, and yet.... Minkie stared more closely at the picture. "She reminds me of ..." Then stopped, because it was too preposterous.

As Marija returned the pictures to her bag, Mike's voice called "Hey, there you are." He loped towards them carrying a clutch of potted plants. "I've found a treasure trove to liven up the garden." He put them gently on the ground and picked one out. "Look at this camelia – a beauty. I fancy putting it by Justin's gardenia. What do you reckon, Minkie?"

For half an hour Mike had been so totally absorbed in the garden and finding and choosing the plants, he had completely forgotten the present. Now he noticed a small frown on Marija's face and Minkie's non committal response to his question. As she went off in search of a loo, Marija said worriedly "I was so stupid, wasn't thinking. I showed her photographs of my family. I think she saw some likeness."

"Hell."

"I'm so sorry."

"Perhaps you imagined it."

But she hadn't. That evening as Mike walked her back to the cottage, Minkie said in that disconcertingly direct way she had, "Is... was Sonja your daughter?"

"Yes." They were crossing the village green. Mike drew her across to the seat under the chestnut tree and sat down. "It was long before I met Sara."

Minkie sat beside him. He reached out and took her hand. "But Sara doesn't know, Princess. You know she couldn't have children. I didn't want to hurt her."

Minkie withdrew her hand gently. "I shan't tell her," she said. "It's none of my business."

Mike returned to Abel's Yard thoughtfully. Sara had not

yet returned from an evening meeting. Marija was watching the Six O'clock News. She switched it off as he came in.

"Well?"

"You were right. I couldn't read her mood. She seemed very detached about it."

"She is a very sensible young woman."

"It's difficult to see why it should matter to her."

Marija looked at him in silence. Began to say something, then changed her mind. Men could be very dense at times.

Oxfordshire : summer 2004/Minkie

"Remember our first meeting?"

"Never can I forget. Never."

Minkie and Shan had taken sandwiches down to Whirling Wood. They sat on the bank of the river dividing their spoils.

"I was lying just over there," Shan said, "thinking there was no reason to live any more."

It wasn't only his English that had improved. Soon after he moved into the cottage, Minkie took him for a tour of Banbury's charity shops. They found jeans, several tee shirts and then went to M & S for underwear.

"Underwear very expensive," Shan commented.

"No, it's that everything else you got was very cheap."

Franko had bequeathed to him his denim suit, a bit big, a bit worn, but still with some life in it. In return Shan had springcleaned the cottage and Luke's semi-detached, still puzzling why he felt it necessary to have both. He had also dug over the garden, cut the lawn once a week, repaired some broken fencing. Then he said "Now I valet your car."

"You mean clean it? Yes please."

"No, I mean valet. Inside and out."

From the house Luke watched him washing and polishing and buffing and hoovering, and had an idea. He made a couple of phone calls. One of them was positive. So Shan set up with his little mobile trolley of cleaning materials in the big car park by one of the main supermarkets on the edge of town. It had a slow start, but within a month he had more work than he could cope with. Through Franko he found and trained two more Polish assistants.

"I am entrepreneur," he announced happily to anyone who would listen.

The only one who didn't entirely fall for Shan's charms

was Mike when Minkie took him round to show off her new friend. "Bit on the young side, isn't he?" Mike suggested as they made tea while Shan roamed the garden.

"Young for what?"

"To be besotted with you as he clearly is. Why, I don't think you've even noticed, Princess."

Minkie decided that she'd never get it right. They were either too young or too old, too brash or too dull. "But it's not about what Mike or anyone else thinks," she heard Justin's voice say, and felt a sudden flicker of deep sadness.

A recent incident had brought him unexpectedly to the forefront of her mind. She had returned home to find Rowena engrossed in sheafs of papers covered with small neat writing: so engrossed that it had taken several attempts to get her attention. At last she looked up "Sorry, Oh, I didn't hear you come in."

"Clearly not." Minkie peered over her shoulder. "Good Lord, that's Justin's writing."

Rowena looked a bit uncomfortable. "Some old diaries."

Minkie frowned. "You think it's all right reading someone else's diaries? I gather Luke does, too, but at least he's inherited them."

"The ones Luke had are recent ones. About Daerley Green. These are really old and Luke doesn't know about them. I found them by chance in that den he had by the patio." Rowena paused. "And I'd rather Luke didn't know. At least not yet. I'm trying – and just beginning to understand that special relationship between Justin and his twin brother James. You know, Luke's Granddad."

"Hmmm. Well, I won't tell Luke as long as you let me read the diaries too."

"That's blackmail."

"Yes, isn't it?" Minkie said cheerfully. "But try and think of Justin as my equivalent of your Grumps."

"OK," Rowena agreed. "I'll try."

Shan was joining one of his mates at a disco; Rowena

was spending the week-end with Franko. Before she left, she produced the plastic sackful of Justin's diaries and gave Minkie a summary of what she had read so far.

Curled up in the armchair she had adopted as her own, Minkie skimmed through the earlier years anyway. After a while she had the strangest feeling that Justin was there reading them to her. What she had said to Rowena about Justin being her 'Grumps' was true. She had never had a close relationship with either of her grandfathers, but from the way that Rowena spoke of hers, it seemed very like the easygoing way she had related to Justin. And because she felt she understood him at a level that had some of the intuitiveness he had always shown towards her, she began to feel with him the disappointment when his brother could not manifest the empathy he had come to need. She tried to imagine how she might have felt if Mike had in any way downplayed her own urgent need to return to Sarajevo. And then recalled so vividly that she could feel again the pain of that terrible row they had had when she spat at him that he had no right to try and control her like a daughter.

Come to think of it, there had been some similar incidents more recently, but she was now better equipped to be her own person. Whoever that was.

She returned her attention to the diaries, noticing that it was nearly midnight but nowhere near ready to give up yet. As Rowena had said, there was a lot of rather dull stuff about his career progress, sometimes linked with contemporary events which ranked as history in her own terms, mainly to do with the Cold War. For two or three years there were few references to James, except echoes of his seeming return to a normal life. Luke's parents moved to Canada for a couple of years and it was agreed that Luke should move in with his grandparents for that period.

And then Minkie came to the page in 1972 which made her catch her breath in disbelief and then read it again and again. The brothers had reunited. James had triggered it by inviting

Justin to Charlbury. Mary had died a few months earlier and James was clearly struggling. Justin, due some leave and going through a difficult patch himself, stayed with him for a month, old wounds were healed, a new relationship formed with his great nephew. Luke, now seven, was clearly put out by an intruder's presence, or more particularly by the attention he was getting, but Justin made great efforts to be as unobtrusive as possible. It was half way through his visit that, on the way to collecting Luke from kindergarten, he overheard a conversation between two women that was to cast ripples, eventually and especially changing Luke's life.

Suddenly he realised they were talking about Luke, saying what a shame he had to live with those two old men while his parents were abroad, what a pity his grandmother had died. Then one of them said quite clearly, "Have you noticed how you quite often see him hanging around the school playground?"

In his diary Justin had raged at such a disgusting insinuation, yet that evening had found himself observing in a quite new way how James acted with Luke. He had questioned James as to when the boy's parents were due back and commented on how much of his growing up they were missing and what a tie it must be for James.. Tetchily his twin had riposted that he didn't know what he would have done without the boy since Mary's death.

It was clear from the diary that Justin was angry that he had allowed the women's conversation to affect him as it undoubtedly did. His stay in Charlbury was due to end the following week after which he was on some Board of Trade mission to Moscow; but before leaving he made a date to come back to Charlbury the following month and on his return to London he also made a call to Vancouver. It was a relief when cheerful extrovert Penny answered the phone.

"Justin! There's a surprise." A small pause. "I hope that doesn't spell problems back at the homestead?"

He had reassured her, reporting a good visit to Charlbury

and the pleasure at how well James seemed these days. Penny agreed, adding how amazing it was that Luke had appeared to provide the original catalyst. In fact it seemed to be mutual since Luke became a much more amenable child when he was with his grandfather.

Justin had suggested the boy was perhaps rather lacking companionship of his own age, but Penny disagreed, pointing out that he'd always been an unsociable little tyke when it came to his peers. Anyway, she added, they would be home in a few weeks, unwittingly echoing James' "more's the pity."

It was then that Justin had come out with the idea that had been forming in his mind since his visit to Charlbury. "I sometimes wonder," he said, "if boarding school wouldn't be the best answer for that boy."

There was a pause at the other end of the line. Then "It would certainly be kill or cure," Penny said. "Maybe that's just what he needs." Justin guessed that Luke's step-dad would have no objection to having the boy out from under his feet..

Back in Daerley Green 2004, Minkie slipped the pages of the diary back into the appropriate folder and leaned her head back. Her mind swirled with thoughts and tiredness, but even when she went to bed the swirling didn't stop and when she came out of a restless sleep a few hours later, it was with an uneasy sense of doom she had not experienced before: as if all the safe reliable parameters of her life so far had blurred and shifted, like quicksand. All she knew about child abuse she had gleaned through horror stories in the media. That it could be remotely connected with anyone she knew was hard, no impossible, to take in. Least of all someone so closely associated with Justin.

She went down to make a pot of strong coffee and sat over it reviewing all she had read the previous evening. She could not, would not believe there was anything to justify the insinuations, yet was afraid to read more of the diaries in case she learned something she did not want to know. But there was something odd, something that did not add up in all this.

Minkie poured herself another coffee and said aloud, "Oh Justin, why couldn't you have kept it all to yourself?"

"Because," she imagined him answering, "there is no truth that is not better for being out than hidden."

The phone rang. "I have terrible head," said Shan's voice. "You meet me in Wood for talk?"

Any excuse to postpone getting back to the diaries.

When she met him half an hour later it was to find he wanted to declare his undyng love.

"No Shan," Minkie said firmly. "It's not undying love; it's affection and gratitude and a feeling of security after feeling lonely and vulnerable for so long. Believe me, I've had all these feelings, too. Think of me as your sister."

"It is not right that I should have such feelings for a sister."

Oh dear. What a tiresome obstacle sex could be, intruding where it was not wanted, and sometimes not where it was. She decided to change the subject. "So where were you last night?"

"This new disco near the canal. I drink too much. Your cousin was there, with Rowena. I think they have very good feelings together."

No doubt. Unexpectedly Minkie felt a wave of nostalgia for Jesse, and the two or three years they had together, a couple of them as girl/boy friends, and then a year living and working together in Oxford. It had been a wonderfully uncomplicated relationship – mutual affection, good sex, a natural ability to work together. What would have happened if 9/11 had not triggered in Jesse an urgent need to return to his roots? Would they have married, moved to America, become absorbed in that American dream which had become so volubly lauded and applauded in the surge of revulsion at everything the destruction of the Twin Towers represented?

"What are you thinking about Minkie?"

"About my American boyfriend Jesse and how I nearly went to live in America with him."

"I am very jealous of him."

"He was not the one for me, though I did love him very much."

"And I am not the one for you?"

"No Shan." She ruffled his hair. "I haven't yet met the one for me."

She sometimes wondered whether she ever would.

Oxfordshire : autumn 2004 – Sara

Sara stood at the kitchen window of Abel's Yard watching Mike rake up the leaves. And felt troubled. Since Marija's visit she had sensed something was wrong. Not that she thought for a moment that their old affair of 30-plus years ago had been re-ignited. Indeed she'd been surprised how relieved Mike seemed when he saw her off at Banbury for the airport bus. For a few days he had seemed more his old self. Then he had called on Minkie one evening to take her out and returned almost immediately tense and clearly unwilling to discuss it except to snap "She's apparently too busy."

"Have you two quarrelled?" Sara asked.

"Of course not. But she does seem to be going through a self-centred phase."

"Oh, that's not just Minkie. It's her generation."

"Well, I'm not yet ready to put a whole generation in the same box," Mike said. "I'm off to The Trumpet. Want to come?"

"I think I can resist such a charming invitation." Sara watched him stomp off, hoping that a jar of Hook Norton and a bit of solitude might mellow his mood.

Now, watching him through the window she could read his tension by the hunch of his shoulders. When Mike came in response to her "Coffee's up", she poured him a mug, waited a few moments before saying "I'm not prying, just concerned that something's amiss."

"Too much time. I need a project."

She allowed a smaller pause. "Do you still fancy a trip to France?"

It was as though a light had been switched on behind his eyes. "Are you suggesting one?"

"No, I'm insisting on one," Sara said.

He got the maps out that evening. "North, south, east, west?"

"I rather thought 'unplanned' – sort of follow our noses, or rather our car bonnet."

"Great. How about the week after next?" Mike fished a diary out of his pocket "October 4th – that's a Monday."

"Perfect. Fits in with a lull at Cyber Inc. And the website will have to tick along without me. I'll get Minkie to keep an eye on things and water the plants."

"If she can find the time," Mike muttered.

Sara dropped in to see her a couple of evenings later. Minkie and Rowena were just finishing supper and Rowena had a date with Franko.

"Funny, I wouldn't have thought he was her type."

"You're putting people in boxes. Like Mike."

"I didn't have that down as one of his failings." Sara followed Minkie into the kitchen with dirty dishes. "You two haven't quarrelled, have you?"

"Did he say we had?" Minkie's voice was flat with lack of interest.

"No, on the contrary. But he's not himself." Sara grabbed a tea towel. "Still, that's not what I came to tell you. I wanted to ask if you'd keep an eye on Abel's Yard, water the plants, check the answering machine for a week or two. From October 4th. We're taking a trip to France."

"Oh?" Minkie paused momentarily in her scouring of a saucepan. "Where?"

"Unplanned on this occasion."

Minkie made coffee and they went back to the living room. Sara asked "Remember that trip to the Dordogne all those years ago?"

"With Azzie. Yes, it was a great trip. I still miss her. The wretch has stopped writing."

Sara said thoughtfully, "You've had a pretty fragmented life, poor Minkie. Azzie, Jesse, your mother, Justin."

"You needn't feel sorry for me," Minkie said sharply. "Just sometimes I wished I belonged – really belonged somewhere. On the other hand being a misfit stops you putting other people in boxes."

Just as sharply Sara retorted "Don't be absurd. You've never been a misfit and you've always belonged . Here, at any rate. Though I know there was a time when I didn't make it easy for you."

Minkie reached across, put a hand on her arm. "I guess having a stroppy foreign kid dumped on you couldn't have been easy."

"It was the best thing that could have happened for Mike."

"Yeah," Minkie said non-commitally.

Sara stated a preference for travelling by car ferry rather than using the Channel Tunnel. "It feels more like a proper journey," she explained. "Watching the white cliffs recede and continental Europe get nearer."

Mike said that fitted in with her Europhobic tendencies. Sara absorbed every media niggle about regulations that would turn carrots purple and straighten bananas, and Mike gave up pointing the positive aspects of freer trade, better conservation laws, not to mention well over half a century of peace.

In the end they abandoned a first idea that they would take alternately left or right turnings to see where this might lead, calculating it could well lead to the middle of an industrial estate. Instead they bought a considerable number of Michelin maps and traced an initial series of scenic routes, marked in green, and linking up across northern France. They already knew that at the entrance of each community the French had the laudable habit of erecting a sign which not only gave the times of church masses (Minkie and Azzie had giggled uncontrollably when they saw that in French this was spelt '*messes*'), but also some nuggets of information about local sights. These could be as scant as listing a XXXIV century church or castle, or reveal quite unexpected treasures. Thus at a cross roads they found and followed a sign announcing '*source de la Seine*'. They found it watched over by a robust nude reclining on a rock and balancing a cornucopia of fruit between her thighs.

"A bit more elegant than old Father Thames," judged Mike.

The next day, at the entrance to Domrémy-la-Pucelle the sign announced that this was the birthplace of Joan of Arc. They parked the car near the church. Sara couldn't get over it.

"You read about these amazing people who change history, but somehow they stay trapped in the pages of a book. Then you find they were born, lived and died liked the rest of us. Well no, not died. Nobody could wish that kind of death on anyone." She looked sad. "And we did it. The English."

"Maybe there's something to be said for Europe after all," Mike teased.

"Oh, you."

The inside of the church was dark and simple. A curator spoke some English. "Jeanne, she was baptised here. There is another church built on the place where the voices spoke to her." He looked disdainful. "But it is rather modern – 19th century. They have also restored the house where she was born."

They found a bed and breakfast place nearby. Over a *ragout de mouton* and a bottle of red they reviewed their day with satisfaction. Mike had visibly relaxed over the past few days, the tension gone from his face. He leaned back in his chair and gave a contented sigh "Would that life could always be so simple – lingering decadently over a good meal with your best girl."

Sara smiled. "That's nice." She reached out for the bottle, topped up their glasses, paused to read the label before putting the bottle down. "Colmar? - that's quite local isn't it?"

"Mmm. It's a main centre of the Vosges and its vineyards."

"Which are only a shortish drive away? And this will be the wine harvesting season?"

"So why don't we go and have potter around there,

indulge in a little wine tasting, a soupçon of gastronomy, the odd bit of culture."

"You've read my mind."

"There was a time when I was quite good at that. And vice versa."

"We've just got a bit out of practice."

They made love that night: not with passion but with mutual concern for each other's pleasure, and then lay companionably in the huge double bed catching up on some of the minutae of each other's lives.

Mike said at last "What do you reckon has got into Minkie?"

"I've been thinking about that. I just wondered whether seeing you with Marija she began putting two and two together and realised you had once been closer than friends. Though it's difficult to see why this should affect her."

There was a longish silence. "I think you're right, love. And, as usual, very perceptive."

"There was a time when you were quite proprietorial about each other," Sara went on. "Not surprising really when you think you had extricated her from that hell hole of a civil war. But there were times when you both seemed to have a little club of your own going from which I felt quite excluded." They had talked about that once before when they were in Sarajevo and, during the course of a mutual house cleaning, Mike had admitted his student-time affair with Marija and Sara had told of her affair with Beresford Tremayne. Later it seemed incomprehensible that they could have drifted so far apart.

"Well, that's all in the past," Mike said firmly, "as I think is underlined by this trip."

"Second honeymoon," Sara muttered drowsily snuggling against him, and promptly fell asleep.

And so it proved to be for the next week as they followed the sinuous roads of the Vosges mountains close to the border with Switzerland, dropped into an assortment of wine growers to sample their wares, get their recommendation for a local bistro where they had a light lunch and imbibed more of the local products before finding a quiet corner to sleep it off. The villages and small towns were delightful, their older districts quaint with half-timbered houses and narrow cobbled streets. Their nights were spent in small inns where they sometimes made love but just as often talked for hours. It was almost like a courtship, a getting to know each other but with a maturity that brought more meaning to the knowledge.

"So what are you going to do when we get back?" Sara asked on what they had mutually agreed would be their last day.

"I've been thinking for a while about a series of features on the changing face of the EU. Have you noticed the contrast between the French country scene and ours? Dozy villages where nothing stirs – just think of Daerley on an average week-day evening. The pubs busy, people coming and going…"

"The kids smoking pot round the war memorial…."

"Yeah, well. On the other hand, think of the number of butchers and bakers and candlestickmakers we've seen here compared with home."

"Not to mention greengrocers selling veg that really look as if they've had contact with Mother Earth. Yes, it's a good idea. But you'll have to range wider than France. So I suppose that means more trips away and more lonely hours for me." Sara put on a mock anguished expression.

"'Fraid so. As long as I have your assurance you won't immediately start setting your cap at the Beresford fellow again."

"Oh, p-lease!"

They arrived back in Daerley Green on a Sunday early afternoon. Sara had telephoned ahead and their mail was piled up neatly on the dining room table beside a vase full of russet-coloured chrysanths.

"Good girl," Sara said, noting there was fresh milk and bread in the fridge and a beef casserole in the microwave ready to be defrosted. "Goodness that's a big one – I'll invite her to share it with us and we can catch up on all the gossip." She reached for the phone.

"Sorry," Minkie said in reply to the invitation. "I'm going out with Shan this evening."

"Pity. Never mind. Come over for coffee tomorrow morning and I'll tell you about the really great time we had."

Mike grunted in response to Sara's report of the conversation. "Would have thought she could have seen him any evening. I really wonder at Minkie's taste in men these days. Shan is far too young for her."

"And Bozo was far too old. And Flip far too brash. Poor girl will never get it right, will she?"

"There wasn't much wrong with Jesse," Mike said, adding quickly in response to Sara's raised eyebrow "once you got to know him."

"Perhaps you'd better wait to get to know Shan. Anyway don't start getting grumpy as soon as we get back."

"Sorry." Mike began riffling through the mail, pausing at one envelope with a pleased grunt, opening it and then letting out a loud "*Great!*"

Sara came to perch on the arm of his chair. "Come on, tell."

"That idea I mentioned about the changing face of the EU. Someone's interested – a new outfit but very good reputation."

"I'm so pleased." Sara leaned over and gave him a hug.

"I'm ecstatic and my heads absolutely buzzing with ideas. But let's get our priorities right," He reached up and stroked her cheek. "Let's go to bed."

Oxfordshire October 2004/February 2005 - Minkie

For days after Marija had shown her the photographs, Minkie kept seeing the picture of Sonja and hearing Marija's words "She would have been a bit older than you by now." And later Sara's words in respect of Minkie's transplanting from Sarajevo to Daerley Green "It was the best thing that could have happened for Mike."

Sara did not know about Sonja. So it seemed she, Minkie, had become in Mike's mind the daughter he had lost. He transferred on to her all the love and sense of responsibility he would have felt if it had been Sonja instead of Minkie he had chanced upon in that children's home.

What began as a shock transformed, the more she mulled it over, into something that became increasingly hard to accept. She had always regarded her relationship with Mike as special. Now she found it was based on some false idea that she had merely acted as a kind of daughter replacement. It accounted for a quite a lot of his earlier reactions.

She desperately needed to talk to someone about it. Franko and Rowena were so wrapped up in each other, she dismissed them. She turned to Shan, who may not have understood much, but so adored her he listened to every word, his dark eyes fixed on her face, ready to say anything he thought she wanted to hear. She became intolerably restless. Rowena commented on it and, eventually, even Pippa at Cyber Inc., especially after Minkie had forgotten to convey two quite important messages.

"Take a break," Pippa advised, "until you've debugged whatever is bugging you."

So Minkie transferred the hours she spent at Cyber Inc. to the forecourt of the supermarket where Shan ran his car cleaning service with growing success, and in due course began to do some of the cleaning herself. She found there was something quite satisfying about making a streaky exterior clean and gleaming, and converting an interior full of discarded sweet wrappings and toys into a wholesome family conveyance.

"I've never seen anyone shine wheel hubs like you can," Shan said admiringly.

Wheel hubs became her speciality, and so one afternoon a familiar voice said "Good God, Minkie, what *are* you doing," and she looked up to see Beresford Tremayne watching her with astonishment and amusement.

"I'd have thought it was fairly obvious," she said briskly.

"I'll rephrase it then. *Why* are you doing? And you have a massive oil smudge on your nose."

"It goes with the territory. As to why, I'm helping Shan. He's – he's my boyfriend." Minkie waved an arm in Shan's direction.

Amanda appeared wheeling a laden trolley. "Good Lord, Minkie. What on earth are you doing here?"

"We've just been through all that," Beresford said. "She's helping her boyfriend clean cars. What does Mike think of that?"

"It's none of Mike's business," Minkie said sharply.

Beresford opened his mouth, closed it, then opened it again to say "I think we could offer you both something more congenial and probably a good deal more remunerative." He saw that Shan had stopped work and was watching them curiously. He raised his voice "Shan, come over here."

Minkie said defensively, "He looks much better when he's cleaned up."

Shan stood before them, like a friendly puppy. "I not shake hands," he said, holding up his filthy hands by way of explanation.

"These are my friends Beresford and Amanda Tremayne," Minkie explained. "They want to offer you a job."

"I can do many things," Shan assured them.

"I'm sure you can. What I have in mind is gardening and odd jobs round the golf club accommodation block, and may be some reception work for you Minkie."

"This I like," Shan said.

"Oh, and we can offer live in accommodation. Not luxury – one of the early chalets built before we added some of the later refinements."

"This I like very much," Shan said.

"And you Minkie?"

"I think," Minkie said thoughtfully, "it could be ideal. But it would be good to come over and see just what is involved."

"How about this evening? Seven o'clock. We can have a bite to eat in the restaurant."

Back in Daerley Green, Minkie and Shan showered, changed, examined each other critically.

"You look more better with hair free," Shan said.

"Better, not more better," Minkie corrected automatically, but she removed the band which tied her hair back in a pony tail and shook her head until it fell in loose curtains round her face. Jesse had always preferred her hair long. And Mike. She looked at Shan's jazzy shirt. "Your grey-stripe would be more appropriate. Cleaner, too."

While he was changing, Minkie went to get Robbo out of the lock-up. Rowena had roared with laughter when she first saw it. "Time you joined the 21st century," she had suggested several times recently. Yes, well perhaps it was time to move on.

It was a lovely evening, autumn colours still glowing through the half light as they crossed into Warwickshire. It was curious that Minkie had only once visited the golf course before and that was for tea with Berry and Amanda before she left for Sarajevo. There had been a lot of changes since then, she noticed as they approached it down the long drive from the main road. A modern wing, a swimming pool and tennis courts had been added to the solid Victoriana of the main club house. The grounds were beautiful and immaculately manicured.

"This is very fine," Shan said, clearly impressed.

Amanda and Berry were waiting for them in the bar with a bottle of sparkling white. Berry explained that Shan would be working under the Head Groundsman who was unlikely to let him loose on the golf course itself but would welcome his young muscles in keeping the landscaped gardens round the accommodation and tennis courts area in good trim. There would also be a certain amount of maintenance work on the chalets themselves. Minkie would be required to present a cheerful, welcoming face at reception, deal with any complaints from guests, make sure any special requests were met. It didn't sound too taxing.

"And who am I answerable to?"

"Me. But you won't find me too hard a taskmaster." Beresford topped up her glass. "Now, how about showing you your love nest before we eat?"

It was one of the older chalets. There was a living/dining area, a small but well-equipped kitchen, shower and loo, a twin-bedded room with wardrobe and dressing table, and a smaller room with two bunk beds.

"It is perfect," Shan said.

"Minkie?"

"It's OK, thanks. When do you want us to start?"

"Let's see. Today's Thursday. Come over the week-end to settle in and start on Monday?"

"Never am I so happy," Shan carolled as he packed his sparse belongings.

"Good. And I'm pleased too." Minkie looked up from ironing one of his shirts. "But one thing we must get clear right from the beginning, Shan. We cannot sleep together."

"Cannot?"

"OK. Will not."

"Why 'will not'? You sleep with Flip."

Damn Rowena. "Yes, but I was crazy for a time."

"You cannot be crazy for a time with me?"

She switched off the iron and went to sit on the sofa beside him. "Of course I *can*; but I don't want. I want to stay your friend. Sex and friendship aren't a good combination. Perhaps in marriage."

Shan opened his mouth, saw her expression and closed it again, and finally said "I do not understand."

"No, well, you'll have to take my word for it. May be it's OK for other people, but not for me. I like you very much. Like a brother. Think of me as your sister."

"You ask much." He looked at her mournfully. "But I will try."

They settled into a routine. Shan worked hard from after breakfast until supper time and sometimes later. Minkie's hours at the reception desk alternated with those of a pleasant middle-aged woman who lived in a nearby village. Her work was hardly taxing. She had learned to be good with people from the time of running the travel agency with Jesse. Everyone told Beresford how charming she was.

In the evenings they would read, watch TV, or Minkie would help Shan with his English, eventually retiring to the bedroom and firmly closing the door. She only had to rebuff him once before he accepted the situation, if not with good grace. On their days off, they explored the Warwickshire countryside on foot until the days became too short when they took the occasional trips into Stratford-upon-Avon queueing up for last-minute seats at its theatres. Life settled into a comfortable cocoon, undemanding and separate from all that had gone before.

Sometimes Minkie found it hard to believe in the past reality of Sarajevo, of her teenage years as a refugee child, of that short intense period of her return to Bosnia. And then she remembered the photograph of Sonja, Mike's dead daughter and the realisation of her own role as Sonja's replacement, and she slammed her mind shut on anything other than the easy-going present. Sara had once told her that was a favourite trick of hers, too, slamming her mind shut against unwanted thoughts. "Trouble is," she'd added, "it gets rid of the pain for a while, but not of what has caused it."

Occasionally Rowena would join Minkie and Shan, giving them the latest Daerley gossip. Quite early on, when Shan was out of hearing, she commented "Mike doesn't seem too pleased about your new life style."

"None of his business," Minkie said sharply.

Rowena looked at her thoughtfully. "I don't know what's happened or what's gotten into you, but I once had the impression you adored Mike, as well as being grateful for all he and Sara did for you."

"Of course I'm grateful, but you don't know the whole story. Anyway, people change." She paused. "So how is Franko. I assume you're still an item?"

"As much as we have ever been. I could never imagine him as a life-long companion. Nor him me I guess. But we're good together in most of the important way."

"Isn't that enough?"

"Not for me. One day Franko will suddenly get some new wild whim and follow it, and probably not want any emotional encumbrances to hold him back. And I'll be broken hearted for a while, but not too long. Anyway I can't stay here forever. Home calls."

Minkie nodded, recognising the sense of such a realistic attitude with regard to her cousin. She had hardly seen him since her move to Warwickshire, any more than she had seen the Hennessys. And then one day, Mike called. She was in reception, on the phone taking a booking from a regular golfing guest from Germany when she looked up and saw him crossing the foyer towards her. He waited while she recorded the booking, looking round distastefully at the plush upholstery and reproduction Oriental artefacts that Beresford had chosen as imparting quality and comfort.

"Hi," Minkie said, annoyed because the sight of Mike had

put her on the defensive.

"Hi yourself." Mike leaned on the reception counter and looked at her impassively. "It would have been good to hear of your plans from you rather than a garbled version from Rowena."

"Yes, sorry. I suppose I guessed you wouldn't have approved, and took the easy option."

"You're part of the family, Minkie. We're concerned for you."

"Yes, I owed you that, I can see. Like I owe you a lot of other things."

"That's not what I meant," Mike said sharply. "You don't owe us anything, except perhaps a bit of loyalty. But you're right – I don't approve. Is this really fulfilling your ambition? What about your art?"

"It's providing me with what I need: space to sort out the next part of my life."

"And have you?"

"For the moment I seem to be enjoying treading water."

Mike grunted. "Well, how would you feel about treading water at Abel's Yard over Christmas? Shan, too, of course, if he wants to come."

Minkie couldn't imagine anything more awful. She said "That's nice of you both. But we'll be working on Christmas and Boxing Day – at triple rates. And after that we've planned a belated celebration with Rowena and Franko."

"Oh? She hasn't mentioned it."

Minkie felt her cheeks flare. To her relief the telephone rang and she turned to answer it. "Sorry Mike. This is what I'm paid to do." And when she looked up again he had gone.

When she'd finished dealing with the call, Minkie sat behind the reception desk pretending to sort out some paperwork and feeling miserable. She had once felt so at ease with Mike, she couldn't bear the alienation that seemed to have grown between them, and loathed the clumsiness of her lie. And his reference to her art had given her an uncomfortable reminder of how important it had once been to her and how she had vowed to herself she would get back to it once she had settled back in England. OK, she'd make a serious New Year Resolution.

She rang Rowena. "If anyone asks, Shan and I are celebrating a late Christmas with you and Franko."

"Fine, though I'm not sure about Franko. He's being very difficult to pin down these days. But there's always Luke, that inimitable bundle of laughs."

Soon after a friend of Amanda turned up from New York. According to staff gossip they had once been more than friendly and certainly Amanda at times became positively skittish. Beresford, on the other hand, became increasingly sour.

"Why Mr Tremayne so angry?" Shan wanted to know.

"I think he's jealous of Mrs Tremayne's friend from New York."

"So it is not same sauce for goose and gander," Shan said, pleased with his new phrase and then looked hurt when Minkie burst out laughing and replied "It is never the same sauce for goose and gander."

Beresford started drinking more heavily at lunch time and went through a phase of hail-fellow-well-met before becoming grumpy and then morose. He was in his morose phase that evening when he chanced upon Minkie delivering a message to one of the guests in the older annexe.

"What a delicious surprise," he slurred. "You are the only one that can help me." He pulled her into a nearby room and on to the edge of the bed where he began a long and barely coherent monologue on how Amanda was being unfaithful to him, not for the first time. There was something about Luke, and then he tailed off and suddenly grasped her closely and fell back with her on the bed, his hands fumbling over her.

"Get off," Minkie shouted, but she was also in a panic of fear as, with Beresford's weight on top of her, she could hardly move.

"You can help me, precious Minkie," he said, his mouth

wet against her face. His hand moved over her and down to her waist where he began fumbling with the zip of her trousers.

Minkie was now sick with horror and from long ago heard Franko's voice instructing her on how to deal with difficult men. With an enormous effort she wriggled partly free and with a sharp movement kneed Beresford in the groin. As he gave a yell of pain, clutching himself, she ran out of the room and back to their flat, gasping and sobbing with shock and humiliation. She could hear Shan was in the shower and flung herself on her bed, crying uncontrollably. And the wrenching sobs were not just for the swamping sense of disgust and shame, but also for the loss of a friendship that had once been important to her.

At last Shan must have heard her and came in astonishment, a towel round his middle, his hair wet from the shower. "What is it Minkie? Tell me, tell me."

But she could not barely speak and he could not make sense of the few words he could understand. He just held her, rocking her like a child and when eventually the sobs began to subside, he lay down and wrapped himself gently round her.

Next day Minkie told Beresford she would be leaving after Christmas. She made sure Amanda was there and, addressing Beresford, said "It would be kind if you could keep Shan on a bit longer. He's nearly saved enough to go back to Poland." Without meeting her eye, Beresford muttered something which seemed to mean 'yes'.

Shan could not understand why she wanted to leave, but she managed to convince him she been offered a good opportunity for a research job with one of Cyber Inc's customers.

In the meantime there was Christmas which bore no resemblance to any past Christmas of her experience, and was hard work from every point of view. Beresford and Amanda had decided to pull all the stops out, both for those staying over and for day visitors. There were gala meals, a live band from Birmingham, Santa Claus and magicians for the kids, cabarets for the adults. Minkie acted as receptionist, general information clerk, occasional child minder; Shan was porter, assistant barman, general factotum, even providing the occasional taxi service to Banbury railway station as required. They fell into bed exhausted in the early hours and were up again all too soon..

It was a huge relief when it was all over and they could head back to Daerley in the knowledge they had four clear days off before the razzmatazz of New Year. Rowena was in good form having accepted the disappointment that Franko had been obliged to leave for 'major business affairs' in Germany. She had consoled herself with a long telephone call to Grandfather Jake. Luke, compared to his usual standards, seemed almost ebullient, catching Minkie under the mistletoe, twirling her round and giving her a kiss on the cheek.

"What's happened to him?" Minkie asked Rowena. "Has he fallen in love?"

"If he has he hasn't told me. But I agree there have been subtle changes for the better in recent months."

As the house was rather full, Luke chose to commute between the cottage and his house on the edge of the village. They made no set programme. Minkie and Shan slept a lot, breakfast was a movable feast and they took it in turn to cook main meals. Luke astonished them all with a star curry, and surprised them even further by telling them he had acquired some cooking skills as kitchen boy while working his way through college. They went to a choral concert in the church, a panto in Oxford, and a craft fair in Banbury. And they went for walks. Feeling a sudden imperative urge for solitude, Minkie headed one afternoon for Whirling Wood. She loved the stark winter shapes of the trees, and wandered slowly along the grassy trails admiring the wistful curve of a willow here, the tall assertiveness of an ash there, and the spiky blackthorn which within a few weeks would produce clouds of white blossom. And as usual, she ended up on the bench by the wildflower meadow.

"Would you prefer to be left alone?" asked Luke's voice. "We seem to make a habit of coinciding here."

“It’s where I met your great uncle.”

“Yes, I remember you told me.”

“I was too young to appreciate it then, but I suspect there were times he needed solitude too. Perhaps you're more alike than you think.”

Instead of bridling as he once would have done, Luke gave a small smile “It’s amazing to think you could be right. Maybe Daerley has a spell that re-invents those who come here.”

Oxfordshire : spring, 2005/Rowena

Rowena put the receiver down and felt worried. There hadn't been an opportunity to meet Minkie since the New Year when she started working for a department of Warwick University which provided accommodation with the job. She had never heard her so depressed and negative. At first she had tried to jolly her out of it, and then realised she was serious.

"I don't feel I belong here any more," Minkie said.

"You're being absurd," Rowena had responded. "What about Mike and Sara?"

"They disapprove of everything I do. Especially Mike."

"I guess he feels responsible for your well being."

"Well, he's not, is he? I made my choice years ago."

"Which didn't work out too well I seem to remember," Rowena had pointed out.

"A fat lot of support you are. Anyway, maybe I'll go back to Sarajevo."

Rowena ran her fingers through the short spikey hair style she had adopted recently. "Let's talk about it properly. Come for a drink – next Tuesday, say. It's one of my evenings off. But it'd be better if you came on your own."

"OK. I'll come at six-ish next Tuesday." And Minkie rang off.

After their initial mutual wariness, the two young women had found a lot of common ground: both a long way from the familiar, in Rowena's case in geographical terms, in Minkie's in cultural terms. Both agreed the British could be difficult.

"If only they'd come out with what they really mean instead of being so anxious to seem nice."

"Yeah, and so ready to compromise you lose track of which way they're facing."

In recent months Rowena had had plenty of opportunity to

observe the Brits at close quarters, at least those of the bit of middle England in which she lived. In order to boost dwindling funds she had taken a part-time job at the local Co-op, doing the early morning shift three times a week; and worked behind the bar at The Trumpet three evenings a week. When she reported this to Grumps, he said "Watch out for family ghosts," and Rowena realised with a small shock that both her father and grandfather had spent their childhood in that place. But the strangeness of the thought soon wore off and, in addition to improving her solvency, she also gleaned a lot of Daerley gossip and a couple of times a week she saw Mike Hennessey.

"Sara's told me to go and chill out," he told her early on. "Apparently I'm turning into a grumpy old man."

A less regular visitor was Amanda Tremayne, in recent weeks accompanied by a quiet and rather dishy American called Rus, with whom Amanda announced she had shared a pad in New York some years back. According to gossip, Beresford's nose was much put out of joint.

On another occasion when the bar was quiet, Mike confided sadly "I worry a lot about Minkie. She seems to have got far too involved with the Polish boy."

"I think you're worrying unnecessarily." Rowena hesitated. "You know she thinks you disapprove of everything she does."

"It doesn't seem to make much difference."

"Well, I think Minkie's far too bright to jeopardise the rest of her life."

"I hope you're right." Mike shrugged. "Anyway tell me about you. You're not leaving us soon I hope."

Indeed that was the most testing current dilemma. She felt very much part of Daerley, quite apart from her relationship with Franko. In any case she was well aware that this was past its peak. When you had been with someone that long you recognise instinctively the small subtle signs that eagerness has mellowed into comfortable familiarity. There was the slightest change of tone, the more casual attitude towards cancelling an arrangement, the ever so slight criticism. Rowena was aware of it in herself, too. It was saddening that good things weren't guaranteed to stay good.

On top of that there was Grumps. "I'll come home this year," she had promised him during their New Year call.

"You've found out about Pete?" he'd asked eagerly.

The pang of guilt had been sharp and uncomfortable. "Not exactly, but I'm getting there."

She was embarrassed by her own dishonesty. Why not admit she had found out precious little, but she was having a fine time and would be home when she was good and ready.

"Well remember I'm not getting any younger." Grumps had sounded as querulous as she had ever heard him.

Her researches had so far led to a blank wall. She had been in touch eventually with the National Archives at Kew where there was the possibility of finding the records of the various squadrons operating in Germany at the time of the friendly fire incident. The cost of commissioning someone to do the research for her would be astronomic. If she did it herself she would need to stay in London and devote many days to the task. And then what? Supposing she found the right squadron, the right pilot – he'd be extremely old, probably dead by now. And, even if he were alive, what would she say to him. *You killed my granddad fifty years ago and changed the course of my life?* It had become easier to postpone the resolution of so many imponderables.

But they couldn't be postponed forever.

She talked to Mike about it one evening when he came into The Trumpet. He considered it seriously for some time. "Perhaps if you actually went to the place where it happened, it would make it easier for you to share with your Grumps."

Why hadn't she thought of that?

She was poring over a map of Germany when Luke called in soon after.

"Here's the Luneburg Heath," he said when she explained what she was doing and they searched it together until Rowena was able to pinpoint Gresse. It looked a long way away.

"We could take the car across to Hook of Holland and be there in a couple of days."

"Why would you want to go to Luneburg Heath?"

"I could do with a break, and it'll be pretty in the late Spring. Unless you think Franko would object."

She could hardly say Franko would probably regard it as a huge joke. Pity he hadn't suggested it himself. So she merely said "I can handle Franko. Let me sleep on it. And thanks."

Although it was half expected it was still devastating when it happened. The day after Minkie's call Franko suggested meeting Rowena at a pub on the outskirts of Banbury before going to his flat. This was unusual for their normal routine was to cook something simple in his tiny galley of a kitchen and eat it sprawling on his foutons. The meal then seamlessly evolved into flirtation and then into love making from which they emerged in the early hours amongst a scattering of plates, cutlery, morsels of food and discarded clothing.

Now, he eyed her over his glass of lager in the small booth furthest from the bar and said, "You are very special friend Rowena."

She eyed him back over white wine spritser. "But….?"

"But nothing. It will always be so. It is only that I must go to Germany for longer time. Tomorrow I go."

"Must?"

"Yes, must. There are many, many people, especially from Lithuania, Latvia, Estonia who wish to work in Germany, in England. I can help them. But I can help them better from an office in, say, Hamburg, or Lubeck."

"And do you have an office in Hamburg or Lubeck?"

"I have feelers out."

Rowena stayed expressionless as her heart nosedived towards her stomach. "And do you have a very special friend there, too?"

Franko had the grace to lower his gaze. "I tell you from first I do not two-time. But there is someone I like to become very special." He raised his eyes. "Are you angry?"

"No, not angry. A bit sad." She had never been any good at dissembling. "We've had good times."

"We could have good time tonight?"

"No, Franko. I would like to go home."

"OK, I take you. I will write from Germany. Perhaps come to Australia."

She knew neither was in the realms of the likely. With a huge effort she managed to hold the tears back until he dropped her at the cottage. Fumbling with the key, she pushed open the door, slammed it closed behind her, and burst into tears. And then saw Luke lounging in an armchair reading the paper.

He got up, steered her gently to the sofa, went over to the sideboard and poured her a large brandy, put it in front of her and returned to his chair and paper. Rowena was so surprised by his lack of reaction that she gulped "Don't you care about anything?"

"Not really. Or rather I prefer to grieve in private and assume other people do, too."

"Have you ever cared to the point of grief?"

"Yes, when my grandfather left me. And inconsolably when he died. And there was a girl once. A fellow student who didn't feel the same way but didn't manage to say so until she found someone else. After that I decided caring was an unprofitable emotion."

"That's sad."

He shrugged. "It's also less painful." He paused. "And have you slept on it yet?"

Puzzled Rowena said "On what?"

"On the Luneburg Heath proposition. It might provide a temporary palliative to a broken heart. I assume it's Franko at the back of this?"

Rowena nodded, feeling suddenly bone marrow weary.

“”I think you’re probably right. Give me a day or so to get back to sanity.”

“How about a meal out on Tuesday?”

“Minkie’s coming over. I think she has problems.”

“All right, I’ll call you.” Luke folded the paper, shrugged into his coat and headed for the door.

“Luke.”

“Yes?”

“Thanks.”

“No probs.” Luke grimaced. “Good Lord you’ve got me at this absurd modern jargon now.”

By Tuesday, the sharp edge of grief had blunted a little. It would be good to talk to Minkie who would say exactly what she thought. But when she opened the door to her and saw the pinched anxious face, Franko went right out of her mind. And then she noticed something else.

“Minkie. Oh Minkie. You’re not…?”

“Yes, I am.”

Rowena drew her into the cottage and stood looking at her aghast. “But how?”

“The usual way.”

“Are you going to get rid of it?”

Minkie’s face flared. “Absolutely not, she snapped. “No way.”

Sarajevo/Oxfordshire : Spring 2005/Mike/Sara

From the café terrace overlooking the old town, Mike gazed down on to the medley of roofs punctuated by minaret, towers, spires, and wondered if Minkie had stood in the same spot. From here the city looked quite whole again, though he was well aware of the tower blocks of apartments pitted black by mortar shells. In the strangest way, despite its violent history both past and recent, the place gave him a feeling of calm he had not enjoyed for months.

"For God's sake go and sort yourself out," Sara had said desperately after their last fall-out. He couldn't even remember what it was about except that it was related to his insatiable restlessness. Was it something to do with his age, and a sense that he had achieved nothing, left nothing to mark his passage? Women seemed to cope with these things better. Sara had got stuck into some major cyber project – something to do with providing a central record from which to access all the community-run websites in the UK, and was as tied up with meetings and phone calls as she had ever been.

There seemed to be a permanent state of contention between them and he recognised his own tolerance was mainly at fault. A typical example was Sara's recent apologetic return from Cyber Inc, saying "Sorry, love. Do you mind if we eat a bit late? I promised to give Jane a lift to the History Society meeting. She's still very wobbly after that knee op."

He remembered snapping before he could stop himself "Doesn't it get rather tiring having a new mission a day?"

She had looked surprised and hurt, and then done what Sara usually did in order to avoid conflict. She ignored him and headed for the door where she paused and said over her shoulder "Tell you what – let's eat out at The Trumpet. I'll meet you there in an hour. My treat. Rowena's on duty there tonight. She'll cheer you up." Which left him feeling more of a heel than he already did.

He'd just finished his latest writing project, editing a translation of Balkan folk tales, and hadn't an original idea or thought left in his body. He'd followed Sara's suggestion and started dropping in at The Trumpet a couple of times a week; but even with a pint of Hook Norton in his hand he didn't seem to fit. He'd been too little involved with village affairs to discuss with any authority the changes of the local cricket team or the fluctuating productivity of the village allotments.

He began emailing Marija in Novi Sad, enquiring about her and Bogdan, and Bogdan's feisty daughter Snežka. Her name meant 'snowy' though anything less chilly than this mercurial youngster was hard to imagine. He remembered how she had demanded of him several years ago "Why did you bomb my country?" much to Marija's embarrassment. He still felt great affection and admiration for Marija but rarely thought now of their brief affair three decades ago. The fact that she had borne his daughter belonged to another existence; the memory that his daughter had died in the siege of Sarajevo long before he knew of her existence was still knife-sharp when it caught him unawares.

And then Marija emailed "Bogdan and I are going to spend a short time in Sarajevo next month. Maybe even think of moving back. Bogdan has never really settled in Serbia, and Snežka still wants to get involved in the city's rebirth. Could you and Sara join us for a few days? And Minkie, of course, if she is free."

He had told Sara after a couple more stupid fall-outs and that was then she had said wearily "For God's sake go and sort yourself out. You'll be better on your own."

Marija and Bogdan were staying with old friends in the suburbs. They insisted there was a spare room for him, but Mike preferred independence and found the bed and breakfast place they had used four years ago was still operating. It brought the memories flooding back of those days so soon after 9/11 which had triggered Minkie's boyfriend Jesse's return to his roots in

America; and Minkie's decision to stay with hers in Sarajevo.

Since their last meeting, Bogdan's English had improved enormously. It was now possible for the two men to have a sustained conversation, and Mike took an even greater liking to this ex-lorry driver, ex-nightwatchman, built like a tank and as gentle as a lamb. It was Bogdan who had taken charge of Marija, bereft of her husband and both her children, and loved her back to sanity. He had no idea, of course, that one of those children had been fathered by Mike.

Mike walked tirelessly round the old city, re-visiting the places Marija had first introduced him to and to which he, in due course, had introduced Sara. He took Marija and Bogdan to see Bozo. It was at Bozo's restaurant so many years earlier that he had first recognised he was in love with Marija. Bozo had lost a leg in the siege, worked for a while for a charity trying to bring the ethnic groups together, but now he had opened another restaurant specialising in Bosnian food. He shouted with joy at seeing Marija again, greeted Bogdan enthusiastically, and then bombarded Mike with questions about Minkie.

One day Marija took him to the place where his daughter Sonja was buried with her brother and adoptive father. They stood together in silence for a while, then Marija said "Now you must let her go, Mike. She was happy while she lived, but she was not the budding angel that I think you have created in your mind. I think Minkie fulfills that role better."

"Minkie has changed a lot."

"And this she must as she grows up. Neither are we the same people as when we first met. I think the trouble is you have burdened Minkie with more hopes than you can reasonably expect from a young girl. What about Sara?"

"It's quite different for her. Sara took a long time to get used to the idea of Minkie. I admit I was selfish in foisting the child on her. By the time she had decided to stay in Sarajevo, though, the two had become really fond of each other."

"Women adapt to change more easily than men."

"I'd already figured that out. Except Bogdan seems to be an exception. I'm really glad for you both that you found each other."

"Yes, happily a few gems can be thrown up by even the worst upheavals."

One day they drove to Mostar to see friends and Mike went off on his own to revisit the city he had not seen since the war. It had always been a favourite, its quintessential Bosniak bank facing its Croat counterpart across the tumbling green waters of the Neretva river. The two had been linked by one of Europe's most elegant bridges: a single span arch built in the 15th century. It was from the top of the arch that the youth of the city traditionally proved their manhood by diving the 70 feet into those waters. It had taken the Croats minutes to destroy this treasure.

Recently it had re-opened after reconstruction. Mike explored it from every angle. They had made a wonderful job of it, but it remained what it was: a fine reconstruction. It would take another five centuries for it to acquire that patina that incorporated the passage of uncountable feet not to mention the accumulation of joy, tragedy, storm, sunshine, snow and a score of generations of boys finding the courage to dive from its highest point to prove their manhood.

Towards the end of the stay, Marija and Bogdan took Mike to their old home not far from the old bazaar quarter. The house had been badly damaged and boarded up, but Bogdan had absolutely no doubt that with a bit of help they could make it habitable and, in due course, restore it to something close to their ideal. They were discussing the options when there was a urgent knocking on the door and a man and a woman brandishing a bottle, burst in excitedly.

"So it's true you are here! How long are you staying? Where is Snežka? How are you? Marija you look so well. Oh, we're so happy the rumour is true and you are really here."

Mike could have roughly guessed what they were saying

even without Marija's translation. She hugged them both and introduced them. "Mike, this is Osman and Mirja, our old neighbours." Somehow this mixed marriage of Bosniak and Serb had survived, even strengthened, he learned.

On the last evening, he and Marija went for a stroll along the Miljica river while Bogdan met Osman to discuss work possibilities should they return to Sarajevo.

"You really are coming back?" Mike queried.

"It's like a door has opened on hope," Marija said. "I never thought it would be possible to think of being happy again."

Mike put an arm round her shoulders and squeezed them gently.

"And you, Mike. How can we give you hope?"

"Things will work out," he muttered. "I've got a bit unsettled and must find my way out."

Marija stopped on one of the bridges and looked down at the Milica's waters, red with the soil from hills. "Perhaps it's Minkie who unsettles you? Mike, you gave her so much. Now you must let her go, too." Then she turned and studied him gravely. "Or perhaps you can't. Have you ever thought, dear Mike, that perhaps you are just a little in love with the young woman who has grown up from your foster child?"

Mike stared back at her, shocked. "Don't be absurd," he said.

Back in Daerley Green, Sara surveyed Minkie across the breakfast table. By now she was much more obviously pregnant. She still refused to say who the father was, but Sara had little doubt. Her main relief was that she was sure it wasn't Beresford. God, how appalling that would have been. But the grapevine had by now established that he had made so many passes at so many female members of staff – been surprised in bed with one of them – that Amanda had walked out on him. Minkie admitted he had made a pass at her, but that was all, thank you very much. On the other hand, Shan had returned to Poland and telephoned every week to see how Minkie was.

She was now back in her old room, accepting Sara's invitation only once she knew Mike was away.

"What is it between you two?" Sara challenged her once.

"I don't know," Minkie said miserably, and she really didn't. "For some reason he doesn't like me any more."

"That's absolutely not true."

"Well, that's how it feels. And the truth is I don't much care for him."

"It would break his heart to hear that."

"Huh. Well, what do you expect? He's done nothing but criticize everything I do since came back from Sarajevo."

"You've done a few pretty crass things," Sara pointed out.

"You mean the drinking and stuff.?"

"Particularly the 'and stuff'"

Minkie was silent for a while. "I suppose I must be a mega disappointment to you both."

Sara reached out a hand and put it over one of hers. "We know – we both know you can't expect anyone to be an image of what you want them to be."

Minkie thought of Mike's dead daughter and said soberly "No, you can't. Just sometimes I wonder what my Dad, my biological Dad would have hoped for me. Certainly not this." She patted her belly. "And the awful thing is that I can't even remember what Dad looked like."

"Is that why you want to go back to Sarajevo when it's born."

"Not it. She. Yes, partly. Being near where he was feels right. And after all her father is also a …" She stopped.

"It's all right, Minkie. You were going to say 'is also a Slav'. I guessed Shan was the father."

"It was only once when I was feeling particularly down."

"It only takes once. I was just a bit surprised that you decided to keep it … her."

Minkie said fiercely "I'm not going to destroy a bit of me. And Shan is a good man."

Sara said wryly "If she has your idealism and Shan's energy, she'll be in for a hard time, poor girl."

Minkie grinned. "You have a great way of making the impossible seem manageable, Sara. Would you be my daughter's honorary grandmother?"

"It would be an honour. On condition I have grandmother's rights to have her come to stay on at least an annual basis."

"You're on."

Sara poured them each another coffee. "Seriously Minkie, how are you planning out the next few weeks? I'd love it if you stayed here."

"Under Mike's disapproving eye? No thanks. Rowena's full of imaginative plans, like whisking me off to Australia…"

"Oh, please, not."

Minkie shook her head. "I've had enough of running away. Maybe that's been my main problem. And I can't run away from this." She patted her belly again. "At least not in any way I could remotely consider."

"So?"

"This'll probably surprise you – but Amanda offered to put me up. She's renting a dear little cottage on the outskirts of Cambridge and is teaching at a local school."

"I'm jealous."

"You can come and stay. And she's got a woman doctor friend who'll keep an eye on me."

"And after the birth?"

"I'll go back to Sarajevo. If it's true that Marija and Bogdan are moving back there, that would be marvellous."

"I hope you're not thinking of marrying Bozo. Even Franko didn't think much of that idea."

"Franko is hardly the best source of advice on marital partners – for himself or anyone else. But no, it would be another form of running away, or rather taking the easy option, and not fair on Bozo. I shall get a job, take up my art again – that's one thing at least Mike would approve of…" She broke off as the phone rang.

Sara reach over to take it off the wall, listened a moment and said "Hello, love."

There was a long monologue from the other to which Sara reacted with the occasional "Mm," "Great," "Really?" Then glancing across at Minkie she mouthed "Mike" and said aloud "That's good news. I'm so pleased for them. But what about Snežka?" She listened again for a while before adding "OK, I'll meet you at the airport. I can check the arrival time at this end."

She replaced the receiver. "Mike's coming home early next week."

"I'll ring Amanda and check when is convenient for me to move in."

"Do you really have to go, Minkie?"

Minkie came over and gave her a hug. "Yes, Sara, I really do."

Oxfordshire/Germany : Summer 2005/Rowena/Luke

"I'll worry about you." Rowena was sitting on the edge of Minkie's bed while she packed her bag to go to Amanda's the following day.

"I'll be fine. People are having babies all the time."

"Especially women." Rowena plucked at Minkie's duvet. "What I meant was that I'll want to know you're all right; and also to see it… her."

"You can come and visit. Sara is."

"Without Mike?"

"Without Mike."

"Is there no way you two can kiss and make up."

"Absolutely no way. I bumped into him in Banbury the other day and he as good as told me I was a slut and what a pity he hadn't put all his time and energy into someone more worth while."

"I find that hard to believe."

"Please yourself."

Rowena bit her tongue. There was no way she wanted to fall out with Minkie on the eve of her journey, so she quietly asked, "And how is Amanda going to feel about this invasion of your well wishers?"

"Amanda is ecstatic to be free of that creep and be her own person again." Minkie looked up from folding tee shirts. "You're not planning to disappear to Oz yet, are you?"

"No, but I can't leave it very much longer. I may be in Germany though."

"Germany, for heavens sakes?"

"My grandpapa, remember?"

"Sorry, of course. So you've decided to go and see for yourself."

"Yes. It was something Mike said. And Luke offered to

take me."

Minkie paused in her packing. "Luke offered to take you? Now, that is seriously weird. Why would Luke want to go to Germany?"

"He said he wanted a break." Rowena became suddenly brisk. "*I* don't know. Why don't you ask him?"

"Perhaps I will." Minkie returned her attention to her tee shirts. "Anyway, on second thoughts, there's no reason at all why he shouldn't. He's become positively benign in recent weeks. It must be the Daerley Green effect. Look what it did for Franko."

"Franko's in Banbury," Rowena pointed out. "And I think he's immune to benign effects."

"Oh dear." Minkie went over to the wardrobe and returned with a couple of voluminous dresses, surveyed them wryly and bundled them into the suitcase. Rowena removed them, folded them carefully and replaced them smoothing them flat with her hands.

Watching her Minkie asked "Did you ever finish Justin's early diaries?"

"No. All that Civil Service stuff got a bit boring unless you were planning a thesis on red tape."

"Well, my friend, I strongly recommend that you have another go. Skip the war years – though of course historically they're very interesting – and concentrate on 1972-77. I think you'll be surprised – and so, eventually, might Luke."

"OK," Rowena said. "I will.

She was on early shift at the Co-op next morning and by the time she got home at lunch time, Minkie had left. To check, Rowena called out "Hi!" as she closed the front door behind her, but the answering silence seemed to emphasise the emptiness of the house.

From the fireplace, the eyes of her koala bear Bunbury glinted at her. "OK, so it's just you and me," Rowena said.

She heated up a slice of quiche and made a salad for

lunch, and then remembered Justin's diary. Well, there was nothing vital on the schedule. She found the plastic bags in Minkie's room, riffled through to find the 1972-77 batch and brought the relevant wadge of papers back to the living room. Then she reached out and pulled Bunbury on to the sofa behind her, curled up and began to read. And read. And read. And when she had finished, she went back to the beginning and started again.

Then she leant her head back against the cushions and thought about what she had read. Poor James. Poor Luke. But eventually she thought especially how hard it must have been to come to the conclusions, make the decisions that so radically affected two lives: in one case not for a few months but for a lifetime.

Sometimes, Justin had written, *when you deeply care for people you must bear the burden of such uncertainties.*

Poor Justin.

"Has anything happened?" Luke asked a couple of days later. He and Rowena were have a pre-dinner drink at The Trumpet.

"No, why?"

"You seem pre-occupied."

"I'm concerned for Minkie. It's probably that."

"Mm, poor kid."

"She's not that much younger than I am."

"Well, she certainly seems it. Certainly not old enough to have one of her own."

"I just wonder how on earth she's going to cope."

Luke looked up from the menu. "Minkie is a coper. After all she's coped with a civil war, living with strangers in a foreign land, even living with you."

"Thanks a bunch."

"Anyway, Minkie is one of those people who everyone will always rush to help. In the past, Mike, Sara, even old Justin. This time Amanda." He paused, looked thoughtful. "Good for her. Have you seen her since she left Beresford?"

"Spoken to her: an uncharacteristic outburst on the phone. Not for his unfaithfulness. After all, she's hardly in a position to cast blame on those grounds. As you should well know."

"Indeed I do. But surreptitiousness has never been one of my faults. Beresford almost turned it into a master class."

Rowena fiddled with her glass. "Amanda's a star. But it's afterwards. The idea of trying to start all over again back in Sarajevo. I can't understand how Mike can let her do that."

Luke began "But don't you see…" changed his mind and said instead, "How about going home and getting seriously down to planning our journey into your granddad's past?"

In the end they settled on the beginning of July. Luke was keen to make a day sea crossing from Harwich to Holland which meant they could leave Daerley very early in the morning and be near the German border the same day.

On the eve of their departure Rowena telephoned Minkie. She said she felt much more relaxed and sounded it. "It's not needing to worry about tripping over someone I know round every corner and coping with the raised eyebrows and the unspoken '*I always thought she was such a nice girl. Poor Mike and Sara – after all they did for her*'."

Rowena laughed. "You think that they are all so bothered about you?"

"Am I being paranoid?"

"A bit."

"Anyway, for the moment life seems blessed. Amanda couldn't be nicer – most of the time it's hard to remember she was once my teacher. In fact, my life seems to consist of a succession of surprises about how all my expectations of individuals have been turned upside down."

"You think too much."

Minkie sighed. "So I've been told. You have a great time. Have you read those diaries of Justin?"

"Mm. Absolutely gob-smacking."

"You could do a great thing for Luke if you could persuade him he doesn't need to be a victim any more."

"You'd make a better job of it."

"He thinks I'm too young. Don't argue, I know he does."

"He doesn't know you like I do." Rowena felt suddenly wistful. "I miss you already. Take care of yourself. Don't give birth before we get back."

"Heaven forbid." A pause. "Will you be godmother?"

"I thought you'd never ask."

On the eve of their departure, Rowena rang the Hennesseys to say goodbye. Sara was away shopping in Banbury, and about to leave for a few days in London. Something to do with the Villages Together project she was involved in. Rowena was pleased to hear Mike sounding rather more upbeat than he had for a while.

"I hope you get everything you want out of this trip," Mike told her, adding "I'm pleasantly surprised to see such positive changes in young Luke. You seem to be a good influence."

"Minkie says it's the Daerley Green effect."

"Hm. Perhaps it will start working on her again," Mike commented and Rowena had a feeling he had not really intended to say it.

The North Sea was in unfriendly mood, and Rowena was extremely sick. And furious with herself.

"Island people shouldn't get seasick," Luke pronounced, looking infuriatingly well.

"I'm not an islander. I live on a bloody great Continent."

"Which is surrounded by water," Luke pointed out. "So why are you cross with yourself?"

"Because I'm a really good swimmer."

He looked momentarily perplexed, then burst out laughing.

"What's funny?"

"Do you think either of those arguments makes more sense than the other? Would it therefore mean that people who are never seasick must swim like fishes? I'm hopeless in the water."

Rowena grinned. "It's a pretty silly non sequitur," she agreed.

"That's better. Now that you've surfaced I'll get you a brandy which should see you through the rest of the crossing."

Almost the first sip made her feel warm and woozy so that when Luke said quite seriously "While you were incommunicado, I did some thinking," she had difficulty in controlling her giggles, reflecting his seriousness and prompting with "And?"

"I've been thinking about accommodation. I think it is better if we have separate rooms."

Rowena's bubble of seriousness burst and she giggled "What a relief! You mean you don't fancy me?"

"I think you eminently beddable," Luke said. "But I just feel that sex gets in the way of friendship. And we are, after all, on a serious mission."

"We can agree on that. As for the sex versus friendship argument, I'll need to consider it when I'm cold sober, and the earth stops moving under my feet." She put her head on one side. "But you are the funniest man."

"No one's ever found me funny before," Luke said, and looked pleased.

In the end they found a guest house close to the border. Over a tavern meal Rowena said "Have you ever thought, Luke, that Justin may have thought he had a good reason for talking your mother into sending you to boarding school?"

"I've thought and thought without coming up with anything remotely plausible. Once I even thought of writing to him and asking him. But by then I didn't want to renew a contact that I had decided to break for good."

"It's just that he reportedly had a good relationship with kids. Minkie adored him."

"Mm, so I gather. Maybe he just mellowed with old age. I can't explain it, and I don't think I really want to waste time talking about Justin."

"OK."

"Let's talk about you instead, and what you expect to find when we reach Luneberg Heath?"

"I've tried to imagine many times. For a long time I suppose I thought I'd find his grave and have a place where I could maybe try to talk to him. But Grumps explained that initially there was a mass grave for all the victims. Then in due course many were re-interred."

Luke nodded. "Yes, I did a bit of research on that myself. The Commonwealth War Graves Commission people were very helpful."

"Grumps said he couldn't understand why he hadn't thought at least of bringing Granddad's remains back to England. But he was disorientated himself for a while, and then he was trying to sort out a new life for Gran and for my Dad. Anyway, I guess what I really want to get out of this trip is a proper sense of what the place was like where he died."

"It'll be a great deal different now. From what I've read, Europe was a criss-crossing network of lost souls: p.o.ws, refugees, defeated armies, people released from concentration camps desperately trying to find their way home."

"Yes, I did realise that peace time sixty years later would make a difference," Rowena said testily.

"I just don't want you to be disappointed."

She smiled. "It's hard to get used to this new, caring Luke."

In bed that night, she lay thinking about the day and not least what a good companion Luke had been. If anyone had told her a few months, even a few weeks ago, that she would look forward to a few days exclusively in his company, she would have referred them to a psychiatrist. It was amazing how much he had changed. Then she found herself wondering whether things might have been very different if Franko had changed as much. And found she really didn't care.

Her last thought before she drifted into sleep was that there was one important thing she needed to tell Luke.

It would have probably been better if she had rehearsed what she was going to say. As it was, the next day they crossed into Germany and had been driving for some time on the autobahns. There was something almost hypnotic about counting the number of '*ausfahrts*' ("doesn't that sound rude!" Rowena giggled) until they reached the right exits for Münster-Osnabrück, Hanover, Lüneberg, or watching a distant speck in the side mirror swell to a truck or car catching them up at feverish speed.

"There's something I need to tell you," Rowena blurted out suddenly.

There was a responding questioning grunt.

"You'll probably be mad."

"Try me."

Rowena began to wish heartily she had not embarked on this conversation. "It's about Justin's diaries."

"What about them?"

"I've read some of them."

There was the slightest wavering of the car's direction. "But how? They're all tucked away in my office."

"Not all of them. There were much earlier ones. We… I found them in that room Justin used as a den."

"And you didn't think of mentioning them to me?"

"I didn't see you very often at that time. And you didn't exactly encourage confidences. Anyway these were from his early years in the Civil Service…."

"And hideously dull I guarantee."

"… and about your grandfather's return from the war."

Luke made a sort of gulping sound. "Rowena, please stop there if you want to avoid an accident. There's a *restplatz* a few miles ahead."

They continued in silence until he had come to a stop in a wooded parking area. Luke switched off the engine and said, without looking at Rowena. "You said 'we'. I take it Minkie was also in on this bit of snooping."

"Yes."

"It was unforgivable of you both."

Rowena nodded miserably. "Yes it was. It's no excuse, but it was just that Minkie was so fascinated to know more about Justin's life before he came to Daerley. And it didn't seem anything to do with you at first."

"At first?"

"And then it did, but by then we were sort of hooked."

"Like reading some kind of soap opera."

"Not at all like that. It just seemed to clarify a few things: like why Justin had never mentioned his twin. Or you. Come to that."

"And what do you want me to do with this new-found knowledge? I assume you haven't dragged the diaries to Germany with you?"

"I photocopied some relevant pages."

"You photocopied some relevant pages," Luke mimicked her. His eyes were cold. Suddenly he hit the steering with his first, hard. "You are totally amazing Rowena. I have spent decades trying to put the whole of that childhood rejection behind me and make something of my life. And then you arrive from the other side of the world, dig up some dirt, and fling it in my face."

"It's not like that," Rowena said miserably,. "Minkie said you don't have to go on being a victim forever."

"Oh, bully for Minkie. Especially given that she's made such a dazzling success of her life."

Rowena had expected him to be angry, but not so cruelly bitter. "Stop it, Luke. If you want to carry on wallowing in self pity, go ahead. But if you could put aside your judgmental arrogant, inflexible opinions, you might...." She stopped as Luke burst out laughing.

"What a magnificent display of self-righteousness!" He leaned back, stretched his neck and shoulders to ease their stiffness, and turned to look at her. "OK, give me those wretched papers and I'll look at them." He started the car again.

Rowena fell silent. Occasionally Luke glanced at her as she sat staring out of the window, her face half turned away from him, shutting him out. He was sorry. He liked Rowena more than he had liked anyone for a long time. He liked her scattiness, but especially her openness, her lack of pretensions. It had been a shock to discover she had been reading the diaries, perhaps finding out things about him that he didn't know himself.

He swung off the autobahn some distance out of Hanover and drew up outside a tavern. Rowena said she had a headache and would give dinner a miss. "A real headache, not a pretend one," she said, "though I guess our falling out has something to do with it. We're not going to stay fallen out, are we?"

Luke muttered something non commital as he headed down the corridor to his room which was full of heavy furniture in the Jugendstil. It smelled of furniture polish and something else. Luke sniffed. It was b.o. and it was coming from him. He wrinkled his nose and headed for the shower.

Then he settled at a table by the window, and looked at the wadge of photocopied pages Rowena had handed him, tapping them into a neat pile, and stared at them for a long time. She had clipped them together in chronological order, the earliest at the top. He couldn't resist the temptation of looking at the last date in 1973, when the decision to send him away to school had been made. It began in the middle of a sentence:

.....Penny and Stephen have at last agreed that my suggestion is for the best," Justin had written. *Perhaps Luke will never forgive me; James certainly will not. It is the price I shall have to pay. When you care deeply for people, you sometimes have to bear the burden of such uncertainties.*

"Oh," Luke said aloud.

Oxfordshire, : summer, 2005/Mike-Sara

Mike watched Sara cutting up peppers for a *ratatouille.* A chance meeting with Minkie in Banbury a few days earlier had left him gutted, and it did not help to know that it was probably entirely his fault. He had seen her in the High Street and called out. She turned like a startled fawn ready to bolt, and just for a moment he thought he had made a mistake. Then he took in the significance of her considerably thickened figure and full breasts and had no control over the words that he spat out.

"Why, you slut!"

She seemed totally unfazed. Looking at him coolly she said "What a pity your Sonja did not live. She would certainly not have been such a disappointment."

"I miss her every day," Mike said.

Minkie did flinch then, and turned to scurry into the narrow entrance of Church Passage. Within moments he profoundly regretted his words, called her name and hurried after her. But she was nowhere to be seen, and he could not search every shop.

Now he asked "Would you ever consider leaving Daerley?"

Sara stopped, knife poised in mid-air. "Every time I think you can't surprise me any more, you go ahead and do just that."

"But what's your answer?"

Sara put the knife down and came to join him at the counter where he was reading the paper over the remains of lunch. "There has to be a motive behind a question like that."

"No. Well, yes – the motive is that I would like to know the answer."

"But why? And why especially now?"

"Darling, we're on the brink of middle age. There's a good deal of life left in both of us. I'm not sure I want to spend it in Middle England."

"Do you mean in terms of geography or life style?"

"Both."

"Have you any alternatives in mind?"

"You haven't answered my question."

"And you haven't properly answered mine. My answer in brief is 'no'. But I'd need to know what the options are."

"The main requirement would be to be somewhere where I wasn't constantly tripping over an acquaintance round every corner wanting to know how my book was coming on."

"You mean you want everyone to be indifferent?"

"And what that charming young Minkie is doing these days?"

"Ah!"

"What do you mean 'Ah!'?"

"You've grown ever more morose since she came back here."

"No I haven't."

"Yes you have." Sara got up and filled the kettle. "What a futile discussion. What is behind all this, my love?"

He shrugged, sought the right words, couldn't find them and said helplessly "I'm just horrendously restless."

Sara reached over for a couple of mugs and the tea caddy. "It often happens to men around your age." She grimaced. "Sorry, that sounds abominably patronising ."

"Explain to me, then, about men of my age."

"Well, mostly they will have been concentrating on their careers to varying degrees, have brought up families; and suddenly this empty expanse of time stretches out just ahead and they don't know what the hell to do with it."

"So what's so special about women that it doesn't happen to them?"

"Well, it probably does – especially successful career women. But on the whole women spend a lot of time working what they want around other people's needs: husband's, kids', ageing parents, school terms. If they're sensible they'll develop some special interests or skills during those years and, hey presto, comes the time when they can actually do something about it: writing, crafts, voluntary work…"

"…computing, looking after strays," Mike continued for her.

"Those, too." Sara warmed the teapot, spooned the tea in and reached for the kettle. "But I get the feeling I'm not getting the whole story here."

He pushed the paper away. "You always were too intuitive by half. OK, I'll come clean. I've been offered a place on a team preparing a documentary series on the aftermath of the Ottoman Empire. Or rather its downfall. The Balkans would be my territory."

"Nobody better. But what has that to do with moving away from Daerley?"

"It'll be a six-month assignment. I hoped you'd come with me, we'd sell up here and start all over again somewhere new where you could launch a local magazine, website and start a whole new collection of strays."

"And what would you do?"

"Hopefully get the motivation for a new book. Maybe try my hand at fiction."

Sara went to the lean on the kitchen sink and look out over the garden which Mike had turned into something of a showplace. "You'd give up all this?"

"And start again somewhere else."

She felt anger rising, fought to control it and said evenly, "You can be a selfish bastard, Mike. This is all about what you want."

"It's all about doing things together – something you used to accuse me of having forgotten how to do."

"But on your terms."

"Oh, forget it."

"I will. I have no intention of leaving Daerley. Least of all when Minkie needs support."

"What's wrong with Minkie?"

"She's pregnant." Sara clapped a hand to her mouth Unforgivable to have betrayed such a confidence.

"So you knew. I had to chance upon her in Banbury to find out." In his distress Mike sent a plate flying. "How? Who?"

"The usual way. And I imagine it's Shan. He calls her every week."

Mike dabbed at the spilt coffee. "How could she!"

"Oh, get real Mike, and join the 21st century."

"Why didn't you tell me before? Why didn't she tell me?"

"She was probably afraid of your reaction. And I'm beginning to see why."

It was as though she had hit him. She saw his face flinch and crumple as he got up and left the room without another word. A few moments later she saw Mike at the bottom of the garden, furiously digging over a patch of rank vegetation that had been scheduled for replanting for some time. As always, the garden was providing the balm that hopefully healed.

Sara had never had a comparable balm, unless it was other people. She reached for the phone and punched in Amanda's number.

"I've just done an unforgivable thing," she informed Amanda's voice.

"Hello, I'm fine thanks and how are you?"

Sara told her what had happened. There was quite a long pause, then Amanda said "I'm not sure why you're telling me, but I'm certainly not passing it on to Minkie. Anyway I gather Mike already knew as she had a rather unpleasant encounter with him the other day. She's just stopped being frightened of what's happening to her and started enjoying the high jinks this baby seems to be enjoying." There was a smaller pause. "How are you really, Sara?"

"I'm fine in most respects. Just finding Mike difficult.

He's very odd at times nowadays. How about you?"

"Simply marvellous. Thrilled to be doing a job I've always loved. Ecstatic at being my own person. I used to wonder if that really meant anything. Now I know. In due course I suppose I'll forgive myself for getting involved with a Grade One slob. Didn't you feel the same?"

Sara swallowed hard. "You mean, you know?"

"Oh yes, it all came out in a spiteful stream while Rus was here."

"I'm sorry Amanda. I hoped you'd never find out."

"I'm sorry, too. After all you were first."

"You did me a favour, though I didn't think so at the time." Sara went to lean on the sink, look out at Mike still furiously digging. "He could be quite exciting, couldn't he?"

"Let's spare ourselves the details." Amanda's tone changed. "I see Minkie arriving back from the shops. Must go. Stay well, Sara, and go and kiss and make up with that man of yours. He's worth a battalion of Beresfords."

"You can say that again." Sara smiled as she put the receiver back.

She cleared the lunch things, made the bed, tidied the bathroom, hoovered through downstairs, thinking hard all the while. Then she went down the garden to Mike.

"Pax?"

Mike grunted and went on digging.

Sara watched for a few moments before saying "You'll have to meet me at least part way. I know it was a beastly thing to say, but it was true and I don't understand it any more than you do."

"You said you could."

"That's because I was cross and thought I was being manipulated. Anyway I have some proposals."

Mike jammed the garden fork into the ground and looked at her expectantly. "Perhaps better discussed in The Trumpet?"

"Gracious is it that late?"

But it was still too early for the usual evening time regulars and they found a quiet corner in the garden bathed in early summer sun.

"Tell me more about the time scale of this project."

"Six months will be the minimum, starting around mid-September. A lot of it will be London-based, but also several weeks on location. I thought of staying with Plum in Canary Wharf while we're working in London. It's an age since I saw him and we were once best mates. The Balkan shots and interviews, as far as I'm concerned, will mainly be in Belgrade, Bosnia, Montenegro, maybe Bulgaria. I thought you might enjoy being part of that. And more particularly I'd want you to be there." Clearly he meant it.

"OK, so here's the proposal." Sara sipped her g. and t. "By all means stay with Plum, but you really don't need me sitting around while you both go off on boyish sprees. When it come to the Balkans, I'd love to be there, especially if you can try and work it in with my commitments. Then when the project is finished, let's re-assess the situation and take it from there."

Mike opened his mouth and closed it again.

"It's the best I can do. I'm so happy you want to take part in this project. But I'm not starting all over again in some unknown dump at the ripe old age of 43."

"Forty-three is nothing, and the dump as you call it will be the place of your own choice."

"As I say, let's think again when it's all over. It's a wonderful opportunity for you to do something you enjoy and do best. Another thing is that by the time we get to Bosnia, Minkie will be settled back in Sarajevo with her daughter."

"Daughter?"

"She's convinced that's what the baby will be. Also that Marija and Bogdan will help her to get established. I think she's expecting a lot, but Minkie has a way of falling on her feet."

"And what about Shan?"

"Shan is a very confused and bemused young man,

anxious for Minkie and hoping to have all the rights without the responsibilities." Sara smiled. "But I like the idea of Marija being involved with Minkie's daughter."

To her astonishment and distress, Mike's face crumpled; he stumbled to his feet and hurried away, muttering he must go home. When she followed him minutes later, she found him in the kitchen, leaning on the sink, the tears streaming down his cheeks.

"For God's sake what's wrong? What did I say?" But unable to speak, he was only able to wave a hand at her.

Sara poured them each a stiff brandy, put one on the draining board beside him and took the other through to the living room. She heard the sobs pause, a series of nose-blowings, a short silence, and then at last Mike came in, saying without any preliminaries, as though continuing a long conversation he had been holding with himself, "It's been such a burden all these years and yet I couldn't find the words. Still can't. You don't know how cruelly ironic that will be if it happens, Marija taking care of Minkie. You see …" Mike paused, fighting for control. "You see, Marija bore my child, a daughter, Sonja. I had no inkling of her existence until she had been dead three years, killed by a mortar in that bloody civil war. And I couldn't tell you."

Sara felt her own tears welling, for the baby she had lost herself, for the repercussions it had had. "She did for you what I couldn't, Mike. I'm so very, very sorry."

Mike told her how he had found out about Sonja, what Marija had told him of her, how he had found no trace of himself in all he could glean about his daughter until he heard about her passion for wild flowers. He spoke quite calmly until he said "Then Marija said how wilful she could be; how she refused to go to a safe place the day she was killed because she was watching a video." Then he broke into tears again until Sara caressed him back to calmness. She thought again of her own secret – that abortion of her late teens – and longed to relieve herself of the burden of it. But she couldn't add to the grief that still convulsed Mike.

As though a dam had burst, he talked of his unknown daughter, of the aspirations she might have had, the possibility of grandchildren, of interests shared. In the middle of it he stopped and said "Marija thinks I've transferred too many of my hopes on to Minkie."

"Marija is very wise."

They went upstairs. Comforting turned gradually into love making that had more tenderness than passion in it. Later, cradling her, Mike said "I love you, Sara; perhaps even more for being able to share that burden at last." He had a thought, propped himself up on one elbow. "How about we drop everything and go back to our favourite places in France for a few weeks."

"Not sure about 'a few weeks'. Otherwise, yes. But it'll have to wait a while – I have that meeting in London– you know, about our Villages Together programme in a couple of weeks."

"Ok. After that."

She snuggled against him. "I love you too, Mike. It's all going to be all right, you'll see."

"Better than all right," Mike murmured in the seconds before he fell asleep.

On the road : summer 2005/Sara

Sara left London before nine o'clock that morning, responding to an urgent need to talk to Mike. The meeting on Villages Together had gone well the previous day but left her mind hyperactive. At some point in the course of a restless night she made the decision to tell Mike of her abortion all those years ago. Then she spent much of the rest of the night profoundly regretting the abortion and those periods of alienation from Mike when she had allowed herself to be drawn into an intermittent but protracted affair with Beresford Tremayne while Mike was on assignments abroad.

At that hour of the morning most of the traffic was coming into London and she made good time. She slipped one of her favourite cassettes into the player – an early Beatles miscellany – and played it through twice before switching on the radio. By now she was within half an hour of Daerley, speeding comfortably up the M40. She frowned as the radio emitted an oddly dissonant combination of ambulance and police sirens over which an announcer's carefully controlled voice emerged with increasing clarity. It would be some time, it pronounced, before the death toll and numbers of injured would be known, as there had been at least three explosions on the underground and one on top of a No. 30 bus in Tavistock Square, but the figures were likely to be high.

Automatically Sara turned off the M40 at Junction 10, soon turning on to the road for Banbury. Twice she swerved badly and, shocked by her own lack of concentration, slid into the first lay-by and switched the engine off.

For the next half hour she listened to the succession of reports as new details were acquired of scenes of carnage and courage.

Dear God! Mike!

Her hand was shaking as she fumbled for her mobile. There were three messages from Mike, the last one shouting "For God's sake ring." She punched in their home number. Mike's voice yelled "Who is it?"

"Your wife, darling."

"Where are you?" he said, and burst into tears.

"In a lay-by about 15 minutes from home."

He was distraught. "I was so afraid. I thought … I didn't know your movements…" She had told him but he didn't always listen. "You're not driving using that bloody mobile."

"I told you, I'm in a lay-by a quarter of an hour away. I've been thinking about Sonja and Minkie, and that we must look after the one as we would have looked after the other."

"We'll talk about it when you get back." His voice was steadier now. "Sara? I love you."

"I love you too, Mike." She rang off, slipped the mobile back into her bag.

She was not using it as she drew out on to the road again, but she did not check her mirrors. The express coach approaching round a slight bend didn't stand a hope of avoiding her.

In the nano second before the impact, Sara's last conscious thought was *I'm so sorry, Mike.*

Cambridge, : summer 2005/Minkie

That afternoon, as they sat in the garden indulging in strawberries and cream, Amanda had gone in to the cottage to answer the phone. Through the open window Minkie heard her say "Oh no, oh God", and then a series of "Mmms" and finally a subdued, "I'll have to find a way".

She came back into the garden, her face pale, her chin trembling. "There's no easy way to tell you this."

Minkie felt her face drain. She stared up at Amanda and whispered "Mike?"

"Not Mike. Sara."

They had been so absorbed in plans for the baby, in the loveliness of the day, in a phone call from Shan excited at landing a landscape gardening job in Gdynia, that neither of them had switched on radio or television. Amanda outlined that morning's tragic events in London and how Sara had contacted Mike when she was nearly home.

Minkie stared uncomprehending. "But if she was nearly home..."

"It happened after the call." Amanda was crying now. "She was my best friend."

"Mike couldn't speak to me?"

"He could barely speak to me. He's distraught." Amanda drew the back of a hand across her eyes. "I'm very fond of you Minkie, but you can sometimes be amazingly self-centred."

"What can I do?"

"Stay here, write to Mike. It will be a b-big f-funeral." The tears were streaming down her cheeks. "Sara was a one-w-woman D-daerley institution."

"But I must be there."

"Mike will need all the strength and concentration he can muster. On top of everything else, he doesn't need to have to worry about you producing the baby at any minute."

They switched on the television and watched a re-run of events, appalled by the sight of so much twisted metal, so many stricken faces, so many shattered bodies. Later Minkie wrote to Mike, tearing up a dozen sheets of paper before she settled on: *don't know what to say, except I loved her, too.*

She had nightmares that night of being involved in one of the incidents and running through a tunnel with her baby searching for Sara. She was awoken by the baby's kicking and lay quietly, calming her mind by focussing on the feel of it.

Mike called her next day. It didn't sound like Mike, but a tired stranger. He said "I think it would be better if you stayed in Cambridge until after the funeral. There will be a lot of emotional upset and it may not be good for you and the baby."

"I want to be there."

"It would help me more if you came afterwards, Princess." His voice broke.

He hadn't called her that for a long time. "OK, Mike, I'll come afterwards.

"Oh, and do you know how to get hold of Rowena? She and Luke ought to be told."

"I have her email and she checks in at cyber cafés quite often. Leave it to me."

"Thanks. Good girl."

So at least there was something she could do for him, though when it came to it the words were not easy to find. She sat at the computer for an age, composing sentences, deleting them, over and over again. In the end it came down to a short stark message: *Devastating news. Sara was killed in a car crash returning from London after the bombs. I wish to God you were here.*

Germany : summer 2005/Luke/Rowena

Luke turned back to the top page, leaned his elbows on the table, cupping his chin in his hands, and continued to read.

He read most of the night, crouched over the pages of Justin's diary, remembering the man of his childhood, not the silver-haired old man who had won the hearts of Daerley Green. Though goodness knows he had seemed old and dreary enough to the boy Luke.

He read quickly at first, skimming the pages, then as he began to register the ramifications behind the words, he slowed down and went back to re-read earlier passages. It was the nastiness of the innuendoes of the women outside the school that made the first impact, as it had done on Minkie. He frowned, re-read their comments and frowned more deeply.

How could people be so sick as to read such disgusting motives into the actions of a loving grandparent. True there had been some high profile cases of child molesting around that time. He buried his face in his hands in distress and immediately conjured up a vivid picture of his grandfather's face leaning over him, blue eyes gentle as the boy Luke looked up earnestly to explain some point he wanted to make.

Once again he re-read the earlier pages that Rowena had selected and which summarised Justin's thinking on what now appeared as a developing situation. Justin affirmed that he could detect nothing untoward in the way adult and child interacted. It was true that James, though now restored to as near normality as he was likely to get, still suffered from short term memory loss and a certain carelessness with regard to his dress and person that could be embarrassing. Several times he had drawn his brother's attention to the fact his clothing was not properly adjusted. Luke remembered doubling up with laughter, shouting 'Look Granddad wants to pee'. But others would be less likely to share his schoolboy lavatorial humour.

Remembering, Luke smiled, and then found he had a catch in his throat.

And for the first time he also found himself considering the kind of dilemma Justin must have faced.

How could people be so disgusting as to impute the worst interpretation on such a perfect affection across the generations. The trigger had been set by the women heard gossiping outside the school. If they gossiped among themselves, how long before they dropped hints to teachers and then the head and then higher authority.

Justin had suggested to Luke's mother and stepfather that it might be advisable to send the boy to boarding school. His stepfather jumped at the idea and his mother who, it must be admitted, was beautiful but totally selfish, soon agreed. His grandfather had been horrified and spent a week-end teaching him army holds that might protect him from bullying. They had stood him in mighty good stead.

He loathed the school but survived because of a sharp intelligence and the skills learned from his grandfather. It was in the second year that he returned home for the summer vacation to find his grandfather had moved to a retirement home in Cornwall. He had left a note for Luke. *Seems my ticker needs a bit of rest, old chap. But your mother will bring you to see me.*

She did: on a day trip. His grandfather had shrivelled into a stranger and died six months later. Luke had blamed Justin entirely and decided never to speak to him again.

Now he read how rumours had begun to circulate. Someone from Social Services had come to question Luke's mother who challenged Justin rather than have her son interrogated. The woman was kindly enough, wanting only to have matters clarified in Luke's best interests. In the course of lengthy agonising, Justin had decided the shock of his grandfather being involved in such a scandal, however groundless, would be worse than a few years' separation. He admitted he had miscalculated: both the depth of the attachment between the two and, of course, what he could never have foreseen. The separation was to be not for a few years, but forever.

After James' death, Justin had gone to see Luke at school. He was in the sick bay, stricken by a bug that had raged through the school but which had probably affected him the more because of the shock of grief of his grandfather's death. Luke was facing the wall when his great uncle arrived. "Shall I come and see you later, old man?" Justin had asked. "I'm fine," Luke remembered saying, meaning "No thanks, I don't need you." Just then he didn't feel he needed anyone. And mostly it had gone on like that.

Wearily he tided up the pile of papers and stared out into the German night. At this early hour of the morning there was little traffic about and nothing moved in the pools of street lights. He thought of Rowena asleep just down the corridor and wished he had the courage to wake her and share some of his thoughts; but knew he hadn't.

He leaned his chin on his hands and thought back, trying to prise out of his memory what it was that had made his Granddad so special. They shared the same absurd sense of humour and perhaps therein lay the key. With the hindsight of his own adult experience, Luke recognised his grandfather had tapped into the essence of his own childhood to escape the appalling things that adulthood had inflicted on him. He saw now that there had never been anything pragmatic about James. He never did anything either for altruistic or for selfish reasons. He did them because he regarded them as the clear and only course of action. He had created a world of his own, as children do, peopled with humans and other creatures who interacted without aggression, had adventures that could be exciting but never threatening. He got on with Luke because he, James, was just another kid – bigger and older and with some useful wisdom, but nevertheless another kid.

Luke suddenly thought how hard it must have been for

Justin to find his twin and soulmate had retreated to another planet to which, however hard he tried, he could not go.

"I should have given you the benefit of the doubt," he said aloud. "Sorry, Justin."

And knew that he had missed out, too.

It would have been unkind to ask him whether he had had a good night for one glance showed that Luke had probably not slept at all, so Rowena said instead "It's a fabulous breakfast buffet."

"Not very hungry."

"It's a long drive, so do your best!"

In the middle of picking at a bowl of muesli and yoghourt, he asked "I assume you had a good night."

She decided to come clean. "Ghastly actually. I spent most of it wondering where you might have got to in the diary. Around 3 a.m. I nearly called you to find out."

If only.

"You're a witch," Luke said, meeting her green gaze steadily.

"Is that good or bad?"

"I don't know as I have yet to reshuffle my life in the light of new knowledge."

"Surely it's better to know than not know."

"It depends whether you've been basing your entire adult life on the wrong assumption.

"Oh dear."

"Maybe it's a subject better discussed when the knowledge has sunk in. We have a mission to complete." He pushed his plate away, reached for his coffee. "But first tell me, Rowena. You have a special relationship with your grandfather. Have you ever worked out why?"

She thought about it hard, wondering why she had never questioned it herself, wanting to give the right and true answer. At last she hazarded.

"I guess it's partly because right from the first memories

we both seemed to be on the same level, almost the same age. Only he knew much more than I did, and shared it with me so we'd be even more equal. Then there was a patch when I really fought this .. co-dependence I suppose you'd call it. I wanted to be a free spirit, find out about the real me. So for a bit I went wild."

Luke nodded. "I missed that bit. Granddad had gone by then."

"It wasn't funny any of it. I kept telling myself it was, only it wasn't. Then I met Greatgrumps – that was Granddad's dad."

"Only he wasn't was he. Your Granddad's dad I mean."

"But I didn't know that at the time. Oh dear, what a muddle it all is."

"Come on, let's get on with the real purpose of being here. Have you packed?"

There were some pretty tedious hours of autobahn speeding across the undulating heart of Germany, stop-starting past the occasional road works, grinding to a long halt in tailbacks caused by a couple of accidents. They reach their agreed destination as the northern day faded into eggshell tones. Lauenburg on the right bank of the river Elbe had somehow retained its original charming medieval style.

"I remember Grumps saying this is where they crossed the Elbe before the bridges were blown up," Rowena said, sounding and feeling subdued. "It's not very far to go now."

"Definitely not now," Luke said firmly. They parked with difficulty in the narrow cobbled streets and he marched into the best hotel he could find, overlooking the river. They looked out across its wide, grey waters next morning during another fabulous buffet breakfast for which neither of them had much appetite.

Suddenly Rowena wanted to delay this culminating point of their journey. "I'll check my email – perhaps it'll help anchor me in reality. There was a cyber café round the corner.

But it was a reality she could have done without. When

she opened Minkie's email announcing Sara's death, she cried out in such distress that Luke, who was collecting coffees from the counter, hurried over, spilling the coffee on the way. Rowena pointed to the screen wordlessly, and by unspoken agreement they left the coffees and went out into the cobbled street where they stood, their arms round each other, like bereft children.

"She was one of the few people who didn't appear to disapprove of me," Luke said.

"She always had time to listen. I can't imagine how Mike is taking it."

"I reckon he's a pretty strong guy emotionally. Now, Minkie, that's another matter."

As Luke tightened his arms round her, Rowena thought how very pleasant it felt; if only the circumstances had been different. "We must telephone. And get back as soon as possible. What the hell do I say?"

They returned to the hotel and put a call through. Amanda answered, said Minkie would be incoherent, gave them a few more details, and promised to email as soon as the date for the funeral was fixed. Then they loaded the car and pored over the map. Gresse, the village near which the friendly fire incident had taken place, was about 15 miles to the north-east on the edge of Luneburg Heath, itself criss-crossed by narrow unnumbered roads. Her grandfather must have stumbled along some of them, scarecrow thin. And Grumps with his septic foot. It had been April, and thankfully fairly warm. Mostly they had slept out in the fields, lived on root vegetables scavenged along the way. A cargo boat on the Elbe had been sunk and disgorged its load of herring roe. Somehow some of it had reached the hungry marchers who had feasted on it. The roe was diabolically salty, Grumps reported, and water sources were mainly limited to ditches and animal troughs.

Gresse, until the downing of the Berlin Wall, had been behind the Iron Curtain in Eastern Germany. As they approached it along a peaceful, wooded lane, Rowena said "Stop!". She got out of the car and wandered along the verge, studying the grassy bank. "They were sharing out a Red Cross parcel somewhere along here when it happened," she said. She raised her head to the sky, now blue and clear except for a few puffball clouds and the white jetstream of an airliner en route for some distant destination. "It's so peaceful. Grumps said he wouldn't have had time to know anything about it. It seems so utterly futile."

Luke joined her and put a hand on her shoulder. "Not futile." And without any warning he crumpled on to the grassy bank, head in hands.

Rowena sank down beside him, not understanding. "I'm the one who should be doing that."

"At least you'd know why you were doing it," Luke managed, between gulps. "This is distress for the grandfather I wasn't able to know and the great uncle I rejected." He fumbled for a handkerchief, blew his nose vigorously and sat up. "Sorry, this is supposed to be your day."

"It wouldn't have happened without you. I'm very grateful." Rowena reached out to pluck a stem of wild geranium and put it behind her ear. Without looking at him, she said quietly "It's possible I could be a bit in love with you."

"I've been a bit in love with you for quite a while." Luke got up, held out a hand to help, and then kept her hand in a firm clasp. "Do you think it might become more than a bit?"

"We'd have a logistical problem."

"No we wouldn't. I fancy a trip to Oz, and meeting Grumps. But let's deal with today first, shall we?"

They drove to the village of Gresse, found the church and its cemetery. A middle-aged couple were tending a grave. They spoke a little English and confirmed that, as children, they had heard the terrible story of the British prisoners who had been killed by their own planes. Nearly all of them had been re-interred, but they directed Luke and Rowena to a line of graves inscribed with the names of the German guards who had died with them.

"Grumps said they were as sick of the war as the prisoners they were guarding. Their main aim in life was to be captured by the Brits or Americans rather than the Russians."

"War's bad enough. Imagine what it must be like to find you're on the losing side. In the first World War, not a lot of the men even knew that until almost the end. All that slogging away in filth and fear to gain a few hundred yards of mud and then lose it again. There's so much I wish I could have asked my grandfather." Luke's voice began to shake again.

"You were only a small kid," Rowena pointed out.

They got back into the car, drove on through rural lanes to the village where Rowena knew that Grumps had finally been liberated. His description of the place was so vivid that she could almost guarantee they had found the right place when they came to a large and ancient barn just beyond a road junction.

"They were here for two or three days before the Allied armoured cars arrived. Grumps was sent back to a first aid vehicle to get his foot properly dressed. The medic who did it had such a broad Glaswegian accent that he was almost impossible to understand, but he was so kind that Grumps just burst into tears."

"Don't," Luke said, "or you'll start me off."

"So what now?"

They followed a track up into the fields and sat on a grassy bank. Luke took her hands in his. "I liked the idea the Hennesseys had – planting a bush in memory of Justin. We'll plant a tree in Whirling Wood for Granddad Pete and take a cutting to plant in Australia."

"You're not allowed to take plants into Oz."

"So it'll have to be a tree bought over there." He released her hands and raised his to cup her face. "You're beautiful Rowena."

She couldn't believe how beautiful she suddenly felt. "Can we sleep together now?"

"Not until we're married."

"How amazingly Victorian you are."

"I don't think the Victorians were above a bit of rough and tumble; they just didn't keeping boasting about it."

"It's hardly as if either of us were virgins."

"I don't know about you, but I was an emotional virgin." He bent his head and kissed her, gently at length.

When at last he drew away, Rowena knew she had wanted it to go on, and on. A little breathlessly she said "By the way was that a proposal?"

"I suppose it was. Don't say you're going to turn me down."

For answer she drew his head down and kissed him, rather less gently. "If that's the only way I get to sleep with you, I guess I'll have to say yes," she said. Suddenly serious, she said "I feel guilty being so happy, when my best friend is so stricken. Let's get back to the hotel and see if there is any news."

They checked their email as soon as they got back to Lauenberg. A message from Amanda gave them the date and time of a memorial service in Daerley Parish Church followed by a private ceremony at the cemetery. She added "*Important: before planning anything else please ring Mike on 338002.*

"You do it," Rowena said. "I don't think I can cope with talking to him at the moment."

"He'd much rather hear your voice than mine," Luke said and handed her the receiver.

Mike sounded weary when he answered the phone, but quite in control. "Rowena, my dear, thank you for calling. I do hope your trip is being successful." But he didn't wait before hurrying on "I'd be so grateful if you could stay with Minkie a day or two over the period of the funeral. I fear on a whim she will come to it although I have asked her not to. In her condition I don't think an emotionally charged occasion is very wise." *Nor in your condition*, Rowena thought. "I know it's a lot to ask, but when you're back in Daerley, we'll go together to the cemetery, and I'll tell you about the service."

"I can understand his reasoning," Luke said when she reported the conversation.

"You can?"

"Well, yes. Minkie going into labour would rather alter the tone of the occasion."

"She's not due for ages yet."

"I was led to believe that some babies had their own agenda. Anyway it would obviously be a relief to Mike and a great kindness to Minkie if you spent some time with her. I'll go to the funeral and keep well out of the way."

"It would be good to have you with me."

"Do you really think it's appropriate that you and I should turned up hand in hand on Amanda's doorstep?"

"No," Rowena said. "Probably not."

Oxfordshire : July 2005 Luke

Luke missed the funeral. He had given himself too tight a schedule and not allowed for the possibility of a puncture or the fact he had uncharacteristically neglected to check his spare tyre recently. On inspection it looked very dodgy. A passing motorist gave him a lift to the nearest garage. By the time the puncture and spare had been sorted out, it was clear he could not make Daerley in time.

In fact he reached it about two hours after the service was over, probably still in time to go to the reception that was being organised at The Trumpet, but it didn't feel right to turn up unannounced. He let himself into an uncomfortably quiet cottage. It was a long time since he had been in it when neither of the girls was there and it felt most strange. But the place was full of their traces. Rowena's oversized Koala Bunbury's brown eyes glinted at him from the corner of the fireplace. Her sketches and painting were everywhere, some framed on the walls, others scattered on the dining table. He picked them up at random. They really were very good – cameo scenes of Daerley – market day, Whirling Wood, the mounds that were all that remained from a medieval castle, streets and individual buildings; and miniatures of gargoyles on the church, a carved door here, a wrought iron gate there. Then he noticed that the miniatures were in a quite different style, meticulous in their detail. Turning them over he saw the initials RJ were replaced by JH. JH? Finally he worked it out as Jasminka (Minkie's real name) Hennessey. What an interesting choice of identity. In a different way they were also delightful, showing an attention to detail that could be Islamic in influence, though Minkie might not thank him for remarking on it.

He picked up one of Rowena's water colours again. It was of a back view of a child hand in hand with an older adult standing in front of the ice cream stall at the market. He felt a sudden wave of affection at the same moment as the choice of subject touched a chord in his memory, and then was aware of the tears streaming down his cheeks The next moment he was gripped by a series of convulsions that rocked him through and through. Rowena had told him he had long needed to express his grief, and he could not now switch it off any more than he had ever been able to switch it on. He cried for a long time, not attempting to control himself until at last he seemed to have cried himself dry. Then he unloaded the car, made himself some coffee, had a shower and knew that he now wanted to make his farewells to Sara.

The overflow cemetery on the outskirts of Daerley was empty as he reached it in mid-afternoon. The new grave was easily identified though of course the stone was not yet in place. There was a scattering of wreaths and bouquets. The waste would have annoyed Sara, he surmised. He dropped to his knees. He didn't remember ever having prayed before and didn't know how to begin. So he closed his eyes and thought of her, seeing her expression of concentration as she gave her full attention to what you were saying. And he found himself crying again.

He fished in his pocket, found a handkerchief, blew his nose and got to his feet. The knees of his trousers were dark with damp and earth and when he looked up he saw Mike Hennessey observing him by the hedge, near the gate.

"I didn't want to intrude," he said quietly as he approached.

"Thanks. I was so sorry to miss the funeral. A puncture, bad timing."

"That doesn't sound like you."

"It isn't. Or wasn't. I seem to be metamorphosising into a new person."

"Is that good or bad?"

"People seem to think it's an improvement."

"People meaning Rowena?"

Had everyone noticed except him? "Chiefly, but among others. It's a long story, and I will tell you, but for the moment I would much rather hear about you and the funeral."

"I don't think I can tell you much about the funeral without making a fool of myself. Except to say the church was 'standing room only', and there were some quite exceptional tributes from half a dozen different people. And the vicar was surprisingly nice." Why was it people so often expressed surprise at the niceness of vicars? "Sara had made it relatively easy by leaving some notes on the music and readings she would like. That shook me because I didn't think of her as someone who thought ahead like that. I sometimes wonder whether I knew her at all."

"You could say that of any relationship between two people, however close." They had begun to walk slowly out of the cemetery to the outskirts of the village and, without consultation, turned down the track that led to Whirling Wood. Luke went on "I'm going to tell you of one which, through misunderstanding, completely wrecked my life. Forgive me, for your mind must be on other things. You don't have to listen, but it'll help sort it out in my head." And slowly, and with frequent hesitations and back-tracking, Luke told the story of Justin's diaries, the ones he had found, and those discovered by the girls. When, after a while, he paused longer than usual, Mike said "Please go on."

Luke turned and saw his companion was looking at him quite intently as though he had taken in every word. He resumed his story and when they reached the bottom of the track, they turned into Whirling Wood and made their way down the main ride to the seat by the wildflower meadow. There they sat as Luke mused aloud on the anguish through which Justin must have lived when coming to the decision he reached, and the self control with which he had refrained from making any further contact.

After a silence Mike said "I can understand how that must

have marked a young boy. Thanks for telling me that. I'd become very self-absorbed in my own perceived failings."

"And I've spent a life time doing the same without realising they were either perceived or failings."

"I think you're too hard on yourself. And it was naughty of Minkie to make so free with someone else's diaries."

"She adored Justin and I think her need to know was just stronger than her usual extreme sensitivity."

"I've rather revised my views on her sensitivity since she returned from Sarajevo. You spoke of metamorphosis – hers came as quite a shock. Her apparent obsession with a good time; her loss of interest in her art."

"You're wrong there. She's done some delightful stuff. I've just been looking at some of it. Come round and have a look."

"Maybe. Well, I'm sorry if I've misjudged her in that respect. But I find it very hard to reconcile myself to her pregnancy."

"That sounds uncharacteristically unfair Mike. We've all – or most of us – made mistakes, had one-night stands, probably quite a few of them. I certainly did and I won't ask whether you did, too. The difference for the girls is that they can lead to terrible life-changing decisions. I admire Minkie for hers."

Mike did not react for a while. When he did it was to say in a tone of bafflement "I can't get my head round this new thoughtful, non-judgmental Luke."

"That's what Rowena said. Ages ago Minkie told me I sometimes sounded like Justin. I'm even beginning to accept that possibility with interest." He looked round at the darkening wood. "I'm even following his custom of coming here to commune, either with myself or a companion. It's where I first met Minkie." He paused. "And Sara."

"It's getting dark. We ought to go back," Mike said, but he didn't move. "I feel just now as though I'm teetering on the brink of a void."

"Don't do what I did and fill it in with meaningless busyness."

"What do you suggest?"

"Minkie needs a home, and my guess is it isn't in Sarajevo."

"Can you imagine her coming here. She's doing everything she can to avoid me."

"That's because she thinks you hate her. She needs to know the truth."

"Which is?"

"That you love her more than you think is appropriate."

Luke waited for the anger which did not come. "Marija said the same thing. I was shocked and angry."

"Wise woman."

"And she's actually here. Came for the funeral. I couldn't believe it when she came up to me after the service. In some strange way she made it all seem bearable." Mike turned to Luke. "And so have you which is even more unexpected. She's at Abel's Yard now. Come back with me and meet her and we'll all go out for a meal."

"And I'll ring the girls to let them know you are more or less in one piece."

"Fine. But we'd better hurry back now or Marija will be worried."

She was. "Where have you been," she scolded, as Mike let them in through the front door half an hour later. "You said you wanted to spend short time with Sara…" She came out of the kitchen, paused as she saw Luke.

"My fault," Luke said. "I distracted him and we went for a walk. I'm Luke Smith, a friend of the family."

She nodded, smiled. "Any distraction is good thing."

"I'm taking us out for a meal," Mike announced. "Away from Daerley, I think."

"Is better," agreed Marija.

As they drove north to and through Banbury and off into a

network of lanes off the Stratford Road, Mike explained briefly to Marija who Luke was. She seemed to grasp an amazing amount of the jumbled story. Mike, Luke decided, had a talent for choosing intuitive women.

"And this Rowena, is she going back to Australia?"

"We may both go. I seem to have fallen in love with her." There didn't seem a better moment to make the announcement.

The car wavered in its course as Mike exclaimed "Well, I'm damned. At least you're an improvement on Franko."

"Thanks."

The pub turned out to be one of those brassy roadhouses with lots of bars and rooms from which they chose a quiet alcove away from the jollity and the music. There was a buffet from which to help themselves and on which Marija treated them to a running commentary on how the various components compared with their equivalents on Sarajevo's market. Despite the difference in age and appearance, Luke could see hints of Minkie in Marija. Perhaps it was that Bosnian quality of inner quiet that seemed there whatever the mood of the surroundings. He wondered whether Mike had noticed it.

"How is Minkie?" Marija now asked. "We are happy to help her, but it is not good idea she come back to Sarajevo."

"Luke was saying the same thing," Mike said. "He thinks she should come here."

"It is only place. This is her growing up home. Sara would want it."

"But first I have to persuade her that I don't hate her."

"How difficult is that?"

"We have not agreed on many things in recent months."

"This happens when people care for each other. You will find a way. When is baby to come?"

"I'm not sure exactly, but it must be fairly soon."

Mike had an idea "Marija would you go and see her? I'm sure Luke would take you. Wouldn't you Luke?"

"Not too sure that Amanda would like to see me on the

doorstep. She was an earlier woman friend," Luke explained to Marija.

"Your living style in England seems very complicated," she commented dryly. "I will telephone Amanda when we get back to Abel's Yard."

What she said to Amanda they never discovered for they were hustled out of the living room while she made the call. But she reported they would both be welcome, though Luke would have to sleep at a neighbour's house.

By the time they drove to Cambridge a couple of days later, Luke and Marija had formed an easy-going relationship. She had visited his cottage, seen Rowena's and Minkie's illustrations, agreed with him about the possible Islamic influences on the latter's; and felt able to confide in him her long-ago affair with Mike and the death of their daughter in the city's siege. What unsuspected horrors lay behind the facades of people you thought you knew. She also told him of her mistake in showing Minkie a photograph of the two dead children and how she had seen the likeness between her daughter and Mike.

"As a result," Marija went on, "I think Minkie thinks she is no more than a replacement daughter."

"It would account for her irritation at Mike's apparent interference in her life. "I don't know how Daerley will come to terms with a *ménage à deux* with such an age disparity."

"It depends on how Daerley interprets it. When you have lived through real tragedy you acquire truer values. I no longer make judgements. When I lost my husband and children I became a crazy person. When you meet my Bogdan you may be surprised that such a person brought me back to sanity. But it is so." After a moment she asked "Do you have music to quieten our thoughts?"

Luke switched on Classic FM. There was a Dvořak concert and they were playing one of his Piano Concertos, and they continued to travel without speaking, allowing their thoughts to quieten.

Oxfordshire : July 2005 – Mike

Plum offered to come from London and stay with Mike until after the funeral. They had lost touch over the years, but Mike accepted the offer, aware that to wallow in the silence of Abel's Yard was to inflict on himself totally unnecessary extra pain. Others had offered, but he and Plum went back sufficiently far to be able to accept each other in all moods.

Mike prepared Minkie's room for him. *You could add a small vase of flowers,* Sara suggested.

"He wouldn't even notice them," Mike said aloud and actually found himself smiling. There was comfort in the imagined presence of Sara being her brisk old self.

Plum arrived the next afternoon. He was working on a marketing project and had brought a pile of documents with him. That was a relief for it reduced the need for conversation after the initial conventional exchange of commiserations and *tell me if there is anything I can do's.*

Mike could only suppose he was still in shock, for he felt no urge to weep, just hollow with a desperate sadness. There were all the basic formalities to go through and, apart from those, all he wanted was the funeral to be over. The vicar, Jon, took the scribbled list of requests Sara had written and planned the service for him, calling to get Mike's assent on this or that detail. Sara had always said he was good bloke in a crisis and Mike had to agree. She wasn't a regular churchgoer any more than he was, but as Jon commented "she had such patent commonsense, sometimes at a premium amongst one's regular congregation." It was Sara who had instituted a panel displaying the help lines of various organisations from addiction to alzheimers. "Obvious really," as Jon said, "only no one else had suggested it."

Otherwise, Mike spent his time in the garden. It was at the end-of-summer overgrown stage, in need of a lot of attention. If Sara had been alive, he would still have been out there, and now it became the complete focus of his days to which he resented any interruption. He stopped only when he was physically exhausted. Plum offered to help, but seemed relieved when his offer was rejected.

Mike flung himself into cutting back a monstrously overgrow *clematis montana,* two honeysuckles, and attempting to uproot a rose of Sharon that had taken over the whole of the bottom of the garden. He potted up three dozen geraniums for the winter; lifted a couple of hundred tulip bulbs, separating them where necessary and laying them out on trays covered with newspaper to put on shelves in the garage. In the evenings, they ate out then slumped in front of the television, Plum happy to watch whatever was on while Mike's head planned the next day's attack on the garden. One evening someone called Alison rang to say that a group of villagers had got together and would like to arrange a small reception at The Trumpet after the funeral service if he had no objection. There had been countless such offers of help, an avalanche of cards and messages through the letterbox. Mike gathered them up and took them under the oak tree where he sat with his back against the trunk reading them. He had always thought such messages written to the bereaved rather meaningless, but now he found himself reading and re-reading these tributes to various aspects of Sara's work in the village or of her character of which he was aware but not always to the depth of these correspondents. He began to wish he had not been so adamant in his request that Rowena should stay with Minkie, though heartily grateful that the latter was safely in Amanda's care.

The day of the funeral became a blur of existing a minute at a time. Friends were making a recording of the whole service so he was able to concentrate on simply getting through it, occasionally taking in some of the waves of warmth and affection that came with the tributes read out. Polly – funny little Polly who had helped Sara with her shop years ago, and was now quite matronly with a small clutch of teenage children – was there. At the end of the service, the children stood in a group and sang *Amazing Grace*, with Polly's penetrating contralto soaring above them all. That nearly finished him.

Afterwards he stood at the church entrance greeting and mumbling to the members of the congregation. And then a miracle. A pair of arms clasped him, a warm voice said, "Mike, Mike, how I feel for you," and he found himself staring unbelievingly into Marija's face. When the procession had finished, he introduced her to the vicar, took her over to The Trumpet and introduced her to Plum. Plum said he'd just had a call from London and ought to go back as soon as Mike really could do without him.

"You go," Mike said. "The worst must be over now, and I'm so grateful you came." By the time they got back to Abel's Yard, Plum had gone. Mike said "Do you mind if I go and have a few minutes with Sara?" and Marija seemed to know exactly what he meant.

And then had come the next surprise in this day of surprises: he had found Luke on his knees by Sara's grave.

When Luke and Marija had left for Cambridge the following day, the house seemed unbearably still. He wandered round it, picking things up and putting them down, noting that already it was showing the effects of Sara's absence. Then he went round it again with a note pad, listing the things that needed doing: a new loo roll upstairs, a clean hand towel downstairs, the watering of plants in almost every room. Having done these small tasks he ended up in their bedroom and noticed that the bed needed stripping. It was as he was pulling it apart that the grief hit him and he collapsed on the bed, clutching one of Sara's pillows sobbing uncontrollably.

When he heard the doorbell he almost ignored it, but went down to find the vicar on the doorstep.

"My dear fellow," the vicar said after one look.

They went into the living room and Mike, still only half in control, poured out two whiskeys, produced glasses, found ice in the kitchen. Though he had never been a churchgoer, there had been times on his visits to Bosnia and Serbia when Mike had found himself in Orthodox churches, watching people light candles, envying the serenity of their expressions. Now he wasn't sure what to expect of Jon or what was expected of him.

Nothing apparently. Jon sipped his whiskey and launched into a monologue on the disadvantages of being brought up as a vicar's son. Mike became intrigued in spite of himself, and also found unexpected fellow feeling.

"At that age," Jon was saying, "you think all your peers are having a perfect time in the perfect family."

"I certainly did," Mike agreed. "In fact, I'd have swapped with you any time."

Jon looked surprised "You'll have to explain."

So Mike told him about his parents who, post World WarTwo, had flung themselves into flower-power in a big way and dragged him off to a commune in East Anglia; how he had loathed it and would have given anything for the sort of ordered life Jon had experienced. "I suppose I must have been an odd child. And to think the one thing I wanted and never got was a daughter of my own to give her the sort of childhood I didn't have. And which she would probably have hated."

"Not the best reason for having a child. Anyway you had Minkie. That was a fine thing you and Sara did."

"I'm afraid I leapt into the arrangement without much consideration for her."

"From where I stood, it looked like a great partnership."

Mike smiled. "So what was so awful about your home?"

"It was ruled totally by timetables and duties."

"I'd have thought that would be a good launching pad for someone destined for the church."

"But that's the point. I had no idea that was my destiny. You may find it hard to believe but one of the attractions – to me at least – of my vocation is its total unpredictability."

"Except presumably for your faith."

"That's the least predictable of all. Many non-believers seem to think that one adopts a faith because it provides a comfortable set of rules which means you don't have to work things out for yourself any more. My faith is forever being challenged. My life is a constant questioning or taking on trust. It seems to me there is nothing easier than to say there is no God, there are no rules and to make them up as you go along."

"Hang on, non-believers have morals too. Besides which I'm not at all sure what I am."

"There's hope for anyone who isn't sure," Jon said. "But I'd better get off my soapbox."

Mike laughed. "You've done a good job, Jon."

"How do you mean?"

"Making me forget for all of a quarter of an hour how dire my life seems at the moment."

"It wasn't contrived I assure you. I like people – well, some people, and I adored Sara in the most proper sense. And wanted to know you a little better. There's only one piece of advice I'll venture to give: don't shut other people out of your life."

"Sara said the same more than once."

"Wise woman. And now I must go."

Mike poured himself a second, smaller whiskey. What a weird old day it had been. If it hadn't been for its harrowing central event, there were parts of it he could actually say he had enjoyed: the pleasure of seeing Marija, the amazing transformation of Luke, the conversation with Jon. Or may be it was just the alcohol. Better get to bed and hope the effects lasted until he got to sleep.

He slept better than he had since Sara's death, but as usual he was wide awake by five o'clock. He made himself some coffee, had a bowl of muesli – that was a first, too. Then he stood for some time at the kitchen window. The garden was looking good. Maybe it was time to start a few changes there, as in the rest of his life. He began to visualise a small shrubbery about half way down. They'd transfer Justin's bush to it, and put something really special for Sara, and may be even for Sonja, for Minkie's mother. "They"? And who exactly were "they"?

He went out and toured the garden as he always did, pausing at length in the area where he was considering the new shrubbery. It would mean digging up quite a section of the lawn and be hard work, but just now he welcomed physical effort. He looked at the lawn more closely. There was an awful lot of moss. He'd have a go at raking it out today, and then may be start some scarifying treatment. It was a bit early, but he could always repeat it in the autumn.

He worked until mid-morning, then had a coffee break. Afterwards he made his first attempt at digging up a corner of the lawn, but there had been no rain for a while and the earth was like concrete. He gave up, got his largest garden fork and started at the far end of the lawn methodically puncturing it, fork width by fork width. Except for the developing ache in his shoulders and arms, there was something almost pleasurable about the rhythmic movement and the slow but visible progress.

He was roughly level with the oak tree when he caught a movement towards the house. A man was walking towards him. No, not walking, staggering. As he came nearer Mike saw he was elderly with a craggy face. Who on earth?

"Who are you?" Mike demanded. He left the fork jammed in the lawn and moved towards the man, reaching him, just as he gave a grunt and collapsed on to the ground. He was unconscious only seconds before he opened a pair of quite vivid blue eyes and said hoarsely "Sorry, it wasn't supposed to be like that."

"Who on earth are you, and how did you get in?"

"Front door unlocked. Careless." He paused to raise himself on one elbow and catch his breath. "Jake Johnson."

Mike stared back at him uncomprehending, then a memory glimmered. "Jake Johnson? You mean, you're Grumps?"

The craggy face cracked into a grin. "Got it in one. I did go to the address where Rowena and your Minkie live, but there was no one at home. So I came along to meet the two people I hear most about: you and Sara."

Mike flinched. "The girls are both in Cambridge at the moment. And, alas, you are a couple of weeks too late for Sara. Her funeral was yesterday."

"Dear God!" Jake did not exactly leap to his feet, but it was a rapid scramble.

"Hey, whoa!" exclaimed Mike. "I don't want you collapsing again. Come on let's go inside and I'll make a drink."

"Don't worry, my head and my insides are all virtually floating. I got a taxi straight here from the airport. What a God-awful journey that is – the flight I mean."

As he settled Jake in the kitchen, washed his hands, put the kettle on, Mike explained how Sara had died.

"And now you're doing what I would do: losing yourself in a frenzy of activity to try and forget. I watched you for a while from the kitchen. So why the hell aren't the girls here to look after you."

So Mike explained about Minkie's imminent motherhood and how it had been his decision that she would be better away from the emotionally charged atmosphere of the funeral, and how he had asked Rowena to stay with her as soon as she got back from Germany. That really stopped Jake in his tracks.

"So she's actually been there, to where Pete met his stupid, unnecessary end? How I long to hear all about it."

"The first thing you're doing my friend," Mike said firmly, "is going straight back to the cottage and having a sleep. I have a set of keys. When you're ready, come back here and we'll call Rowena and give her the shock of her life."

Jake nodded. "I guess I am kind of tired, but if it weren't for the news of your Sara, kind of elated too. I've always wanted to come back, never thought I'd make it."

After he had settled Jake into Luke's cottage, Mike

returned to Abel's Yard and followed his example. The accumulation of physical and emotional effort over the past few days had suddenly caught up with him and he fell into a deep sleep for several hours to be woken by Plum telephoning to find out how he was. Mike showered and changed and wandered over to Luke's cottage. Jake, looking slightly less exhausted, was struggling with the quirks of an ageing water heating system. Mike sorted him out and went to sit in the living room while he showered. From the corner of the fireplace Rowena's koala bear Bunbury fixed him with an unflinching gaze.

"I think we'll get you checked out by the local quack," Mike told Jake when he materialised some time later looking a good deal fresher and smarter. "But for the moment we'll introduce you to some English cuisine."

"I've been here before," Jake reminded him.

"I hope we've improved in the past fifty, sixty years."

They went to The Unicorn where it was still early enough to find a quiet corner. Jake stood in the doorway looking round and repeating "Oh my, Oh my"

"I take it you don't recognise much."

"Not a thing."

"Well, it was taken over by a brewery in the '70s I gather, and more less reconstructed inside."

They took a foaming pint of Hook Norton apiece over to a table away from the bar. Mike asked "Did you know that Rowena went over to Germany with Luke Smith?"

"That cold fish landlord of hers?"

"No so cold fish any more it seems. Sara quite took to him – must say I never saw much charm in him. Anyway apparently, as a child, he had a very close relationship with his own grandfather who served in the First World War. By all accounts the old man had seen terrible sights and withdrawn from the world until Luke came along and then the two became inseparable. When he died, Luke for some reason decided he must be partly to blame."

Jake was quite still a moment. "That's amazing. It's a repeat of what happened between Rowena and her great grandfather – he was in the Gallipoli campaign."

"Anyway, if it helps, I was quite staggered to go to the cemetery after the funeral and find Luke on his knees by Sara's grave. We talked a lot. He's quite changed – in fact, really rather likeable. And talking about going to Australia to meet you."

"Well, at least I've saved him that trouble." Jake finished his beer. "Come on, let's go and ring up the girls."

It was Amanda who answered the phone.

"Something to ask you, and something to tell you," Mike said, trying to keep his voice calm. "If Rowena's there, I have a big surprise for her."

"Not sure we can cope with more surprises," Amanda said quietly. "Minkie has just gone into labour."

Cambridge/Oxfordshire: July/August 05 – Minkie

Nobody slept much that night. Amanda drove Minkie to the hospital and opted to stay with her. Rowena and Luke had gone out for a meal and got back after the exodus to the hospital. Marija was writing to Bogdan and Snežka.

They made some coffee to keep themselves awake "in case there's any news" though Marija advised them against too high expectations. "By the way," she added, "Mike implied he had a surprise for Rowena."

I don't think I can take any more surprises," Rowena said, reaching out for Luke's hand.

"So what are your plans?"

"As soon as we know Minkie and the baby are OK, we'll head for Oz. I *must* see Grumps, tell him all that's happened, about going to Germany, about Luke. And then I must be back here for the christening. And then, and then ….. I don't know, I just don't know."

"I do," Luke said. "We're going to live happily ever after. Here or there, or alternately in both places."

"You are lucky to have a choice to live in a time and a place without war," Marija said.

"Afghanistan? Iraq?"

"It's not likely to affect what you do tomorrow or the next day."

"She's right," Rowena said. "We have no idea –none of our generation has, except the poor devils who've got stuck with the job of clearing up the politicians' messes."

"Hey, I didn't know you were a woolly liberal."

"I'm anti-war if that's being a woolly liberal."

Marija sighed. "Some of us did not have the luxury of being anti-war."

Rowena opened her mouth and shut it again as the telephone rang. Luke reached out for it, said "Oh, hello" in a surprised voice, then shook his had to indicate it was not from the hospital. He said "Mm" a few times, and then "exactly where are you?" and finally "I'll pick you up in half an hour."

As he put the phone down, he said, "The whole world appears to be converging on us. That was Shan."

"Shan!" exclaimed Rowena as Marija enquired "Who is Shan".

Luke headed for the door, leaving Rowena to answer Marija's question.

Minkie stirred and opened one eye. She felt pretty sore, but knew it was nothing compared to a few hours earlier when the pain had reached peaks that were breath-stopping and she had come to realise that the person yelling was her. Then it had stopped and there had been a lot of bustling about followed by a sound like a persistently protesting kitten, and a bundle of something wrinkled and red and damp was put in her arms.

"Hello Branka," Minkie said.

You wouldn't think something so small could make so much noise, but she knew it was a good thing.

"Well done Minkie," Amanda was there as she had been all along. "The staff say that was relatively easy."

"If that was easy, I wouldn't want difficult," Minkie muttered. Amanda took the bundle from her, passed it to a nurse, then sat on the edge of the bed.

"Thank you for letting me be here," she said. "My first birth, and it's true when they say it's something very special. I quite envied you. But it's more than a bit late for me now." She patted Minkie's arm. "I'm off to get some sleep and let you get some, too. I expect the mobs will be in later."

But when Minkie opened both eyes a few hours later, there was only one figure there sitting reading. She didn't recognise him immediately. Then "Shan?" she questioned, and more definitely, "Shan! How did you get here?"

"By train, then ship, then train, and Luke he met me at

station. It was very kind. It was necessary to see my daughter and her mother. I am very proud of you Minkie."

"Such a long way to come, Shan. Where are you staying?"

"Sharing room with Luke." Minkie giggled, imagining there was someone else that Luke might have preferred as a room mate. Luke went on "It was like miracle. My employers sent me here for work experience on a fine property in north of England, so I make small detour, but I must leave tomorrow. I will come back on my way home and perhaps you come with me?"

Oh dear. "No Shan, I can't start again in yet another country. Sarajevo is where I belong."

"My mother, she love you very much. Everyone love you, especially me."

"Branka must have a chance to know her roots."

"Her roots are the golf club near Banbury," Shan said realistically. "Sometimes we have to make our own for the next generations."

"Too tired to argue, Shan. Have you seen our daughter?"

"Of course. She is the most beautiful in the hospital, in the world."

Minkie smiled, "Yes, isn't she?"

When she awoke again, Shan had gone and Branka was in a small cot by her bed. She reached out a forefinger to touch her cheek and a small red fist flailed the air.

"The trouble is," Minkie told her daughter, "that there are only two people whose opinion I would really trust; one isn't here any more and the other hates me."

A small knot of people entering the ward resolved itself into Rowena, Luke, Marija and a cloud of flowers.

"Where is she?" They crowded round Branka's cot, cooing and admiring.

"Hello, and yes, I'm fine thanks," Minkie said after a while. "This baby business is a doddle."

They transferred their attention to her. Marija said

"Amanda said you had a really hard time and were very brave." Really?

Rowena said "Seriously, she's a honey. More you than Shan I'd say. I hope she keeps that turned-up nose."

"Is she supposed to look so screwed up?" Luke asked, then grinned to show he wasn't serious.

"Hooray, Luke made a joke," Rowena said.

"You'd better tell her the latest excitement," Luke said, "before you burst."

Rowena took a deep breath. "Guess who turned up at Abel's Yard while Mike was in the middle of de-mossing the lawn."

Minkie could just see him at it, rake in hand, full concentration on the task. "Someone from this planet?"

"Just about."

Minkie guessed wildly "Must be Grumps," and couldn't have been more surprised to find she was right. When they had all stopped talking at once, she learned the facts including that Jake was driving Robbo over that very day. Couldn't Mike have brought him over at least, and looked in to see her?

"Will he be all right driving a strange car in a strange country?"

"Don't let him hear you ask that," Rowena said, still hugging herself with excitement. "They drive on the left in Australia, too, and he can handle anything from a motorbike to a two-ton truck."

"Many of the important things in my life have happened here," Minkie told Branka. It was a month later and they were on the seat by the wildflower meadow in Whirling Wood. Minkie had taken Branka out of the buggy and propped her up with a steadying arm on the seat beside her, though whether she could see, let alone focus on anything through the small slit in the all-embracing blanket was doubtful. She continued "This is where I met Justin. And Luke. And your father. And where I came whenever I had something especially happy or sad to think about. Like the news of your granny's death, or when Jesse said he loved me; or the news of granny's death before she actually died. I'll explain that to you some time. Justin and I used to come here a lot, too, to chew over the problems of being me. How I wish he could have known you. Sara, too. They would both have adored you." Minkie scooped the bundle up and rocked it. "As I do."

They had returned to Daerley Green a week earlier and were back in Luke's cottage. Marija had moved in too for a couple of weeks. Rowena, Luke and Grumps had made a snap decision to go over to Germany so that Grumps could revisit the scene of the friendly fire which in the end had affected all their lives. Mike had come over one evening to meet Branka and behaved rather like a distant uncle they had not met for a long time. He used the occasion to tell them that he was going to London in a few days' time and then to Belgrade for planning sessions on the new documentary film he was involved with. As he left, he said to Marija "Perhaps we can meet when you get back to Serbia," and to Minkie "Take care of yourself young lady, and the littl'un." He poked at the bundle that contained Branka. "Anyway you'll be all right with most of Daerley Green keeping an eye on you." Which, of course, absolved him from any responsibility.

In particular they had been adopted by Polly Cuttle who had once helped Sara in her shop and was now a matronly Mum with three children. Then heavily pregnant herself, she had befriended Minkie when she first arrived, a bewildered thirteen-year-old. Everyone said she had sung magnificently at Sara's funeral. Polly had recently moved back to Daerley, worked part time in the shop and was delighted to have a new tiny being on which to lavish her maternal instincts. As soon as Marija had left, she announced, she would be looking in every morning. Anyway, Rowena and Luke were due back the next day, and in a fortnight, Mike. Not that he would make any difference.

Minkie put Branka back on the seat. And what about her

own decisions? They couldn't be postponed for much longer. Marija had insisted that she should give much more thought to her original plan to return to Sarajevo. "Of course I help you all I can. And Snežka would be overjoyed. But your growing up culture has all been here. The hopes, fears and, above all, priorities, are so different. At least talk it over with Mike before you finally decide."

"He'll be glad to see the back of me," Minkie muttered.

She gave now a big sigh as she wondered how things could have gone so wrong between them.

"Whenever I see you here, you're looking miserably thoughtful," a familiar voice said, and a moment later Luke sat beside her the other side of Branka. He poked an experimental finger in the opening in her blanket, and said "Well, she's looking a bit more human." At which Branka began to howl. Minkie picked her up again and began rocking her. Luke added sadly "Never was any good with babies."

"It'll be different when it's your own."

Luke looked startled and said "Good Lord," as though the thought of such a possibility had not struck him before.

"You're back early."

"I think Jake was keen to get back, it was quite tiring for him. Marija said she thought you might be down here."

"How did it all go?"

"Emotional as you might expect. And fascinating for us as Jake was able to point out the fields they had slept in, and the tracks they followed. I guess such friendships as Jake and Pete had are pretty rare."

"I suppose everything intensifies in times of fear and urgency. That's why in some ways it's difficult for me to find my place in Sarajevo. I didn't go through those awful years when you didn't know whether your family or your best friend would be alive at the end of the day."

"Isn't that a good reason for staying here, where you have your place?"

"But Luke, that's the point. I don't any more. Sara is dead, my ex boy friend and best girlfriend are in America, you and Rowena will probably end up the other side of the world."

"And Mike?"

"And Mike hates me."

"So you keep saying, though I don't know on what grounds."

"Mike isn't all he seems you know."

"Which one of us is?"

"Did you know Marija had his daughter, and she was killed during the siege? She would have been about my age."

"No I didn't. But so what? It was long before he met Sara. How do you know he didn't tell her?"

"I think it's extremely unlikely."

"Perhaps. Just as it's extremely unlikely, Sara…" Luke stopped. "I don't think rummaging about extracting snippets from people's past is a good guide to current character assessment. Believe me, I should know."

"Anyway, what would I do here?"

"Far more options here than in Sarajevo I would have thought. For example, you could look after Mike for a while."

"Like a dutiful daughter?"

Luke gave up. "Come on, it's cooling off. I'll take you both home."

Back at the cottage, Rowena was introducing Jake to 'proper English tea' and toasted teacakes. Jake greeted Minkie warmly. They had liked each other from the beginning. "You're not as buttoned up as a lot of the Poms," Jake assured her and this was apparently a compliment.

It wasn't quite as awful as she had anticipated having Luke's cottage to herself. Every morning Polly Cuttle called in as soon as she had finished her stint at the shop. She was like a breath of fresh air, full of the latest gossip to which Minkie half listened, beginning to feel that she was part of the community again.

Branka adored her, her face creasing into a big toothless grin as soon as Polly arrived, and Minkie refused to accept Polly's assertion that it was only wind. If Minkie had nothing else planned, Polly would arrange to pick up her mid-afternoon, either for a country drive, shopping, a stroll round the village during which Branka would be introduced to a dozen more people, grinning toothlessly unless she happened to be asleep.

Half way through the second week, Polly rang to say she'd caught some kind of bug and it would be better if she stayed away from Branka. It was a huge disappointment; perhaps it was not a good idea to become too dependent on one person. And then she remembered the bundle of Justin's diaries that Luke had brought round one day. She felt curiously reluctant to read them, which was absurd given that she had read his earlier diaries quite uninvited. Now she got them out, curled up on a corner of the settee with Branka alseep beside her, and began to flick through the pages. Luke had jotted a few dates down and she turned to the first in May, 1994. Justin was describing a small party he had given when Beresford Tremayne first came to Daerley Green. Minkie read:

How truly amazing. It seems that Beresford Tremayne and Sara were at school together. The dear girl did not appear entirely delighted to see him, was quite cool with him. But he was obviously bowled over and, indeed, she looked quite ravishing in great contrast to the rather drawn look of recent months. Not for the first time I wished I were several decades younger myself. On the other hand, I suspect Sara and Mike may be experiencing something of a crisis of confidence in their relationship. A very small crisis I trust, but one that will certainly not benefit from any external complications.

There were some other concerned references to Sara, and a few months later, he wrote *I truly hope that Sara's and Beresford's simultaneous absence from Daerley last week-end is no more than a coincidence. I'm not usually a bad judge of character, but I think I may have been quite wrong about*

Beresford. I suspect the attraction of a woman like Sara will far outweigh any considerations as to whether or not she has other commitments. And when I saw Sara in the Co-op this morning, she was uncharacteristically short with me.

So perhaps Azzie had been right all along. Minkie had had a terrible row with her closest friend when Azzie, who had never taken to Beresford, suggested that he and Sara were sleeping together. It was so awful that she hadn't even been able to talk to Justin about it, but he had realised something was wrong and suggested that perhaps Azzie was feeling a bit left out of things as Minkie was then spending so much time with the young American Jesse. So Minkie had made the first move and patched things up, though they kept off the subject of Beresford until Amanda came back from America and started going out with him. At which point they both decided he must be a bit of a sex maniac. And after that ghastly episode at the golf club earlier Minkie had no doubt of it. Though come to think of it, if it hadn't been for that and how it had upset her, she might never have let Shan into her bed, with the result fast asleep on the settee beside her.

The Lord did indeed work in mysterious ways.

If Sara did have an affair with Beresford, it was worse than the affair Mike had had with Marija because that was way before he had met Sara. Thinking back, she had been aware of tensions in the house, especially when Mike came back from a long session in a war zone. His familiarity with Sarajevo had been one of the things that had made it so much easier for her to talk to him; much easier than talking to Sara who was always so wrapped up in village affairs. Come to think of it, it must have made Sara feel rather out of things at times, and if that were so she, Minkie, was partly responsible for it.

Minkie leaned over to check on Branka. Still fast asleep. She flipped through the earlier pages of the diary again, pausing at references to herself. *Poor, lost waif* Justin had written after their first encounter in Whirling Wood. Later there were comments like *What a transformation. Her English has really come on remarkably. I'm beginning to think she'll be a heartbreaker in a few years' time.* Then, following the news of Minkie's deepening friendship with Jesse, *She seems very happy though I can't help feeling he isn't quite mature enough to handle all those hidden depths. But then who am I to judge youngsters? I didn't make such a good job when it came to Luke.* Good heavens, the very first reference to Luke -–that must have come as a surprise to the man himself. She was surprised herself to come upon a number of comments like *Of course she is still very young but I hope that Minkie will overcome her tendency to regard her own judgments as more sound than others'* She checked the date. It was the time of her disagreement with Azzie over Sara and Beresford. Had Justin had the same suspicions? Oh, if only he were here to ask and to advise. Though perhaps these thoughts from the past and beyond the grave were a substitute, if only they were not so enigmatic.

She felt suddenly very tired, rested her against the back of the settee and was awakened an hour later by demands for attention from the bundle at her side.

With Polly still unwell, Minkie returned to the diaries over the next couple of afternoons. She came to the period in early 1997 when Jesse had returned to the U.S. for a while, and Azzie had also crossed the Atlantic to meet relatives who had settled there after leaving Iran. For a while Minkie had felt quite bereft. Justin commented *It does not bode well for the future if she becomes so dependent on others to give her life meaning.* Minkie thought a long time about that. It was true that her first months, even years, in England had focussed largely on the thought that, despite all evidence to the contrary, her mother was still alive. Very fortuitously she had been proved right just at the point that Jesse had responded to an urgent need to return to America following the events of 9/11. But Minkie herself had not been able to adapt to the changed conditions of her home city, and by the time she returned to Daerley a lot of things had changed there too. Including Justin's death.

At this point she had made the decision that it was her right to have a good time. What would Justin have made of Flip and his friends? But would she have needed them if Justin were still alive? And didn't that just underline his point of her dependence on individuals? Well, hopefully she now had Branka for a very long way into the future. They had each other. They would become co-dependent.

It was on the third afternoon that she came to the last entries in Justin's diaries. His writing had become larger and more wobbly and was sometimes difficult to decipher. There was a long entry about two weeks before his death after he had talked to Sara at length and for the first time about his twin brother James and the terrible sense of guilt he had felt for not being able to rescue him from his awful pit of despair. *But for some reason I could not bring myself to tell her about Luke. Perhaps even now I harbour shame that I could have brought myself to even go along with such suspicions.* Well, at least she knew what that was all about.

It was the entry for a few days later that made Minkie catch her breath in disbelief.

Sara seems to have decided, Justin wrote, *that the confidences I shared with her deserved some kind of reciprocal confidence. I wish to God she hadn't. Not that I think any the less of her. Abortions are almost the norm these days, but of course they were not at the time she had hers. It became clear, though, that it was not the abortion that troubled her so much as the fact it had been the cause of her inability to bear any more children. Knowing how much Mike has always wanted a daughter I can understand that, but there is nothing that can be done about it I have worried for some time about Mike. His skill as an observer which makes him such a good correspondent in the more fragile parts of the world also seems to bar him from letting people into his life in more familiar surroundings. Minkie has been the big exception. Deprived of the possibility of a daughter of his own, I fear that it may reflect on Minkie – I have already noticed Mike treating her with all the protectiveness a father would a favoured child.*

So she hadn't imagined it! Justin had noticed it too. Mike had been a real pain for a while, though she had regarded it more as interference than protectiveness. Poor Mike, cheated of a daughter of his own through Sara's abortion, and because his Bosnian child had been at the wrong place at the wrong time.

And what about poor Sara? What a terrible decision to have to make. She must have disliked the father of her baby very much; perhaps he never even knew about it. Minkie caught up the bundle of blanket and baby that was Branka in her arms and held it close. Thank God she made the decision she had.

Sarajevo : August/September 2005/Minkie

From her favourite viewpoint overlooking Sarajevo, Minkie absorbed the familiar scene now in less than favourable conditions. A heavy high-summer smog filled the head of the valley, shrouding all detail. If you hadn't known otherwise, it could have been the pre-war Sarajevo, somnolent in the murky heat, its scars temporarily invisible. Many of the scars had been healed anyway with rebuilding and renovation; but no amount of renovation could return the city to its former state of easy-going multi-culturalism.

Franko had agreed she should return here before making a final decision about her future. He had turned up on her doorstep at the middle of August, unannounced as usual, handsome as ever, looking affluent, quite unapologetic for his long silence.

"You are more beautiful than I remember," he had said, whirling her round in the entrance. "And I think perhaps also you have put on some weight." Then over her shoulder he had seen Branka on her back in her playpen, struggling hard to turn on to her front. "I see you have much to tell."

She had given him a resumé of her time at the golf club with Shan whom he had already met, omitting the incident with Beresford. When she had finished, Franko said "Well at least she will have good Slav genes. I don't imagine Mike is very pleased. But Sara will always help."

So she had to tell him about Sara's accident. For a moment Franko stood quite motionless, then he reached out for her and held her very tight for a long time, until there was a protesting demand from Branka. Franko let Minkie go and went over to kneel by his ... "What is she?" he demanded. "Cousin once removed?"

"Some sort of cousin," Minkie came to kneel beside him. She had not seen him with a tiny child before, but he had been brought up in a large family and instinctively seemed to know what to do.

"So if Sara is no more, nor your mother, I must take some responsibility for your future."

Minkie stifled a giggle at the thought of Franko taking responsibility for anything, but found she was mightily glad to see him all the same. "There's nothing here for me any more. I've decided to go back to Sarajevo. It's where Branka's roots are. And mine."

"Hm. It is not good to make too quick decision. This affect whole life of your baby." Franko stopped short, clapped a hand to his forehead. "But I am crazy. I am so excited to see you, to meet my new cousin, I forget to ask where is Rowena." He looked round the room. "I don't even see that absurd bear."

"She's gone to Australia." Minkie hesitated a moment before adding "With Luke."

"*With Luke!*" Franko went over to sit on the settee, his expression almost comic in its dismay.

"Well, you can't expect women to wait around for you forever. Anyway, you two were never going to be a permanent item."

"We suited each other. I did not realise how much. When she said she was going to Germany with Luke, I thought it was joke; that she was trying to – how do you say?- get revenge."

"You should never take things for granted, Franko. And Luke has changed – he's a really nice man." Minkie picked Branka up and went over to join him.

"How happens this miracle to Luke?" He put his little finger into Branka waving fist and she clasped it, gurgling. "Never mind about him. You see, this one likes me. She is very beautiful Minkie."

"Yes, isn't she. I'm so sorry Sara never saw her. Or Mother. But it's right that she be brought up in the place of her ancestors. And perhaps help to build it as it once was."

"That would be suit your purposes, not hers," Franko said.

"I think you have to forget that particular dream."

Minkie looked at him sadly. "To think you and I once shared the same particular dream."

"I was always more realistic than you. But now I will make a serious and practical suggestion. We shall travel together to Sarajevo. It is time I saw the family. I now have a very fine motorhome – second hand, but very fine; so it will be very cheap trip. There is a camp site near the city. You can visit Marija and Bogdan. And Bozo. And see the family again."

"Do you think it's a good idea to see Bozo with someone else's baby?"

"I think Bozo has new restaurant and new woman. Older. Much better for him. And we shall not take Branka. Such a journey in hot summer is not good for baby."

"I can't leave her." Minkie was aghast.

"Then I will not take you. Could not Amanda help you?"

"Amanda is in Cambridge." Minkie sat thinking for a while, and then knew who would help. "There is someone called Polly who used to help Sara when she had the shop. She has three children and she loves Branka. I think she will help."

"That is perfect."

And so it proved to be. Rowena and Luke were not due back until the middle of September, so Franko decided they would leave as quickly as possible. Polly was enchanted with the idea, and Minkie took Branka over on the eve of the departure. She almost chickened out at the last moment as she saw Branka gurgling happily in Polly's arms, and fled before she could change her mind. She also asked Polly to tell Mike what was happening in case he tried to contact her.

The journey to Sarajevo was like an unexpected holiday. Franko was apparently "between women" so Minkie had him to herself. They put the autobahn section through Germany behind them as quickly as possible, ambled more gently through Austria and thence through the Ljubelj tunnel into Slovenia. It seemed so bizarre to have to stop for emigration and customs control as they crossed first into Croatia and then into Bosnia-Hercegovina, only a few years earlier all part of the same federal republic. They allowed themselves the luxury of loitering along the Croatia coast, even deviating a little to go to a small camp site Franko knew beyond Dubrvonik. From here they took a motor boat into the old city, despite war scars rising as magnificently as ever from the sea shore. They walked round its massive walls, explored its narrow alleys and steep stairways.

"How it's changed," complained Minkie as they edged their way past the outdoor tables of a continuous succession of restaurants. "The tourists have taken over."

"Someone has to pay for one of the world's treasures."

They retraced their route a little before turning inland, soon crossing into Bosnia-Hercegovina and reaching Mostar. The landmark medieval bridge, destroyed in the war, had been rebuilt as an exact replica. Many of the broken buildings around it still await reconstruction.

"They have done very good job," Franko said.

"It looks what it is: a replica," Minkie commented.

"You have become difficult to please, cousin. You think it would be better to leave it in destroyed state?"

"At least it would remind people what war does."

"I think they do not need reminding."

"But the next generation will, and the next even more."

"I always tell you, you think too much."

But she cheered up as they followed the magnificent Neretva valley upstream. At least the scenery remained unpolluted if you closed your eyes to destroyed farms and villages.

The camp site at Ilidža was almost empty. Once it had been a gracious spa a few miles out of Sarajevo. The Archduke Franz Ferdinand had stayed here on the eve of his visit to the city in 1914 when a student had shot him and triggered off a series of events culminating in World War One. Minkie remembered showing Sara the corner of the pavement in Sarajevo bearing the imprint of the student's feet where he was standing when he fired the fatal shot. The imprints had been destroyed or removed during the war.

They had supper at the camp site restaurant and next morning took the tram in to Sarajevo. Franko, who had not revisited his city for some time, was impressed by the rate of repair and reconstruction. "And just look at the new mosques."

"Saudi money," Minkie muttered.

"How do you know?"

"How often have you seen a multi-minareted Bosnian mosque?"

Not being much of a mosque-goer himself, Franko was not really in a position to argue.

They got off the tram near the National Museum and went their separate ways. "Your Mum and sisters were only just civil when I was here last time, and I see no reason to expect anything different," Minkie said. "I'll go and check on Bozo. Did you say his new restaurant was near the Medresa?"

"Just round the corner from it. I'll pick you up there in a couple of hours."

Minkie took her time, noting the most recent restoration work that added style to the old Habsurg era buildings of the commercial centre. Everyone was out on such a warm September day, and the cafés packed. She thought back to the long-ago of her childhood when she could not walk more than a few metres along this same street without someone calling her name. Now she only saw strangers: smartly dressed – the Sarajevans had always had style – but strangers. She noticed quite a few young women wore the hajib now.

"Hey Minkie! – Minkie!" She paused a moment, shook her head, assumed she was dreaming and continued her amble. The call came again, louder more persistent. Minkie stopped looked back at the pavement covered with crowded tables, identified a wildly waving arm: a young woman with short dark hair. Pretty, but unrecognisable. The young woman got up, wove her way through the tables and finally confronted her. “Minkie – are you going to ignore me after all your promises?”

Her promises? She looked at the smooth young face more closely. Good God.

“Snežka?” she queried. Then “Snežka, it’s not possible that you can have become so grown up.”

She had been fourteen when Minkie last saw her just after the horrors of 9/11. Could four years have made such a difference? Clearly they could, for she would never have recognised this slim young woman, with the gamine haircut, firm jaw, serious eyes. Oh yes, she should have remembered those serious eyes, far too serious for the child she had then been.

Snežka tugged at her arm. “Come and have coffee, meet some of my friends.”

Minkie disentangled herself gently. “I can’t stop now, I’m meeting someone. Perhaps later.”

“I hear you have a baby.” Snežka made it sound almost like an accusation. “You won’t have time any more for changing things like we both wanted.”

“We’ll talk about it Snežka. I assume your parents are here too? I’ll call you.”

She moved on, rather more quickly now, into the old bazaar quarter, and saw the sign she was looking for over an entrance to the courtyard of an old building. It read *Dve bela goluba* – Two White Doves – the same name as the restaurant Bozo had run before the war. She peered cautiously into the courtyard. A dozen tables were set attractively among potted orange and lemon trees. Two of them were occupied, and a man was coming out to clear some recently vacated tables. At first she didn’t recognise him. The last time she had seen him, he still had only one leg; now he had a prosthetic second leg, with which he moved so smoothly that it was hard to realise it was not his own.

“Bozo,” she called.

He look up, hastily put the tray down before he dropped

it, and hurried towards her, his mouth opening and shutting and nothing coming out. Then his arms were round her and he was saying "Jasminka, Jasminka," in a loud disbelieving voice. He had never called her by her Anglicised name.

He pulled her towards the restaurant, calling "Sasha, Sasha come quickly," and a woman with a white unform and white cap over hennaed hair came hurrying out. "A miracle, here is Branka's girl". Not "the girl I wanted to marry" but "Branka's girl."

Sasha extended her arms in greeting. "We close for afternoon siesta," she said and went to close the door out on to the street.

"You can't shut shop like that," Minkie protested.

"Why not, when I am shop owner. Come inside. We will have *travarica.*" So he had not forgotten her favourite tipple flavoured with marjoram and mint.

It was cooler inside and Sasha soon joined them. "Bozo spoke of you so much I became quite jealous," she laughed.

"I was too old for her," Bozo told her fondly. "Or she was too young for me. But now she is mature lady with baby, I hear."

"How did you hear?" Minkie demanded.

"Mike telephoned."

"*Mike!*" Why on earth should Mike feel it necessary to keep Bozo informed on such matters?

"Why not? Our paths have crossed several times. And he told me the terrible news about Sara, and he wanted to know if Marija and Bogdan had already moved back here."

Ah yes, Marija, the mother of Mike's daughter. "Well, as you probably know, they are. I bumped into Snežka on the way here."

"Yes, but the house is still being renovated so they are staying with friends. I haven't seen young Snežka for a long time. By all accounts she is rather like you at the same age."

"By all acounts?"

"By Mike's account." Him again! "I believe you were very passionate and intense in your teens. But now, Jasminka, tell us why you are here."

"I must decide on the future for baby Branka and for me."

"And where is she baby Branka?"

"Franko didn't think it was a good idea to bring her on such a journey in the summer heat."

"I couldn't imagine Franko could be so sensible."

"Mm, I was surprised too."

"I am also surprised you are thinking of returning. I remember you were not very satisfied when you were here before."

"It was very different then. Mother was so ill, I did not have Branka, Sara was alive…."

When Bozo didn't respond, Minkie looked up and saw his expression as he watched her with a small smile. "You seem to need many circumstances for your decisions and your happiness, Jasminka. Usually it has to come from within." He paused as he saw her frown. "I think I have made you angry."

Not so much angry as lonely. There was no one in the wide world who could share with her that sense of being tossed from one set of circumstances to another at the whim of events beyond her control. Azzie would have understood for she had experienced a similar desolation when she left Iran during their war with Iraq. But Azzie was in America with a whole set of re-discovered relatives. Her circle had expanded while Minkie's had shrunk.

There she went again.

Sasha said "I think you're being very hard on her, Bozo."

"Well, you overcame much harder circumstances." He turned to Minkie. "Sasha was brought up in a Russian orphanage and you've probably heard how appalling they could be. Then she was fostered like you – but they were no Mike and Sara. They wanted cheap labour on their farm in Moldavia. In her teens she managed to get across the border into Romania, which wasn't a lot better under Ceaucescu. But she met someone who knew someone in a village in Serbia which was largely Romanian in population. There she worked for a very nice family, who made the unfortunate decision to move to Sarajevo a few months before our war started. The family were killed during the siege, and I found her scavenging in my dustbins."

Minkie looked at Sasha with new respect. She didn't look at all like someone who scavenged in dustbins.

"Perhaps a problem for Jasminka is that her growing up has been in a country where everything is so different, especially expectations. I have been thrown about more or less in this Balkan hotch-potch and am familiar with what to expect and not expect."

Minkie remembered Bozo saying once that he would prefer to stay here than come to England because here he knew how things worked and didn't work. She reminded him of that now.

"Yes, and it is still true. But you, you will always want to mend the things that don't work and be disappointed when you find no one else really cares. You are accustomed to living with people who make things happen."

"Franko makes things happen."

"Now there's a life that would not be suitable for baby Branka."

"He's coming to pick me up soon – Franko I mean. He has a motorhome and we are staying at the camp site at Ilidža. Why don't you come over and have a meal with us there at the camp restaurant; it's rather good."

Sasha went off to prepare a cold dish that was one of her favourites: *pršut*, tissue-thin air-dried ham, accompanied by olives, gherkins, tomatoes, grated cheese, and a bottle of *Dingać,* a red wine from the Pelješac peninsula in Croatia. Her return with it coincided with Franko's arrival and Minkie was heartily glad to have the focus off herself for a while. Franko reported his family were well, overjoyed to see him, and anxious to know more about baby Branka.

"They are very proud of you Jasminka," he said. She thought he seemed unusually subdued.

"Well, that's a first."

"You must try not to be so inflexible. They are changing. Mother has aged so much since the war. She has lost her fire and is now an old lady who needs the help she used to give to everyone else, but does not know how to ask for it. Some of my brothers and sisters, especially the ones who are married and living away, have not understood this and still think she can come and take care of the children, cook meals for them when they are working. I will tell them this must stop. The younger ones are full of ideas for the future, very self-centred as happens at that age, and do not notice how much she needs their support."

"It's the same in England. Probably worse as there isn't the same extended family structure as here."

"So some things are better here?"

"Yes, the vegetables and the fruit and the coffee," Minkie teased him.

"Oh you. Without your Branka you are reverting to type. When are you going to see Marija and Bogdan?"

It was two days later when Minkie joined Marija on the small strip of land behind their home. Bogdan had already ploughed and harrowed it, and Marija was doing a final removal of any large stones, stacking them up at the bottom of the plot with the idea of creating some kind of a wall.

"This reminds me of the time I first met Bozo," Minkie said, tipping a barrowload on to the growing pile. "When and what are you planting?"

"I thought I might start this afternoon, especially if you can stay and help. Bogdan is tied up with builders. A friend is bringing over a whole lot of salad seedlings, and I'm planning on concentrating mainly on root vegetables this first year."

"Yes, I'll stay. Haven't had a chance to get my hands

dirty for too long."

"Sonja used to enjoy that too."

"Most of what I've learned has been from Mike. In Sonja's case, it was already in her genes."

"It was the only thing I ever found she had in common with her father. Otherwise she could be pretty self-centred."

"Marija, she was only thirteen when she died."

"Twelve. And you're right, she didn't have time to develop into a full person."

"I can't imagine you ever being self-centred. Nor Mike, really. Though I guess he thought I was."

"It's a shame you have such negative thoughts about him. He always adored you."

"It's a bit hard finding you that you've unwittingly been taking the place of someone's daughter," Minkie said. She bent to ease a particularly large stone out of the earth.

"It was never like that. Mike didn't even know he had a daughter until 1997 – at least four years after you first came to Daerley Green. He learned about her existence and her death all within a matter of minutes. Perhaps you should stop and think about that sometime."

"In other words I'm being self-centred?"

"Just a bit. Snežka is the same, but she is still young enough to get away with it."

"What am I young enough to get away with?" Snežka asked as she approached them.

"Being self-centred."

"Well, thank you very much. Here am I devoting my life to making the world a better place...."

"Better according to your view of it," Marija put in.

"Do you want my help or don't you."

"We do, we do."

The three of them put in a good few hours of hard work, pausing only for a cold drink, bread and salami in the shade of the only tree, a tired-looking plum, By the time Bogdan returned, they had removed all visible stones, planted two rows of salad seedlings, and three rows of carrots and parsnips. He stood, hands on hips surveying the results of their labours.

"Looks good," he pronounced. "Very good." And it did, the healthy brown soil now punctuated by small green plants.

"Too much like hard work for me," Franko announced when he came to collect Minkie, but agreed it looked fine.

"Why don't we start another scheme like Bozo ran, getting the different ethnic groups working together. Though it wouldn't be very practical for some of the Moslem girls enveloped in all that stuff."

"And how do you think they manage all over the Middle and Far East?" Marija asked. "You're being silly Snežka."

Minkie had been thinking the same things so decided to keep quiet. Anyway, as far as she could see, her generation were getting on with the new circumstances of their lives without a fuss.

Suddenly she ached for little Branka.

"I want to go home," she told Franko as they drove back to Ilidža.

"Not yet, someone is coming to meet me here in a few days."

"What nefarious activities are you up to now?"

"Not nefarious. You are always so suspicious. They are bringing good material you cannot easily get in England."

"Like drugs?"

"Like medicines."

Minkie decided it was probably better if she didn't know. She contented herself with telephoning Daerley Green and hearing little Branka's distant gurgle at the end of the line; which only succeeded in making her more homesick than ever.

"There is one thing clear," Franko said over dinner that evening. "This experience is proving you should be in Daerley Green, not here."

"It doesn't prove anything, except that I want to be where

little Branka is."

"But what will you do if you stay? Help Snežka with the next revolution? What about your art?"

"You sound like Mike."

"I don't think he'd feel flattered. Anyway I can't help you because all your decisions are hemmed in by 'ifs' and 'buts', and I don't understand what has changed."

In the end it was an unexpected thing that led her to postpone her decision.

"Polly wants you to call her," Bozo told her when she visited a couple of days later. Her heart had begun to plummet in fear before he had a chance to add "She said it's nothing to do with little Branka."

Indeed Minkie could hear her gurgling in the background as Polly answered the phone. "I'd just like you opinion," she said. "May be I'm being unnecessarily fusspottish, but Mike came home several days ago and has closeted himself in the house. I thought he'd come for news, but no. Then I saw him briefly in the Co-op. He looked ghastly."

"Well, he has recently lost his wife," Minkie pointed out.

"Yes, but not sad-ghastly; ill-ghastly."

Minkie thought of Justin's words oncerning Mike's inability to let other people into his life, with Minkie being a big exception.

"Franko's just waiting to see someone, then we'll be heading for home. Should be back in a few days."

It was as simple as that.

Oxfordshire : September 2005

Franko said he would drive Minkie back to Daerley, stay the night then go on to Germany. From the way he said it, she knew he was anxious to get his business in Germany over and return to Sarajevo. It was a complete change from the days not so long ago when he ricocheted from one place to another, always busy, always with something new to arrange, new people to meet, new problems to overcome. She preferred this new Franko, and wondered whether Rowena might too. But, it was too late. She had met few couples in such true rapport as Rowena and Luke when she last saw them.

They reached the cottage just before midnight. Polly, bless her, had stocked up the fridge, put fresh flowers on the fireplace where Bunbury usually sat.

"I miss Bunbury," Franko said unexpectedly.

"Well you'd better get used to missing Bunbury's owner."

"Yes, I find nice Bosnian girl. No complications." And Minkie knew that of course he would.

It was Franko who found the letter in the hall. It had skidded under the hallstand.

"For you," he said, "with American stamps."

It was addressed to Minkie at Abel's Yard, so Mike must have surfaced sufficiently to come round and deliver it; or more likely asked Polly to do so.

She recognised Jesse's neat hand and half of her did not want to open it. She prayed *please no more disasters*. But it revealed no disasters, only potential complications. Jesse wrote that he had been following life in Daerley Green through its website, that he was devastated by the news of Sara's death, delighted that Minkie had returned to Daerley herself, that he was taking a small vacation and would be arriving shortly .

"Oh God," said Minkie.

"What now?

"Jesse is arriving any day."

Franko grinned at her infuriatingly. "And I thought my life was complicated!"

She couldn't ring Mike at this hour, but she checked the answering machine and, among several messages, found one from him: *Welcome home, Minkie. I expect you will have read Jesse's letter. He's arriving on Friday. I've invited him to stay here and explained you are at Justin's old cottage. Presumably Rowena and Luke are due back soon.*

Friday. Today was Wednesday.

Another message from Rowena said *Back on the 15th. Can't wait.*

Well, at least there was nothing she could do about anything now.

Franko had made breakfast when she came down next morning. The phone rang as he was pouring out coffee.

Mike said "Jesse's Flights bus is due at Banbury bus station from the airport at half six tomorrow evening. How about you meeting him with Robbo? I'm sure he would rather be greeted by you than by me. You could bring Branka over and I'll look after her until you drop Jesse back here." Whatever had been wrong with him, he was clearly better.

Things felt as though they were beginning to close in. She spent the intervening time sorting through mail, catching up on laundry, freshening the cottage up with flowers in readiness for the travellers' return, bombarding Polly for a minute-by-minute account of Branka's time with her, and in return answering her barrage of questions about her time in Sarajevo.

"Will you go back there?" Polly asked.

And Minkie realised she was no nearer making a decision.

On Friday evening she parked Robbo across the main road from the bus station and went to sit on a bench nearer the Flights arrival stand. The bus was late and her stomach churned with anxiety. What would Jesse think of her? Of Branka? And, equally, what would she think of him?

The bus arrived twenty minutes late and he was the first

off it, his arms open to embrace her and within seconds she was caught up in them, and his mouth was on hers, warm, tender, familiar. Even after all this time, amazingly familiar.

He held her away from him, looking at her with such intensity that they seemed held, the two of them, in a bubble a thousand miles away from the bustle all around.

"You've got a bald spot," she accused. He had also put on a little weight and looked affluent.

"Tact was never your strong point, was it? Thought you might have acquired a little with maturity. Anyway it's only a small round patch."

He went to collected his case and they trundled it across the bus station, over the main road.

"Good God, you've still got that old bucket."

"I know, I know. You'll have a stretch limo and a four-wheel drive by now."

"Neither." With difficulty he fitted his case into Robbo's modest boot. "Let me look at you again."

They stood, not touching, surveying each other. He was still very good looking.

"What happened Jesse? You stopped writing."

"I married my college sweetheart Maddy, and she left me for another. And, hey, you stopped writing, too. Have you left me for another?"

"Yes and no." Minkie got into the car. "And let me remind you, it was you who left me. But I do have a baby now, though no husband."

She was watching his face as she said it. There was a flicker of surprise that might also have held disapproval. "Isn't that rather inconvenient? What does Mike make of it?"

"Mike's thoughts are a bit difficult to read these days. Sara was fine."

"I bawled like a kid when I read about her death"

As they drove back to Daerley, she told him briefly about Shan who had wanted her to return to Poland with him, about

Rowena and Luke and the latter's amazing transformation, about her own restlessness which led to her return to Sarajevo.

"And what now?"

"I'm still not sure. Tell me about you. I'm really sorry about Maddy."

"Yeah, so was I for a while. I thought we had a lot going for us. I'd continued in the travel business – the same sort of tours that you and I were marketing in Oxford. It just went from strength to strength. But Maddy didn't want to work in the office, and she didn't want a kid too soon either, so she had too much time on her hands. She was terribly traumatised by 9/11. Of course you don't know. She was actually in New York and had planned to meet a friend for coffee right by the Twin Towers. At the last moment she changed her mind and didn't go. It was too late to get hold of her friend, who ended up by being very badly wounded and in a wheelchair."

"That's terrible."

"Yeah. Maddy developed some kind of survivor's guilt. I don't understand it, but apparently it happens." No he probably wouldn't understand it, and, yes, it did happen. "Anyway, I guess I helped her quite a bit to come through it and one thing led to another. But the real Maddy was a much tougher woman than the one I thought I'd married and it wasn't working out."

"That's weird. You were the restless one when you were here."

"Yeah, it is weird. Anyway, she met someone else who was equally restless, and I thought it was better if we parted. I guess I had fallen a bit out of love, too."

"Are you on your own?"

"I have an arrangement with a colleague at work. We share a flat, give each other enough space."

They had reached Daerley Green and Jesse's nose was glued to the car window. "Jeez, it's all so familiar, and so different. So small compared with home."

Mike must have been looking out for them, for he was at

the front door as Robbo came to a halt. He came down the path to greet Jesse, and Minkie thought he looked more relaxed than she had seen him since Sara's death.

Jesse gave him a bear hug, as American men did each other. "I don't know what to say, Mike. About Sara."

"You don't have to say anything. I'm just very glad to be able to welcome you back. Do you think young Minkie has changed much?"

"Prettier than ever. Perhaps a little heavier. She's told me about the baby – that was a surprise."

"Come in, come in. I've defrosted a casserole. One of the last Sara made."

Branka was sleeping deeply, but Jesse cooed appropriately in that tentative way that adults do if they had not had much contact with small babies. It was a convivial meal, rather as might be shared between unusually compatible strangers rather than old friends and lovers unmet for several years. Because Jesse had not been directly involved in any of the recent events, had not even met some of the protagonists, it was easier for them all to remain quite detached, at least on the surface. There was even a gust of laughter from Jesse when Mike gave a quite funny resumé of the downfall of Beresford Tremayne.

"Never did see what Minkie saw in him," Jesse pronounced.

"He was always very kind to me," she said. "And that meant a lot."

"Just as well you weren't a few years older," Jesse commented, uncomfortably near the truth.

Afterwards, Mike took Jesse round the garden while Minkie made coffee. From the kitchen window she watched their figures moving through the deepening dusk. Jesse was still undoubtedly a very attractive man, but she was trying to identify a small something that had changed. As they came in Mike said, "Minkie, why don't you stay the night here?"

She was busying arranging the cups on the coffee table in

the living room, felt her face redden as the options flashed through her mind, found herself gabbling. "Thanks Mike. But I think after all the recent upheavals, it's time to get Branka back into some kind of routine again. Come over as soon as you like in the morning, though, Jesse. Perhaps we could do a tour of old haunts."

Jesse picked up on it immediately with "Yeah that would be great, really like old times. You drive and I take care of Branka."

Minkie made her excuses and escaped as soon as she could. And it did feel like an escape she told herself as she let herself in to Luke's cottage and let its familiarity enfold her. What was Mike up to? Was he trying to throw her and Jesse together, and hopefully get rid of her that way? Branka was already fast asleep, barely reacted except with small animal noises as Minkie changed her and settled her in her cot. It took Minkie herself a good deal longer to follow her into a trouble-free oblivion.

"Let's go down to Whirling Wood," Jesse said next morning, "and I was wondering, how about giving Robbo a well-earned rest and I'll hire something a bit more propitious?"

"Propitious to what?"

"Well, I guess this is some kind of celebration, isn't it?"

"Isn't Robbo good enough for you?"

"Will you stop misinterpreting everything I say? You've become so prickly."

"You're right, Jesse. Sorry. You go ahead and hire what you like while I get Branka ready. It might be better if I take care of her anyway, while you drive."

He returned in an hour with the latest Toyota and they drove first down to the main entrance of Whirling Wood. Oddly enough Jesse was one of the few people she didn't associate it with, and indeed he strolled between the trees, looking around appreciatively as if almost seeing it for the first time.

They sat on the bench by the wildflower meadow. "Tell

me everything that happened after I left you in Sarajevo."

So Minkie did her best to summarise all that happened, the difficulty of settling back in the city of her birth, of making that longed-for relationship with her mother, her relationship with Bozo, her mother's death and her eventual return to Daerley Green.

"And then you met this Shan?"

"Not for quite a while. Before that I went wild for a bit." She told him about Flip's gang, though not about the partner swapping, but how for a while she felt she was making up for the teenage years she'd missed out on."

"Hey hold hard. You had a good part of your late teenage years with me."

"Yes, I know. And that was great, but it was all building up towards getting back to Sarajevo somehow. And I think I sensed you were restless even before you knew it yourself."

"So you went wild for a bit. Sounds a bit like Maddy. But then I guess that was as a result of a very big trauma."

"Well having your father shot while he was holding your hand wasn't exactly run of the mill either."

Jesse turned to her, his expression stricken as he took her hands. For the first time she caught a glimpse of the old Jesse she had completely shared her life with for a year or more.

"Forgive me, darling. Such a lot has happened it's difficult to take it all in. So, how did Shan come into all this?"

Minkie gave a small laugh. "We found him, or rather Luke did, over there." She pointed to the river bank where Luke had come upon this human-shaped bundled of rags.

Jesse looked puzzled. She explained how Shan had been exploited and had lost all hope by the time they found him.

"You mean he's an illegal immigrant?"

"Well, he's not here now so he can't be. And he never claimed benefits, always worked his way, earned more than his pay."

"I wish I could meet him. He must be a truly magnetic

guy that he could so win your heart that you wanted to bear his child."

"It wasn't like that."

"How was it then?"

But Minkie knew if she explained for the rest of the day, it was doubtful Jesse would come anywhere near understanding how it really was. They had led such different lives over the last four years; their expectations for themselves and from others bore no resemblance.

"Let's move on," she said.

He wanted to revisit the small furnished flat they had shared in the Woodstock Road. Of course it was occupied, but Jesse said to the young man in overalls who opened the door, "I'm real sorry to disturb you, but my … my fiancée and I shared this flat a few years ago and it would be great to be able to see it again."

The young man said "Come on in" and stood aside to let them into the familiar narrow hall that led into the living room, the only decent-sized room.

"It's a bit untidy," he said. "I'm fixing some shelves and my wife is out at work."

The furniture was much as it had been, but of course it was lacking the knick-knacks and touches that Minkie had spent hours acquiring at craft fairs and in local markets. When they had left, she had given them all to Sara who had put them all in a box up in the loft at Abel's Yard until such time as Minkie decided to settle down. It hadn't happened.

The place seemed smaller than they remembered it.

"Bit scruffy," Jesse murmured as they returned to the car.

"But we were very happy," Minkie reminded him and felt a shaft of nostalgia for those uncomplicated days before 9/11.

"We were, weren't we? I guess it was a mistake to go back home so quickly."

Better not go down that road. "So where now?" Minkie put in quickly.

"I fancy a stroll by the canal. Where that canal shop is."

"Well, there are several, but I think you mean Aynho." It was where she and Azzie had had that awful row over whether or not Sara was having an affair with Beresford, but Jesse had never known about that.

They strolled south towards Somerton. After a while, apart from the hum from the M40, they could have been miles from anywhere. The hedgerows were still summer-thick, alive with bees bumbling lazily, and an azure flash of kingfisher zipped ahead of them,

"I'd forgotten how beautiful it is," Jesse paused while Minkie adjusted the harness that fitted Branka to her back, and then took her hand. "I get the feeling Mike would quite like to see us get together again."

"Really?"

"He's been quite worried about you. That wild patch you were talking about. I explained to him about Maddy and the reaction to the trauma."

"That was kind of you." Minkie meant it ironically, but Jesse squeezed her hand and said "That's all right." Then after a long moment "How would you feel about that?"

Oh good God, she had not anticipated this. "It's been three years, Jesse. We're very different people."

"Are we? Well, yes, I haven't slept with any illegal immigrants to the best of my knowledge. Though heaven knows there were plenty of them about. Different from yours, of course. Mainly Hispanic from South America and especially Mexico; or Asian."

"You sound disapproving."

"No. Of course some panhandle, even steal, but most of them do a good job. Don't know how we'd cope without them in the fruit picking season. You see them in their thousands in the orchards and soft fruit fields. I hear they'll live ten to a room to save money."

"I don't imagine it's through choice. Shan said some of

the living conditions for the immigrant agricultural workers were worse than those they kept their pigs in Poland."

"No, but then no one asked them to come. And it wasn't easy when I arrived home, putting down roots after so long, learning to make my way – well, like Shan did."

"But he was an illegal immigrant as you pointed out. And you always had your parents to bail you out."

"I didn't need bailing out," Jesse said indignantly.

"And I don't suppose any of your employers wanted any sexual favours."

"Sexual….? What are you talking about? And why are you being so difficult?"

"I'm not being difficult, just realistic. As I said we're different people. I've spent much of my time in a wounded city with people trying to put behind them experiences we couldn't begin to imagine." She had now identified the change in Jesse that she had sensed earlier. It was not so much a change, though, for they were now touching on subjects that had never arisen during their time together. What she was identifying was a streak of intolerance, or maybe a lack of compassion.

Abruptly he let go of her hand.. "Well, I'm sorry, Minkie, if I haven't suffered enough to qualify for your affection.."

Don't be absurd. You have my affection and always will."

Jesse stopped and took her in his arms. "I'd forgotten just how much we had together. I know you've had a much harder path to follow, but I'm truly willing to try and understand, willing to change, willing to do anything, in fact.. It would be so very wonderful if I could take you home with me. Both of you. We could work together, build a nice home just as we did before, but bigger. Eventually have more kids. Could you think about it, darling?"

It felt warm and safe standing in the confines of his arms. Branka reached out for a fistful of Jesse's hair and gave a pleased gurgle. It was very tempting. They knew each other so well, could surely adapt to any differences that had arisen.

Jesse bent to kiss her. It was with a tenderness she hadn't felt for a very long time. The kind of tenderness that would make you wake up each morning with a sense of joy. It would be good for Branka, it would please Mike, it would end the interminable uncertainties. Minkie reached up to take Jesse's face in her hands and kissed him back.

"I guess," he said happily after a while, "that could count as a yes."

There had been no way of alerting Rowena and Luke to Jesse's arrival, so when he looked up from reading the paper as they let themselves in, it was to be greeted by "And who the hell are you?"

Minkie came hurtling down the stairs and there was a confusion of "God, I'm glad to see you's" and hugs and "tell me everything's" while the two men stood a little aside.

Luke made the first move, held out a hand, said "Luke Smith".

"Hi. I've heard of you. I'm Jesse Maynard."

"*The* Jesse?"

"I know of no other."

"Then I've heard of you, too."

The young women disentangled themselves. "Sorry, sorry," Minkie said. "I see you two have made your own introductions. Jesse, this is Rowena Johnson from Western Australia."

"Hi Rowena. I've been admiring your paintings. They're enchanting. I hope you'll let us buy some for our home."

Minkie and Rowena exchanged glances. Rowena's eyebrows shot up. "They can be a wedding present if we're talking in those terms."

"I'm entirely in Minkie's hands," Jesse said. "But for the moment I must leave you. I'm meeting Mike over at The Trumpet to which I moved this morning. I really can't go on taking advantage of his hospitality indefinitely. I've invited him over for dinner as a small thanks. And I guess you all have a lot to catch up on."

"Too right," Rowena said, adding as the door closed behind him "Where the hell did he spring from?"

Minkie flopped on to the settee. "He heard about Sara's death, wanted to be with us; his marriage has just broken up."

"And you're planning to fill the gap? Are you demented? Has he always been that pompous?"

"He's *not* pompous," Minkie said crossly. "Well, may be just a bit, but nothing that can't be repaired."

"You mean you're taking on another mission? What has Mike to say?"

"It's Mike who pushing us into it."

"I don't believe it."

"I do," Luke said.

Minkie said "I really don't want this conversation. I want to hear about Oz and Grumps and your plans."

"And I'm just about riven with jetlag," Luke announced. "I suggest we unpack enough for tonight, go for a meal to The Trumpet and then fall into bed."

"Not The Trumpet," Minkie said. "I have no wish to intrude on Jesse's and Mike's tête à tête."

Over the meal, Rowena told Minkie they had decided to ask the vicar if a small memorial could be put in the cemetery in memory of her grandfather, and also to ask Mike if he would add a bush for him in the new shrubbery he was planning. Luke had put out some feelers and discovered his consultancy was likely to find a good foothold in the Antipodes.

"And it wouldn't matter whether we were here or there," Rowena chipped in enthuiastically, "So we are thinking of spending six months with Grumps and six months here."

"Maybe not forever, but for the forseeable future," Luke added.

And what about you?"

"I've got to decide what's best for Branka."

"Are you sure you know what you're doing?" Rowena stood in the doorway of Minkie's room a few days later while the latter got ready to go out with Jesse. Again.

"I need to get to re-know him before I make that final decision."

"Of course you do. Are you getting any nearer?"

Minkie shrugged into a clean shirt. "Yes and no."

"Everything's 'yes' and 'no' with you these days."

"It's not easy Ro. We have such a lot of shared memories. But we do disagree on rather a lot of things, too."

"Such as?"

"Iraq, genetic engineering, single parents. But a bit of disagreement is healthy, isn't it?"

They had become quite heated over the environment. Showing him photographs of Whirling Wood's wildflower meadow, Minkie said, "Imagine if we lost that, not just here but all over the world."

"But they'll be replaced by other wildflowers. Don't you see that one size doesn't fit all? If you maintain your wild flowers and lose the extra food with which you need to feed a growing population, you're shooting yourself in the foot."

"We don't carry guns in this country," Minkie said primly. "Anyway if you really believe one size doesn't fit all, why are you trying to impose your political system on the poor benighted Iraqis?"

When they ignored the rest of the world and went back to the things that formerly preoccupied them – where to go that evening, what to eat, ways of expanding Jesse's business – the sense of harmony was remarkable. He was getting quite good with Branka, too. In the long run, that was the most importanr thing of all.

She wondered what Sara would have thought. She knew what Mike thought.

A couple of days later, Shan arrived on his way back to Poland. That evening, Minkie was in the kitchen peeling cherry tomatoes to add to a Mediterranean casserole when she heard Rowena say "Hi Jesse. Minkie's in the kitchen, Shan is upstairs with Branka."

If she had not stopped to rinse the tomato juice from her fingers, her whole future might have been different. By the time she was half way up the stairs, Jesse's angry voice was saying "What the hell are you doing with my daughter," and Shan replying "Excuse, but she is *my* daughter.

Minkie burst into the bathroom to be confronted by two men, glaring at each other over the tiny bundle that was Branka enfolded in a thick white towel. Shan was gently patting her dry.

"Minkie I do not want that Branka go with this man."

"At least she can be sure of a good home, education, chance in life."

"I can all these things."

"Shut up both of you," shouted Minkie, and Branka raised her small pale eyebrows in alarm and began to cry.

But Jesse had already shut up. He stood, loose-limbed, laconic, watching Shan with a look that said as plainly as if he had spelt out the words *You're a loser; you don't stand a chance.*

It was a look Minkie had seen uncountable times: at school as the ethnic tensions began to take hold; on the faces of interviewees on newsreels in a dozen of other people's wars.

"Is still damp," Shan managed to say as he headed for his room. He turned and said again "I do not like that she go with this man."

Minkie scooped up the bundle in the towel, and shouted at Jesse "Get out of my house!"

"And mine," murmured Luke, just behind her.

"I credited you with more pride. How could you Minkie?" Jesse began

"Get out," Minkie shouted even louder and Branka yelled even louder, too.

Oxfordshire: Postscript – September 2005

The cemetery was empty except for a lone figure standing by Sara's grave. He was dressed in a baggy pair of jeans, a check shirt, a sweater slung loosely over his shoulders, and had clearly come straight from a gardening session. As she approached, her shadow came alongside his until it stopped level with his shoulder.

After a moment he said, without turning "Princess?"

"Mike."

Another pause.

"So when are you going?"

"Going where?"

"To America with Jesse?"

"Why would I do that?"

"He rather gave me that impression. He'd be a good father for Branka. You'd make a handsome couple, and knowing – really knowing someone as you two know each other, makes for the strongest of relationships."

"Branka already has a father who made his own decisions. And I found I didn't really know him at all. Anyway," she added after a moment, "I find him a little immature."

There was a snort that might have been interpreted as a chuckle. "Oh Princess, you are funny. But Justin used to say much the same. So did your mother."

"What, that I'm funny?"

"No, that Jesse was a bit immature for you. Though he's an immeasurable improvement on the riff-raff you've chosen to spend your time with since your return."

Minkie thrust her hand deep in her pockets. "You would be amazed how pompous Jesse could be. How come I didn't 'take precautions'? Couldn't I have chosen someone responsible enough to be a permanent father? And so on and so on."

"All reasonable enough points."

"Yeah, and at least he didn't call me a slut."

Mike turned then, his face twisted with remorse. "That's the most unforgivable thing I have ever said to anyone."

"I'll tell you why it happened and then we'll forget about it. Beresford made a pretty vile pass at me and I panicked. It was such a shock that I rushed back to our flat. Shan found me in hysterics and comforted me the best way he knew."

"I'll cut his throat," Mike was almost shouting, dropping his voice as he saw someone enter the cemetery gate. "Beresford, not Shan."

"You'll do no such thing. Branka is one of the very best things that ever happened to me. I wouldn't marry Shan anyway. I regard him much more as a younger brother."

"Some people would regard that as incest."

Go on, Minkie, Justin's voice said in her head. *Go on, say it.* "How would they regard it if you fall for your foster father?" Minkie asked quietly.

When the silence had gone on for too long, she said "For God's sake say something?"

"How can I when I'm speechless with joy?"

"So that means it's OK?" Minkie took a hand out of her pocket and slipped it through his arm. She glanced down at the grave and saw that Mike had added some more plants and a tiny evergreen.

He followed her glance. "You know I did tell her about Sonja in the end? And her main reaction was that at least Marija gave me something she wasn't able to. Such generosity of spirit. It made me feel even more guilty."

Perhaps the time might come one day when she could tell him about that long ago abortion and dissipate the guilt. But not now.

"How could you love me and be so beastly."

"I can tell you exactly how. That day I came to Sarajevo and Bozo told me you had gone for a walk along the river, I saw you on the bridge and stood watching you for ages before I called you. It was like a thunderbolt, like seeing a stranger and yet with a sense of coming home for the first time. And it was also terrifying. I knew it couldn't be. My first instinct was to go away without speaking to you. But what would I have said to Bozo and everyone else who knew I had come for the express purpose of bringing you back to Daerley? So I tried to distance myself, encourage you to move in with Rowena, avoid you as much as possible and hope things would go back to where they had been. It didn't work. The more you seemed to be making a mess of your life, the more I cared."

"Well you were pretty successful in putting me off."

"And you made it easier by becoming extremely unbecoming."

"I thought the world owed me some fun. It was awful. I was awful."

"Let's be thankful Branka wasn't the result of any of those episodes."

"I was very precautious throughout that period. But with Shan I was so sure I'd not sleep with him that I stopped bothering."

"It's hard to understand why he didn't leap at the excuse to marry you."

"Oh, he did – on condition I went to Poland. I'm tired of running away, Mike."

He put an arm round her shoulders. "Was that why you decided against going with Jesse? He seemed so sure."

"Only partly. But we did seem to disagree on almost everything from the Iraq war to the environment. I was finding a distinct streak of racism in him you know. The final straw was when he walked in two days ago and found Shan bathing Branka. He demanded to know what he was doing with *his* child, I really thought there were going to be fisticuffs." She caught Mike's snigger. "Don't laugh, Mike. It was awful. But it was also a catalyst. Jesse so obviously despised the man who was Branka's father. How long before he started despising his daughter?"

Minkie stifled a giggle. "But you should have seen them: glaring at each other like angry bulls."

"Where are they now?"

"Jesse went back to The Trumpet, Shan leaves for Poland tomorrow. Never mind about them. What about us?"

"Well you know I've started on that documentary series? That means I'll be away for a few weeks very soon; in fact, need to go up to London early next week."

"But that's fine. I'll be a dutiful daughter and Branka and I will look after Abel's Yard while you're away. I'll also do some painting so you stop nagging me. In fact, I may nag you to do some writing to go with my illustrations. Something for children perhaps?"

"And then?"

"I've stopped trying to read the runes. I'll be a dutiful daughter as long as you like."

Mike ruffled her hair. "There'll be talk, some disapproval. Are you sure this is what you want Princess? Gut level sure?"

"I should be sure after trying to find every reason why it wasn't true for so long. There is no one I would rather be with."

He nodded, kissed the top of her head. "By the way where is Branka?"

"With Rowena and Luke. I think they're playing mummies and daddies. I said I needed to see you and would pick her up soon. They seemed unsurprised."

Mike bent down to remove a weed from Sara's grave, and knuckle in a winter pansy more firmly. Then he straightened up.

"Come on, Princess," he said. "Let's go home."

ACKNOWLEDGMENTS

My thanks to all my friends from former Yugoslavia over the past 40+ years who have contributed to my knowledge of their fascinating and often misunderstood country; and especially to Dr. Svetozar Koljević and his wife Ksenija.

Also to Mrs Betty Carter of Perth, for checking information for me on Western Australia.

My thanks, too, to my husband George Spenceley for tolerating ongoing intermittent strife with my recalcitrant computer; but especially for my first chapter from whose circumstances he was, thankfully, a survivor.

As for further conflicts, I strongly believe in the responsibility of each of us in working towards their avoidance. I thank those of you who share in and act on this belief.

Sylvie Nickels, November 2007